ONCE IN A LIFETIME

He grinned, flashing his extraordinary dimples at her once again, making something in her middle inexplicably waver. Before Claire could fathom why he'd smiled, his lips locked onto hers. Shocked, she gasped and he took full advantage, delving into her, taking possession.

How she came to be leaning into him, how her hands had ended up on his massive chest, she couldn't say. She did know that she'd never been kissed in such a fashion in her life.

A
HIGHLANDER
FOR
CHRISTMAS

SANDY BLAIR

ZEBRA BOOKS
Kensington Publishing Corp.
www.kensingtonbooks.com

ZEBRA BOOKS are published by

Kensington Publishing Corp.
850 Third Avenue
New York, NY 10022

All Kensington titles, imprints, and distributed lines are avail-
able at special quantity discounts for bulk purchases for sales
promotion, premiums, fund-raising, educational, or institu-
tional use.

Special book excerpts or customized printings can also be cre-
ated to fit specific needs. For details, write or phone the office
of the Kensington Special Sales Manager: Attn. Special Sales
Department. Kensington Publishing Corp., 850 Third Avenue,
New York, NY 10022. Phone: 1-800-221-2647.

Zebra and the Z logo Reg. U.S. Pat. & TM Off.

ISBN-13: 978-0-8217-7997-2
ISBN-10: 0-8217-7997-4

First Printing: October 2007
10 9 8 7 6 5 4 3 2

Printed in the United States of America

"Magic doesn't come to those who don't expect it."

—Diana Vreeland

Prologue

December 1745
Scotland

"Please, Cameron, *please,* I beg ye, please dinna go." Mhairie Stewart clutched the wolf pelts draped across her adopted son's massive shoulders. "I've seen what will happen, laddie. These battles will all be for naught, and ye ken that I'm rarely wrong."

Truth to tell, she was never wrong but occasionally did pretend to be, else those within the clan think her truly bewitched. 'Twas bad enough that most eyed her potions with suspicion, even when they were in sore need of them.

Her son put down his whetstone and stood. Towering over her, he gently cradled her gnarled fingers within his wide, callused palms. "Minnie, dream or nay dream, I *have* to go. I have no more love for Prince Charles than ye—hell, the man can barely speak Scot, much less Gael—but the MacLeod, Da, has said we go, so go I shall."

He bent to brush a tear from her wind-chafed cheek and his rich raven locks fell forward, framing his bonnie face. Her heart contracted. "But—."

"Minnie, why do ye fash? Ye ken that I'm the strongest among our clan, and truth to tell, of many more."

Aye, he was that, but the vision had been so clear . . .

"I promise to return to ye."

Ack! 'Twas the point! There wouldna be a returning. Thousands would remain on the field, in a glen of blood near Inverness!

Goddess and her son's saints preserve her, she hadna struggled for hours to bring him forth from her poor sister's womb and then spent decades fretting over his every misstep and bruise to have him die so inglorious a death!

She took a shuddering breath, praying guilt would sway him where reasoning had failed. "Son, look at me. I havena many moons left to me. Will ye have me fret them away?"

Tsking, he wrapped his powerful arms about her and pulled her close, making her only that much more aware of how fragile her once strong bones had grown, of how close she was to being no more.

Into her hair he whispered, "Minnie, I love ye with all my heart and would remain if I had a choice." He then leaned back and lifted her chin with the crook of his finger. Dimples bracketed his handsome grin as he looked into her eyes. "I promise to be careful. I shan't take any unnecessary risks."

Augh! He didna ken the meaning of careful! She'd heard the tales despite his trying to keep them from her, knew of the many risks he'd taken over the years in heat of battle. And had she complained? Nay.

From the verra first moment she'd held him she'd sensed that he was destined for glory. In a flash of insight she'd seen his matured countenance as it was now, his startling blue eyes, broad smile and cleft chin, had heard hundreds shouting his name as he waved. And well she understood that such a path often required daring. But to die for this, *this* . . . *impostor*?

Never!

He gave her nay choice. She would now have to do what she thought never to do to anyone—much less to her son—but Cameron *would* meet his destiny. She'd doubtless lose his love in the process, but 'twould be worth the loss and grieving to see him safe, so he might possibly be liege, mayhap even be king, to remarry and, hopefully, to a stronger lass who could birth his bairns.

Her decision made, Mhairie heaved what she hoped sounded like a resigned sigh. "I see that I canna dissuade ye. So be it. But grant me one last boon. Let me bless ye in the auld way before ye go."

Cameron's brow furrowed as he gave her that *'tis all nonsense* look he always managed whenever she insisted that the last bit of the grain be left in the field for the Pooka, but finally he nodded. "As ye lust."

She reached into the deep pocket of her gown and pulled forth the amulet she'd crafted years ago should she ever need it. "Bend down then."

He examined the large hollowed acorn attached to

the leather cord and his grin returned. "Where there's a witch, there's a way, huh?"

Mhairie cuffed his arm and anxiously glanced about. "Ye ken better than to joke about such."

Sister by marriage to their last liege lord, she'd been offered a place within Rubha Castle when she'd first arrived decades ago. Had there been a forest at hand where she could have sought occasional privacy to worship as she chose, she would have happily joined her young sister and new husband within Rubha's formidable walls, but such wasna the case. Her sister's new home sat on a windswept headland with nary a bush, much less an oak, for miles.

Having gained Cameron's acquiescence to a blessing, she patted his cheek. "Ye're a good lad. I dinna care what those silly lasses say about ye."

Cameron cocked an eyebrow as he settled back on the bench before her modest croft and reached for his blade. "And what might that be?"

"That as brawny and fine as ye might be, ye're still too full of yerself by half."

He laughed, causing great dimples to form in his cheeks as he drew his whetstone along the edge of highly polished steel. "Go on with ye. Ye havena much time. We leave at dawn."

Pulling her gaze from the harbinger of death he so lovingly fondled, Mhairie muttered, "Aye."

Her thoughts consumed with the lie she would tell his father and with the sleeping potion and snippets of verse she had yet to fully formulate, she hobbled as fast as her creaking hips and failing heart would allow down the path past Rubha Castle, turned south at the wee stone kirk that she and the rest of the clan attended daily, and then onto the path leading to the firth and its boulder-strewn beach.

At a lone stone croft built into the cliff, she knocked.

Three breaths came and went before the leather-slung door listed open and Tall Thomas poked his shaggy head out. Squinting against the glare bouncing off the choppy sea, their clan's huge light-keeper grumbled, "What do ye—Ah, 'tis ye." He grinned and pushed the door wide. "Did ye bring currants, mistress?"

"Nay, Thomas." She held out a leather pouch. Once firm and tawny but now stained the color of old wood, the pouch she held was too flimsy by half from decades of use so should he not return it—which he more often than not forgot to do—she'd be none the poorer. "I've brought ye walnuts."

"Oh." He snatched the bag from her hand. "Next time bring currants. I'm a wee stove up."

Humph. "Next time." She eased past his formidable bulk into the croft's one-room interior. As her eyes adjusted to the gloom her nose twitched, offended by the acrid stench of mildew, sweat, and old ashes. As Tom leaned out to grab the door, she grumbled, "Leave it open. Please." He scowled over his shoulder at her but left the door ajar. "Have you been applying the ointment to your wound as I asked?"

Thomas caught his lower lip betwixt his teeth and she heaved an exasperated sigh. "Sit down and roll up your sleeve." He did, and she tsked finding a soiled, sloppily applied dressing covering his right forearm. "If you were having trouble doing this, why did ye not come to me?"

"Ye ken why, mistress. They," he cocked his head in the direction of the village and castle high above them, "fear me."

Aye, they did. Misshaped by perpetually growing lumps of flesh, Thomas—desperate and near starvation—had wandered onto MacLeod land some fifteen years past. Their liege, not having the heart to cast him out, had given him this isolated and damp croft that no one else would occupy.

Clever with wood, Thomas had tried to make his way as a carpenter but none, save Mhairie, would barter with him fearing they'd catch whatever afflicted him. So now he earned his keep by tending the fires on their headland whenever their men were out to sea. No easy task given his infirmities and the distance he had to travel to gather wood. Worse, he had no help. His lone brother had gone to the New World—to a place called Virginia.

As she finished redressing his wound, which was healing nicely despite Thomas, he murmured, "How will I ever repay yer kindness, mistress?"

She smiled, glad for the opening. "'Tis simply done. I have need of your croft this evening and for the box ye crafted for me so many years ago."

"When?"

"Just before the moon reaches its zenith."

He nodded. "Good. I dinna feel comfortable wandering about before gloaming." Thomas shifted his gaze to the long, intricately carved oak box resting against the back wall. "I'll miss looking at it."

Mhairie rose and ran her hand along the finely chiseled spirals, crescents, and wedges—auld symbols that meant the world to her—carved into the box's lid. Aye, 'twas truly a sight to behold. Wishing she could take possession of it but knowing the risk, she murmured, "'Twill remain in yer safe keeping, Thomas. I just need a bit of privacy to put something of great value into it." She resumed her seat on his cottie stool and patted his misshapen leg. "Grave trouble is bearing down on us, Thomas. 'Tis verra important that the box never be opened by any, save me. That which I put within must be safeguarded." No one would think to look for Cameron here, but just in case, she added, "Safeguarded with yer life, if need be."

Scotland's future might well depend on it.

He tipped his head and stared at her for a long moment, then held out his hand. "Aye, m'lady, with my verra life."

Chapter One

Boston
December 2, 2007

Claire MacGregor wanted to cry. The biggest shopping weekend of the year had come and gone and she'd only brought in thirty-six dollars and change. Merry Christmas, ho, ho . . . *blah*.

But then Christmas hadn't been the same since her mother had died eight years ago. Had it not been for customer expectations and the hope of luring shoppers into the Velvet Pumpkin she wouldn't have bothered to decorate at all.

The brass bell hanging above her antique shop's door chimed, and Claire looked up from her computer screen, a smile in place for her first customer of the afternoon. Seeing Tracy Simpson crossing the threshold, all hope of her making her first sale of the day fizzled. "Hey, Tracy. How did the job interview go?"

Tracy grinned as she pulled off her gloves. "I didn't go. I went to a cattle call instead."

"A cattle call." Claire glanced at the French banjo-bottomed clock she held on consignment, then out through the wide bow windows fronting her shop. Four-thirty and snowing. No way could Tracy race across town now. "I don't believe you did this."

Tracy dropped her leather trench coat onto the back of a nearby Victorian side chair, then strolled toward Claire's most prized possession, the eight-foot-high baroque mirror that dominated the front half of the Velvet Pumpkin. "I know, I know. I should have gone to the job interview and I will . . . tomorrow, if I don't get a call back in the morning."

God, not again. "And what if you don't get a call-back and that secretarial position is taken? What are you going to do? Swivel around brass poles for the rest of your life? You have no savings, Tracy. You spend every dime you make. Hell, you're only a good case of the flu away from being evicted."

Tracy waved a dismissing hand as she scrutinized herself in the mirror. "Claire, you worry too much. I'll get the call. I'm perfect for the part."

Hating herself for asking, Claire grumbled, "What part?"

Tracy's face lit up like the small Christmas tree standing next to the mirror. "Of Sandy."

"Sandy."

"In *Grease*! You know the musical that starred Olivia Newton-John and John Travolta. You remember. We saw it a dozen times."

How could she forget? Having been an academic geek in bottle-bottomed glasses in high school, never having been on a date that Tracy hadn't strong-armed one of her boyfriend's football teammates into going on, she'd been mesmerized by the film, caught in the fantasy of having a man of her own with flashing blue eyes, dimples, and a cleft chin. A fantasy she was ashamed to admit she still harbored and had yet to experience despite new contacts and having read every *Cosmo* she could get her hands on.

"Ya, I remember. But hasn't the production been here and gone?"

And didn't the role of Sandy usually go to a headliner?

And a young one at that?

"It's summer stock."

"Where?" *Please don't tell me it's some community theatre without a budget.* She didn't have the money to bail Tracy out again.

Ignoring the question, Tracy turned sideways to the mirror and lifted her boobs with her hands. "I think gravity is starting to take its toll. I'm not collecting the tips I did a few years ago, not dating as much either. Tell me the truth. Do I look my age?"

Hell, they both did.

Tracy, the leggy blond star of their high school musicals, had blown off college and run straight for Hollywood. After ten years, three commercials—one for a laxative—and a supporting actress role in a truly forgettable, straight-to-video horror flick, she'd given up on being a film star and headed to New York in hopes of making it on Broadway. But by then, she was well into that no-longer-an-ingénue-not-ready-to-play-someone's-mother netherworld so many middle-aged actresses found themselves in. After a few more fruitless years, she'd returned home, an obsessive name dropper.

Meanwhile, Claire had been hip deep in endless minimum-wage jobs but finally she'd acquired her master's in art history, only to discover after a decade of no sleep, night classes, and shouting "You want fries with that?" that she was but one of hundreds looking for curator positions. Thank God she had an eye for quality antiques and had been able to parlay a few awesome estate and garage sale finds into solid cash. At least she now owned this shabby three-story brownstone and the Velvet Pumpkin, failing though it was. "Your boobs are fine. Leave them alone."

With her gaze still locked on her reflection, Tracy arched her back and pushed out her butt. "You haven't answered my question."

Mentally groaning, Claire assured her, "You look great, could pass for twenty-five, maybe twenty-two." When Tracy grimaced, Claire shrugged. "Stop fretting. And I'll keep my fingers crossed for you."

Looking sullen, Tracy grumbled, "Thanks."

"You're welcome." Claire turned her attention back to her computer screen. Praying someone had put a bid on the Victorian jewelry she'd scooped up at an estate sale, she clicked on eBay and mumbled, "Anything is better than you dancing at the Purple Pussycat."

"I heard that and it's not that bad. The bouncer keeps the creeps at bay."

Finding only two bids for the gold-filled locket and chandelier earrings, neither of which covered her initial cost, Claire groaned.

"I'm thinking," Tracy said as she faced the mirror, "of getting breast implants. Maybe even a butt lift."

Good Lord. There comes a time in every woman's life when she just had to admit she's no longer the cutest kitty in the litter box and go on. "For heaven's sake, Tracy, you've read all those articles—"

The bell over the door clattered, and Claire rose from her stool, a smile again plastered on her face for her Christmas shopper, only to find her mailman clomping snow on her welcome mat. "Hi, Mark."

"Hey, Claire. Howz it going?"

"Slow, but then it's snowing." She took the box addressed to her upstairs tenant from his gloved hands, mindful that his attention had already shifted from her to Tracy, who stood with one hip cocked, twisting a strand of shoulder-length platinum hair between her fingers. Long resigned to fading into the woodwork whenever Tracy was around, Claire muttered, "Tracy, meet Mark Mullany. Mark, meet Tracy Simpson."

Turning beet red, Mark mumbled, "Hi ya, Tracy."

"Hi, yourself."

Tracy's tentative—out-of-character—tone caused Claire to glance from Tracy to Mark, then back again. Did they already know each other?

Mark, forty-something and still good looking in a padded teddybear sort of way, was married last she heard and not really Tracy's type.

As if to confirm her suspicions, Mark tugged at the cuffs of his gloves and muttered, "The kids have been sick and Kathy's been pulling her hair out, so I haven't been getting out much."

Tracy suddenly grinned from ear to ear. "Well, I hope the kids are feeling better soon."

"Ya, me, too." Mark glanced at Claire, apparently realized she was paying attention and turned fuchsia. "Well. Gotta go. Hope business picks up, Claire."

Curious about the undercurrent between her friend and her mailman, Claire mumbled, "Thanks, Mark. Give my best to Kathy and the kids."

"Will do."

With a wave and a final glance at Claire, Mark left, leaving only a puddle on the door mat and a brassy tinkle in the air.

Claire watched her friend fidget with her hair and makeup for a moment before asking, "What's going on?"

"Nothing."

Crap! Claire came out from behind the mahogany sideboard that served as her reception desk, office, and lunch counter. "Talk to me."

Tracy spun, a slight blush gracing her cheeks. "There's nothing to tell. He comes into the Pussycat once in a while, that's all."

"Uh huh. Then why did you light up like that tree when he said his kids were sick?"

Tracy sidestepped left and started rearranging the cinnamon-scented candles sitting on the oak dresser beside the mirror. "He hasn't been in the club in a while and I was worried that something might have happened to him."

"Are you two seeing each other?" Is this what all the talk of boob and butt lifts was about? Tracy wasn't simply worried about her floundering acting career but fearful she couldn't hold a man's attention anymore?

With her face averted, Tracy inched farther away. "We're just friends, Claire, nothing more."

"He's married." Having come up the hard way, Claire didn't live in a black-and-white world, but there were definitely limits on how much gray she'd tolerate.

"Ya, I know." Tracy headed toward the desk and her coat, no doubt hoping to escape.

Pissed, Claire blocked her path. "And he brags regularly about his kids."

"It's not like that! Look, he comes in twice a week, throws back a few beers and we talk. Nothing more."

And pigs fly.

Tracy needed attention to function. Particularly a man's. Insecure at the best of times, she had a long history of choosing bad boys who left her twisting in the wind. Mark, a family man, would be a break from tradition, but then again, he did say something just a few weeks ago about working on his Harley.

Seeing her friend's jaw set and normally full lips thin into a hard line, Claire heaved a resigned sigh. Hey, it wasn't her life. "Sweetie, I just don't want to see you get hurt again."

"Thank you. And you're no one to be shelling out dating advice. You haven't been out with a man in years."

"Have too. I went out just last week."

Tracy snorted. "Going to a comedy club with Victor, your gay interior designer, *does not* constitute a date, Claire. I mean . . . when was the last time you got laid?"

Sensing the accusation worm turning, Claire

reached for the candles, rearranging them back to the way Victor, a master merchandiser, had piled them. "I don't remember."

"My point exactly. I bet you look like a prune down there. You really need to invest in some serious lingerie and then find yourself a boink buddy. You know what they say . . . use it or lose it."

"Augh." True, she hadn't been on a real date in years, hadn't found anyone worth getting dolled up for, much less making love to, but *prune?* Claire shuddered.

Tracy, a look of pity in her eye, wrapped an arm around Claire's shoulder. "Finding someone safe— and in as much need of some healthy, casual sex as you are—would do you a world of good."

Claire grumbled under her breath. The only males in her life were either gay or plain vanilla. No way would she be boinking any of them. She'd done the let's-turn-this-friendship-into-something-more thing with the guy she'd been dating in college. Biggest mistake of her life. The sex went from bad to hopeless and she'd lost a friend when she put an end to it. Lesson learned, she vowed never again. She was holding out for the man of her dreams, one with flashing blue eyes and dimples, one who'd be able to turn her knees to jelly and her blood on fire with just a look or touch. The fact that she was now thirty-one and he'd yet to show up didn't dissuade her. Miracles did happen.

Tracy looked at her watch. "Now that we've made nice, do you want to join me for supper? I haven't eaten all day."

Claire studied the snow falling in fat, dime-sized

flakes that clung like meringue to the lonely parking meters outside her door. Hell, there was no reason to stay open. No one would be out Christmas shopping tonight. And closing early would save on heating oil.

"Only if we go to the Union Oyster House." Clams were her comfort food, and the Union had the best.

"That works for me."

"Let me check something before we leave."

She clicked on eBay. As she punched in her password, Tracy twirled the wrought-iron Christmas card holder sitting on the desk. "Hey, you got another card from that old guy you helped a few years ago."

"Yes." Claire grinned. It had been on a night much like this one that she'd first met Tavish MacLean. She'd been closing up for the night when she heard the crash, rushed outside and found Tavish half frozen, his compact car crumpled against a light pole and sitting crosswise to the deserted street. After he assured her he could walk, she brought him back to the shop, where she'd called the police and tended his wounds.

While they waited three hours for the tow truck to arrive, she'd filled him with cocoa and sugar cookies and he'd entertained her in his lovely burr with tales of his Christmases in Scotland. Since then, he called regularly, always sent her a lovely anniversary card three weeks before Christmas, and drove down from Portsmouth to have lunch with her the day before Christmas.

Reading the card, Tracy grinned. "I think he's sweet on you, Claire."

"Just my luck the only real man in my life is almost eighty and—"

Brrrrringgggg.

Tracy jerked, her head snapping around in the direction of the sound. "What the hell is that?"

"Just the loading dock bell." As it continued to clatter like an ancient firehouse alarm, Claire reached for the cane she kept behind the desk.

"Who'd be making a delivery at this hour?"

"No one. It's probably just kids screwing around."

Every merchant on the street had recently been hit by vandals. Their leader, a pimple-faced kid of about fifteen with a pierced eyebrow and tattooed fingers, had had the audacity to suggest she pay protection money to ensure her windows remained intact. When she told him to go screw himself or she'd call the cops, he'd shrugged and walked away.

At three the next morning, the crash of glass followed by her security alarm screaming nearly gave her a heart attack.

She'd shot out of bed, grabbed her cell phone and cane and headed for the back staircase. She hadn't made it to the first landing when she heard alarmed shouts from her elderly second-floor tenant.

After telling Mrs. Grouse to stay calm, she raced down the stairs and found the glass in her double front doors in shards but everything else intact.

The police came, dusted for prints and said they'd patrol the neighborhood.

And then it happened again.

To date, the little bastards had cost her $1,800 in new plate glass and glazing fees, an amount she could ill afford.

In the backstore room, cane in hand—its lethal inner

blade exposed—she peered through the small window. A moving van filled the alley and a man, dressed in a delivery uniform, stood on her loading dock blowing white clouds into the air. The loading dock—an add-on the previous owner had constructed when he'd converted the first-floor apartment into retail space—had been the primary reason she'd chosen this narrow building over others. That and its rock-bottom price. There was something to be said for leaking pipes, an antiquated heating system, and layers of lead paint.

She pulled back on the steel bolt and cracked open the sliding door. Peering out, she asked, "May I help you?"

The guy stomped his feet as he held out a clipboard. "Are you Claire MacGregor?"

"Yes."

"Good. Sign this, and we'll start unloading."

"But I haven't ordered anything."

"Doesn't say that you did. We're just delivering the stuff from the house."

"What house?" She hadn't been to an estate sale in weeks. Couldn't afford to go. "Look, you must have the wrong—"

"Claire!" Tracy shouted from the front, "The phone—some guy from Brindle, Bailey, and somebody, attorneys at law. He says he has to talk to you."

Shit. Now what? Scowling, Claire pointed at the delivery guy. "Don't you dare unload a thing until I get back."

At the front of the store Tracy held the phone out to her. "Are you in some kind of trouble?"

Chapter Two

Claire shrugged as she took the phone. "Not that I know of."

Praying her vandals hadn't decided to sue her for defamation of character—her language had been scathing the last time they'd called and threatened her—she brought the phone to her ear. "Hello, this is Claire MacGregor. How may I help you?"

"Ms. MacGregor, this is Wesley Brindle, senior partner at Brindle, Bailey, and Sheltonship. I'm the executor handling the estate of Mr. Tavish MacLean, formally of 210 Willow Street, Portsmouth, New Hampshire. It's my sad duty to inform you that Mr. MacLean has passed, and—"

"*Passed?*"

Claire groped for the stool behind her. No, no. She'd just received her anniversary card, had spoken with Tavish not a week ago. He'd called to thank her for the chocolate chip cookies, and they'd made plans to meet Christmas Eve as they did every year. If the weather was nice they'd stroll through the Common, admire the decorations and store windows, then . . .

He couldn't possibly be dead.

"Ms. MacGregor?"

Claire struggled to clear the burning at the back of her throat. "I—I'm here. When did he die?"

"On November 28th, of a heart attack."

Oh, God. He must have mailed his card that day. "Please tell me he wasn't alone when it happened." Please, please. She couldn't imagine anything worse.

"No, he didn't." The clipped voice had softened. "According to the police, he was in a grocery store when he collapsed and the manager called 911. Unfortunately, the paramedics couldn't revive him. The police went to his home in hopes of notifying next of kin. Finding he lived alone, they went through his personal phone directory and found our listing."

Poor sweet Tavish. He'd been the picture of health when they'd last—

"Ms. MacGregor?"

"Yes."

"I know this comes as a shock, but it was very important to Mr. MacLean that his estate be settled as quickly as possible. Since he'd died of natural causes and his affairs were in order, I believe we're close to completing that task. He bequeathed his assets, limited as they are, to you."

Claire's throat, tight with unspent tears, seared as she croaked, "To me?"

"Yes. At his request, you'll be receiving a check within the next week." He asked her to confirm her mailing address, which she did. "I've also contracted a moving company to crate his worldly possessions and deliver them to you per Mr. MacLean's instructions. The truck should arrive in a day or two."

Oh shit!

The delivery guy was still freezing his buns off on her loading dock. "Could you please hold for a moment?" Without waiting for an answer, she covered the mouthpiece and flapped a hand at Tracy, who stood not three feet away pretending not to be listening. "Quick! Go to the back and tell the delivery guys they can unload the truck."

"Okay, but what's happening? Who died?"

"Later." She shooed Tracy away and again tried to clear the thickness in her throat before saying, "Mr. Brindle, I'm sorry. The moving van is here."

"Ah, very good. I feared the weather might delay them. In a day or two you'll receive a certified package containing a copy of the will and a check. Please sign the enclosed forms and send them back in the envelope provided as soon as possible. We can deal with the tax issues at a later date. Do you have any questions?"

Yes, hundreds. "Why did Tavish name me as his heir?"

"He had no family and from what I could glean from our conversations, he was quite fond of you."

"Oh." She'd been very fond of him, too. Imagining Tavish—pink-cheeked, dressed in tweed, wispy tufts of white hair sprouting from beneath his tam—chuckling as the Russian Tea Room fortuneteller told him that he'd live to be one hundred, seeing him grow pensive when the woman had said, "Ah, a secret . . . but you've chosen well," and then to see his broad grin return when the fortuneteller had picked up Claire's teacup and told her that she'd have a strapping son— her tears spilled. Tavish had only been seventy-seven.

"I think that covers it," Mr. Brindle murmured. "If you have any more questions, please don't—"

"Where is he buried?" The opportunity to attend his funeral had passed but she could still pay her respects at his gravesite, place flowers by the headstone. Roses. He'd loved red roses.

"Mr. MacLean requested that his body be shipped to Appin, Scotland. He's buried in a family plot next to his parents."

"Oh . . . I see." Her gaze shifted to the open armoire and the glass case protecting a beautifully crafted miniature sloop sitting on the middle shelf. Tavish, an avid model builder, had told her it was an exact replica of the boat his father had once owned. He'd given the model to her last Christmas and she'd placed it in the shop in hopes that it might garner him a commission or two.

She could wire flowers. Tavish had said Appin was small, little more than a fishing village. Perhaps someone in town or at the church would remember him, might agree to place the flowers on his grave for her. Maybe Teleflora—

"Ms. MacGregor? Are you still there?"

Claire shook her head, felt tears splash her cheeks and dashed them away. "Yes. I'm sorry, this—it's still such a shock."

"I quite understand. If you have any further questions, please don't hesitate to contact me." He gave her the information. "If there's nothing else, I'll bid you good evening."

"Thank you."

How long the phone buzzed in her ear she couldn't have said, but a thud followed by Tracy yelling, "For God's sake, be careful with that!" pulled Claire out of her daze.

In the back room, she found Tracy shivering against the frigid blasts coming through a wide-open loading dock door. Beside her stood four shoulder-high wooden crates. "How many more are there?"

Teeth chattering, Tracy shrugged. "I have no idea. I just know they're heavy. The guys have been sweating and cursing a blue streak."

Claire ran a hand over one of the crates. How sweet of Tavish to care enough to will her his worldly goods. And how painfully sad that she—a relative stranger—had been the only one he could leave them to.

The burly guy she'd left standing on the dock dropped another crate—this one long and low—on the floor, then shoved his clipboard under her nose. "That's it, lady, five crates. Sign here and we'll be gone."

After reading the invoice, Claire signed the bottom, then handed the clipboard back. As he tore off her copy, she asked, "Do you know the contents?"

"Furniture and clothes, mostly."

Great. She was already up to her chin and wall-to-wall in furniture.

She took the copy he held out to her and saw him to the door. "Thanks and Merry Christmas."

The guy waved over his shoulder as he headed for his truck. Ah, apparently a fellow Scrooge.

She closed the door and threw the bolt.

"So," Tracy grumbled, "are you going to tell me who died and what all this is about, or what?"

"Tavish died. Last Monday." Just saying the words caused something around her heart to contract and more tears to well up.

"Oh, Claire, I'm so sorry." Tracy wrapped her arms around her. "I hadn't realized he'd meant so much to you."

"Thanks." Her relationship with Tavish had been a special secret, one she'd kept close. She'd never known her grandparents and Tavish had somehow filled that gap. And knowing how ridiculous it was for a thirty-one-year-old woman to long for such a connection—much less cry over its sudden loss—she stepped out of Tracy's embrace, forced a smile and tapped on the closest pine crate. "He willed the contents of his home to me."

"You're kidding."

"No." Claire gave the crates a final glance, noting that the last crate the men had brought in looked like a coffin. She headed for the front of the store.

"Hey! Aren't you going to open them?" Tracy's high-heeled boots clicked against the shop's warped oak flooring as she followed. "I'll help."

"Thanks, but I'm not ready to open them just yet. Let's find something to eat."

"Oh, okay." Brow furrowed in obvious confusion, Tracy donned her coat as Claire shut off lights. "Are you still up for going to the Oyster House?"

Claire shook her head, doubting she could eat, but knowing she should try or she'd being dealing with the mother of all headaches before too much longer. "Let's just go to the Cocky Rooster." The neighborhood pub was a lot cheaper.

She flipped up the hood of her down jacket, tugged on her gloves, activated the alarm and closed the Velvet Pumpkin's front door. Inserting the key into her newly installed deadbolt, she mentally cursed the hoodlums who'd forced her to change out her shop's pretty but useless antique hardware.

As Tracy tottered on her four-inch heels down the broad granite steps coated in as much snow, she said, "Wouldn't it be cool if he left you millions stuffed in a mattress?"

Claire, moving just as cautiously but in sensible rubber-soled boots, guffawed. "Dream on."

Tavish, for all his affection toward her, had been a bit of a recluse and almost as poor as she. She'd be lucky to not find a body in that long narrow crate.

"Shit."

There was only one thing Wesley Brindle loathed more than dealing with his ex-wife and that was lying—even by omission. Which was why he handled only civil litigation cases.

His caseload wasn't as sexy as the criminal work his partners handled, but to his way of thinking, he walked the higher ground. Cranking out mountains of documents, creating ponderous witness lists, and filing delay after delay in the hopes of wearing down an opponent beat the hell out of standing before twelve jurors, good and true, and bending the truth—to the point of dislocating Lady Justice's arm—all in the name of a fair trial for a guilty-as-sin bottom feeder.

And still he'd just lied by omission to a client—or better put, a potential client—and all because Tavish MacLean's will stipulated that upon his death Wesley was to deliver $2,000 to Ms. MacGregor and to place the rest of the man's liquid assets—$12,000—into an escrow account to cover any future legal fees the lady might incur.

Never having imagined that Tavish would die before explaining why the lady might need a lawyer, Wesley ground his teeth, the calzone he'd eaten for lunch souring in his stomach.

Well, there was no undoing it now.

Thank God he'd taken the precaution of hiring a private investigator to do a background check on Ms. MacGregor when his friend had named her as his sole heir. Other than having an incarcerated thief for a father, a few questionable friends, and a hefty mortgage she was hard-pressed to pay, Ms. MacGregor appeared to be a model citizen. So, he really had nothing to worry about.

He drummed his fingers on the polished surface of his rosewood desk, his gaze shifting from the broad Charles River twenty-one stories below to the glass case sitting on his bookcase. Within it was Tavish's parting gift to him, the beautifully rendered half model of Admiral Nelson's *Victory*.

Ya, he had no reason to sweat and Clinton never inhaled.

* *

Dressed in her favorite after-hours outfit—an over-sized T-shirt, fleece robe, and teddy bear slippers—Claire took a healthy swallow of merlot and stared at all that was left of her friend Tavish MacLean.

Only five moving crates after surviving a polio epidemic, two world wars, a loving but childless marriage, and too few golden years. What the hell was wrong with this picture?

There should be more.

And children or grandchildren should be inheriting his treasures, not her.

Sniffling, she put down the wineglass and grabbed a claw-toothed hammer. She'd postponed this long enough.

Half way into the first box, a thump sounded behind her and the door at her back flew open with a bang. Heart in her throat, she spun, her hammer raised and ready to clobber. "Oh! Mrs. Grouse." Claire lowered the hammer and blew through her teeth. "Good God, woman, you scared me half to death."

Her bathrobe-clad tenant lowered her rolling pin and patted her own chest. "And you, me! I heard this awful screeching noise and thought those young thugs had broken in."

"So you came down here alone?" The woman was insane.

Mrs. Grouse shrugged her plump shoulders as she looked at the boxes. "Why are you working so late?"

"Tavish . . . died last Monday. These are his things."

"Oh, no." Mrs. Grouse waddled toward her, her arms

out, her pink sponge rollers bobbing, and her worn satin robe swishing. After giving Claire a cologne-drenched hug, she murmured, "Such a dear man. And so young."

Claire nodded, deciding age must be relative. Mrs. Grouse was eighty-five.

"Dear, is there anything I can do to help?"

"You're sweet to offer, but no. I really need to do this on my own. I'm sorry I woke you."

Mrs. Grouse waved a dismissing hand. "I wasn't asleep. Don't need much at my age. Thank heaven for the *Your Shop* TV and CNN. They're on day and night." She clucked as she surveyed the mess Claire had made, then gave her arm another pat. "Well, don't work too late. They'll still be here in the morning."

Yes, and Claire would be tripping over storage crates and packing material for weeks if she didn't get the mess out to the dumpster by eight tomorrow morning . . . for her neighborhood's monthly bulk pickup.

With a final wave, Mrs. Grouse headed for the stairwell, where she'd doubtless have the devil's own time making it back upstairs, thanks to arthritis. Why the dear woman remained in her second-floor apartment instead of moving into a retirement home with an elevator remained a mystery. But Claire didn't complain. Her company and modest rent—not to mention Mrs. Grouse's world-class coffee cakes—were worth the inconvenience of Claire having to run out to the grocery or pharmacy whenever the old dear needed something.

Hearing Mrs. Grouse's door finally close, Claire turned her attention back to the crates.

Three hours later, she collapsed onto a stack of books—most of which dealt with ships or model building—poured the last of the wine into her glass and stared at the necessities of one man's life.

A collection of plaid sports coats, shoes—their toes curled and scuffed from wear—slacks with shiny seats and creased knees, a few hats, socks, and underwear. Added to the mix: a toaster with a frayed cord, a clock, battered kitchen utensils and pans, a few pieces of chipped English bone china with a delicate pink rose pattern—probably a wedding gift—stained stainless steel flatware—she'd like to know how he'd managed that—shaving gear, canned goods, a vacuum cleaner as old as dirt, hundreds of small woodworking tools, and dozens of delicate ships and boats trapped in green-tinted bottles. Next to those items stood a full-sized pine headboard, dresser and matching end table, a harp-backed rocking chair with more layers of paint on it than she had years on her, and a spindle-legged maple kitchen set straight out of the '50s. And there was still a box yet to open; the one that looked like a coffin.

Yawning, she picked up the gold-leafed picture frame she'd placed on the end table and ran a gentle finger over the glass. Over Tavish and his love, Margaret, as they stood grinning, he young and dressed in a formal military kilt and she, blond tendrils flying in the wind, dressed in a lovely Victorian wedding gown and clutching a bouquet of wildflowers.

"I'll miss you, Tavish, I truly will." She clutched the picture to her chest and closed her eyes. She shouldn't be angry with him for leaving her like this. His wife had waited long enough.

Heaving a sigh, she placed the picture back on the end table, picked up the hammer and knelt before the long, narrow crate. Nails bent and screeched. If the fates were kind, she'd find a lost Rembrandt. Maybe the bridal gown she'd seen in the photograph. Or better yet, maybe she'd find a complete service of Waterford stemware with a matching footed punch bowl and twelve perfect cups. Now that would be lovely.

When the last nail gave way, Claire closed her eyes and grasped the lid with both hands.

Please, God, don't let it be a perfect scale model of the Queen Elizabeth II.

Heart tripping with anticipation, she gave the lid a shove. It hit the floor with a resounding thud and she opened her eyes.

Chapter Three

"Crap." Another box. This one secured in yards of bubble wrap.

She tried to lift the box out and failing, picked up the hammer again. When the crate sides fell away, she hacked through the tape and then pulled back the bubble wrap.

"Oh. My. God. Thank you, Tavish MacLean." She ran a gentle hand over the Celtic carvings imbedded on the lid of the smooth-as-silk, tea-colored oak chest before feeling around the edges looking for a latch or hinge. Finding none, she decided the lid simply sat on the base and lifted, only to almost drop it seeing a large white envelope addressed to her resting on a mound of dark green felt. Muscles straining, she carefully set the heavy lid aside and opened the envelope.

My dearest Claire,
I hope to discuss this delicate matter with you when we meet for our Christmas lunch, but in the event the

fates are unkind, I'm placing this letter with my most prized possession.

Dear God, how long had he been ill?

Please forgive me, but I truly believe you're the only person on whom I can rely, the only one with the mettle to carry on as I have sworn to do, but now no longer can.

This chest and its contents once belonged to Lady Mhairie Stewart, sister-in-law to Laird Malcolm MacLeod of Rubha, who died in December 1744.

My family lore holds that just prior to the MacLeod clan joining the Jacobite uprising, Lady Stewart entrusted all before you to our forebear Thomas MacLean, asking that he never open the chest but protect it with his life until such time as she returned for it or until Scotland was once again secure. Since neither occurred, Thomas brought it with him when he fled to America.

This chest has since crossed the Atlantic three times as it passed from father to son, from uncle to nephew, and each caretaker has pledged to guard it with his life. I, having no children, am entrusting this treasure to you and ask that you, too, protect it with your very life if need be.

The contents are not fully understood and some items—a white lawn shirt, a pelt, and boots—have disintegrated. I have enclosed a translation of the parchment found within the chest. Should you come to understand its meaning, I have no doubt that you'll know how best to proceed.

I wish you a long and happy life, my dear.

With great affection,
Tavish

"Damn it, Tavish." A thousand questions careened around inside her head as she wiped the back of her hand under her nose. "Why did you have to up and die before telling me about this?" And what in hell was she now pledged to protect?

She set the letter aside and lifted the felt. Finding a long, kite-shaped bundle wrapped in shrunken wool and tied with a velvet cord, she tugged on the cord and the layers of wool parted.

"Holy shit."

Scattered on a large mound of dark green plaid sat a fist-sized brass brooch inscribed with a bull's head, a studded leather belt, a hammered brass cuff, a small square box, an elk-handled short blade and a five-foot-long leather scabbard holding a bejeweled back sword gleaming in the glow of the bare-bulb chandelier above her.

"Oh my God, this is so totally wicked." She ran a shaking finger along the oiled and supple leather, marveling at its state of preservation. Anxious to see the blade, she slid her hands beneath the sheathed sword and with no small amount of effort lifted it out of the box and onto her lap.

To her surprise the broad blade slid from the scabbard as if it had been used yesterday, its dual edges sharp and gleaming, not a speck of rust anywhere. Phenomenal.

"There isn't a curator or antique dealer in town that wouldn't give his or her eyeteeth to hold this."

Gripping the hilt with both hands, she swung the weighty sword in a figure eight before her. Within seconds her wrists and forearms burned, ached from the weight, and she had to set it back on her lap. "Damn, I'd hate to meet the original owner in a dark alley."

She tipped the sword toward the light to better read the engraving on the worn hilt. *S Ca on M·od.* Hmm, the lettering appeared to be seventeenth to eighteenth-century English, but that didn't mean the language necessarily was. Latin, French, and Gael were all in common use in Scotland for centuries. Squinting, she examined the scratches between the legible letters. Damn, she needed her loupe and it sat on her bedroom dresser two stories above. But even without the loupe she'd bet her next commission that the huge cabochon in the center of the Celtic cross decorating the hilt was an amethyst. The smaller, mottled green stones surrounding it were Connemara marble from Ireland. Both gave credence to the provenance Tavish had provided, which indicated its owner—and not likely the Lady Stewart, unless the woman had been an Amazon—had been wealthy. Had it belonged to her husband? Her father?

Claire examined the bull's head brooch, then picked up the short sword and discovered its six-inch blade was as sharp as that of the back sword. As she turned the four-by-four-inch decorative oak box examining the myriad of hieroglyphs, something rattled inside. Ah ha! A puzzle box. What fun.

She pushed on each surface, hoping to find a pressure point—a lever—but finding none, set it down and picked up the second envelope and scroll. "Maybe these hold the key."

Mindful of the vellum's fragility, she took care

unrolling the scroll only to be disappointed, finding the message written in Gael.

As she opened the envelope, the clocks out front started chiming. How could it be two in the morning already?

She had to get to bed. The envelope and the trash could wait until morning.

She draped the plaid over her shoulders, slid the back sword into its scabbard and clutching it to her chest, pocketed the rest of her treasures.

Two hours later, Claire kicked off her down comforter and reached for the art deco lamp sitting on her nightstand. There wasn't a chance in hell she'd get any sleep until she'd solve the mystery of the puzzle box.

The moment she'd gotten upstairs she'd grabbed her loupe and learned the original owner of the back sword had been a knight named Sir Cameron MacLeod. One puzzle down, one more to go.

She reread the translation Tavish's ancestors had made of the scroll. Several hands had made notes along the edges questioning a word or two. The final consensus read:

> *Within essence, within soul*
> *If nay mater, then mate behold*
> *For only thee doth hold the key*
> *Tis how he kens*
> *To set aright and future be*

"Well, that's helpful. Not." With the loupe pressed to her right eye, she studied the hieroglyphic symbols and discovered tiny depressions at the center of each. "Hmmm, I wonder . . ."

She scrambled off the bed, opened the cedar chest that sat at its foot, and hauled out her sewing box.

"Needle, needle, my soul for a fine needle."

Finally, fine needle and loupe in hand, Claire, her legs folded beneath her, began poking the needle into the tiny holes in numerical sequence starting from left to right and then in degrees of geometric complexity. "Damn, there has to be a sequence, a pattern."

"*Tis how he kens . . .* thinks." Well, most men thought with their heads and then with their hearts. No, first a guy thought with his penis and then with his head. She hunted but found nothing that even faintly resembled a phallus symbol.

She turned the box again and spied a pair of tiny concentric circles with pinholes at each center that could represent breasts. Hmm. She stuck in the needle. At the outer edge of one side, she found two crescents that faced each other that could—if she held the box just so—loosely resemble a vagina. Nothing ventured, nothing gained. She stuck the needle into the tiny hole at the center and shuddered. Now what?

She turned the box again. Ah, those swirls. They sort of looked like ears and there was lots of space between them, save for that one almost-invisible pin hole.

Claire pushed in the needle, something clicked and one side popped out a quarter inch. "Wahoo!"

How many generations of MacLean men had tried and failed? Ha!

Turning the box so the loose panel faced up, she lifted it and with breath held, peered inside. "Huh?"

She tipped the box and a large acorn fell into her palm. "Odd, feels warm." The acorn had been inscribed and drilled to allow for a leather cord that was now brittle with age. She grabbed the loop and studied the inscription on the acorn.

Anail. Tha gradhach. Wonder what that means?

As she examined the acorn, the cap came loose and silvery sand fell into her palm. It felt slick, almost silky. Oh well, at least the sword had been worth the loss of a night's sleep.

She clapped the sand from her hands sending it flying. "*Anail. Tha gradhach.*" Wonder what it—

CRAAACKKKK

Claire jerked as her hands flew to her ears and an incandescent glow turned night into day within and without.

"Damn, that was close."

Augh! Her tree! The sugar maple standing before her front door had been on its last root when she'd bought the townhouse. After three years of fertilizer sticks and water it had finally come back to life last spring.

Car alarms were whoop-whooping as she jumped out of bed, pulled open her plantation shutters and hauled open the window to look outside.

Hanging over the windowsill, she looked down and found her tree whole and lovely, snow decorating its black, leafless branches. She then craned her neck to look at her roof and finding no smoke rising, looked right and left, praying her neighbors' buildings weren't on fire. But all appeared normal. There was very little wind and the sky, rather than roiling, was simply a calm, luminous gray. And the snow had slowed to a flurry. Hmm, so what had caused the lightning?

A chill slithered down her spine, making her shudder. She pulled back in and closed the window. As she reached back for the shutters, a large callused hand clamped over her mouth.

A scream rose in her throat as she frantically clawed at the hand. "Eeeee!"

A steely arm encircled her waist, pulling her back against a formidable male body. Hard, hot, naked flesh pressed her from shoulders to quaking naked thighs.

On a wisp of clove and musk, the stranger hissed into her ear, *"De' an t-ainm a tha ort?"*

She keened and the hand slid from her mouth and encircled her neck, long fingers catching her under the jaw and lifting.

"Who . . . who are you? What do you want?" *Oh, God, please, please, please, don't let him hurt me.*

"Who are ye and what," a deep baritone asked, "in bloody hell is going on here, Sassenach?"

Oh God! How had he gotten in? Oh please God!

Screeching, Claire lashed out, her fingers curled like talons in hopes of hitting the man's eyes. When her fingers caught a long strand of hair, she yanked, heard a grunt, and the arm encircling her waist rose and squeezed the air out of her lungs.

The hand slapped over her mouth again. "Cease! I willna harm ye."

Her lungs frantically tried to draw air while her heart tried to break through her ribs. Formidable body heat penetrated the thin cotton of her T-shirt. Oh, God, he was going to rape her, why else would he be naked?

Black spots formed before her eyes as she began kicking. Before she could connect, he spun her so that she faced the mirror opposite her bed.

As her gaze locked on his, the arm locking the air out of her lungs eased.

"Look."

She couldn't have pulled her gaze away to save her soul. The man holding her life in his massive hands stood a good foot above her, outweighed her by one hundred pounds, and was, in fact, stark naked.

Staring into her eyes, he murmured, "Do I appear a man who needs to rape a woman?"

Unable to speak, she shook her head. No, in fact he looked like a cover model, bronzed and buffed to the extreme. If she'd seen him on the street, she'd have thought him a body builder or gay. Or maybe an actor. His hair was blue-black and wavy, hanging well below his collar bones, his brow broad but furrowed, his eyes an intense blue, his jaw square. No, he definitely didn't look like he needed to rape women, but then again . . .

With his gaze still locked on her reflection, he leaned forward so that his lips brushed her ear. A chill raced down her spine as he hissed, "I need answers, woman, and need them now. Ye willna come to harm if ye be truthful and dinna screech. Do ye agree?"

Claire nodded. She'd have agreed that the moon

was on fire had he asked it of her. The hand covering her mouth fell away but not so far that he couldn't grasp her again within a heartbeat.

"Yer name."

She took a deep shuddering breath. "Claire."

His head tipped as he studied her reflection, his gaze raking over her body before settling on her breasts, which thanks to her terror were disgustingly perky, her nipples making twin steeples of her nightshirt. "Yer surname."

Sur . . . oh. "MacGregor."

"MacGregor."

The way her last name cleared the back of his throat before rolling off his tongue left little doubt as to what he thought of it. Augh.

The hand keeping her pressed against his massive chest slipped away and grasped her upper arm. Before she could bolt, he spun and she had no choice but to follow. As his gaze raced from her partially open closet, to the overhead ceiling fan to the lamp and digital clock on her nightstand, a rumbling deep within his chest started and grew louder. Not good.

"What place is this?"

"It's my apartment." Idiot.

He gave her arm a jerk, pulling her up onto her toes and still he loomed over her. "That I ken. But what place? Where precisely am I?"

Cringing, she whispered, "In Back Bay."

Eyes narrowing, he hauled her higher and bared his teeth. "What bay?"

"Dartmouth Street, Boston. Boston, Massachusetts."

"Aack!" Muttering what sounded like curses, he

dragged her to the window and pulled open the shutters to peer outside.

As he examined the street below, Claire leaned as far back as possible. The muscles she'd seen in the reflection as he stood behind her looked twice as large now that she was staring directly at them. As did his chest and—my God, the thighs on the guy! She wouldn't stand a chance if he decided he wanted her. Worse, from what she could see from the side, he was really hung.

Shuddering, her gaze settled on the back sword and small blade on her bed. If she could just get to one of them, maybe, just maybe. . . .

At her side, her intruder muttered something unintelligible again and suddenly she was free and careening sideways. She tripped over her sewing basket and fell ass over teakettle onto the floor, her butt in the air.

Damn the man!

Scrambling to her feet, she jerked on her night shirt in an effort to cover her ass, only to turn and discover the hunk's attention had shifted to Tavish's gifts lying on her bed. He'd already flung the plaid about his hips and over his shoulder and was reaching for the belt.

"Hey! Don't you dare touch those."

Furious, she jumped onto the bed and snatched up the closest weapon. The short blade wasn't much bigger than a paring knife but anything was better than nothing.

The hunk snorted, and with a firm tap of his hand, the scabbard and claymore flipped off the bed, airborne. Then *swoosh,* his arm thrust out and the sheathed claymore settled over his right shoulder.

Claire gaped. How had he done—

Augh! Who cared.

Fearing he'd lunge at her, ready to dodge, she shifted her weight from side to side, the blade clutched in her right hand. "Give it back!"

He shook his dark mane, the corner of his lip curling up as his gaze shifted from the blade in her hand to her legs. "Nay, 'tis mine."

"Like hell it is."

"Humph!" He placed his hands on his hips. "Dinna call my integrity into question, woman. If I say 'tis mine, then rest assured 'tis mine."

Before she could respond, he reached back, the claymore sang through the air and was suddenly pointing at her chest. "The sgian duhb. Please."

She shook her head, having no clue what he'd said.

"The blade, lass, hand it over."

No, no. She backpedaled until her back slammed into the cold brass of her headboard, the short blade wavering before her in a sweating hand. "Leave!"

He huffed and stepped closer, bringing the tip of the gleaming broadsword to within an inch of her heart. Shocked, she yelped and dropped the knife.

Without taking his eyes off her or moving the broad sword, he scooped the knife up. "Thank ye."

The claymore then disappeared into its scabbard and her intruder was securing the brooch to the plaid on his shoulder. "Have ye a ribbon?"

Why would he need—good God, did he plan to tie her up? She contemplated lying but then feared he'd trash the room and find her jewelry pouch hidden in the lowest drawer. "Top drawer behind you. Take the damn ribbons and go, but leave the swords. There's no way in hell you can pawn them." She'd file a police report and then call Shields, the president of the local pawnbrokers association. She'd have everyone in town on the lookout for them.

Keeping her in his peripheral vision, her intruder pulled open the top dresser drawer and ran a careless hand through her collection of so-not-Victoria but definitely Discount-Mart secrets. To her embarrassment, he hauled out her lime green push-up bra and black boyshorts.

Staring at them as they dangled from a long finger, the furrow between his eyebrows deepened. "Humph."

"Put those back, take the damn ribbons and get out of here!"

To her relief, he dropped her underwear back in the drawer and hauled out a handful of ribbons. Selecting a length of wide, black velvet, he surprised her by tying it not around her as she'd expected but around his bulging left bicep. He then slipped the short blade through the ribbon, securing it to the underside of his arm. "Twill do."

Oh good. Now please leave before I have a heart attack.

He cocked a finger at her. "Come."

Oh, no. No, no. Not happening. She shook her head hard, causing beads of sweat to trickle down between her breasts. She wrapped her fingers around the brass spools of her headboard. As she opened her mouth to scream, he smiled, flashing great dimples at her.

"Lass, I mean ye na harm."

"Then leave. Please—"

Buzzzzzzzzz!

"Good morning, Boston! This is Chopper Dan high above the Fenway with your morning traffic report," her radio bellowed. "Southbound 1 A is a parking lot from the Saugus rotary to the Mystic River Bridge thanks to an oil tanker that jack-knifed—"

"What the bloody hell—" Her intruder's hand flew to the hilt of the claymore.

Claire yelped, her cry strangling halfway up her fear-dried throat. Before she could slam the snooze button, shutting off the vibrating voice of Boston's high-flying traffic reporter, a steely arm encircled her waist and she was hauled off the bed and again plastered against the man's chest. As she gasped for air, the sword's hilt crashed down, turning her radio into sparking black splinters.

Mouth agape, Claire glanced up. The man holding her was ashen beneath his tan as he snarled something unintelligible at what remained of her radio.

Please, God, please make him go away.

"Ye're safe now. Come." Without waiting for a response, he shifted his hold to her wrist and marched into the living room where he came to an abrupt stop. The rumbling started again deep within his chest as his gaze careened around the room, hopping from her modest flat-screen television to her vintage eight-track stereo system to the tall, bow windows she'd draped in vertical, green-and-white striped sheets because she hadn't the money for more plantation shutters. Finally, he shook his head, sending ebony waves that smelled of male, wood, and musk dancing about his shoulders and across her face.

"The passage out?"

Claire pointed a shaking hand to her right. "There, down two flights."

He strode to the door as she stumbled behind. She flipped the deadbolt—anything to get him out faster—and he jerked open the door.

Without loosening his grip on her, he peered into the hallway, listened for a moment and grunted in apparent satisfaction. He then hauled her up against his chest again, his hands pressing her to him from hips to chest. A sob shook her as his right hand tipped up her chin.

"My apologies, lass."

Something in his expression, the softening about his mouth and glimmer in his eyes, made her believe that he might actually mean it.

She nodded, her throat too tight for speech, and he grinned, flashing his extraordinary dimples at her once again, making something in her middle inexplicably waver. Before she could fathom why he'd smiled, his lips locked onto hers. Shocked, she gasped and he took full advantage, delving into her, taking possession. The firmness of his lips quickly softened, rocking her to her core and turned her knees to jelly.

How she came to be leaning into him, how her hands had ended up on his massive chest, she couldn't say. She did know that she'd never been kissed in such a fashion in her life.

He grinned, gently tapped the tip of her nose with his index finger and crossed the threshold, only to stop and look over his shoulder at her. "Ye've splendid hurdies, lass, makes me loath to kiss and run but . . ."

What the hell were hurdies?

And then he was gone as silently as he'd come.

Her knees and thighs shaking, her fingers pressed to her still tingling lips, Claire stumbled into the hall.

What the hell—?

She leaned over the banister and caught a glimpse of plaid as he flew on silent feet down the stairs. She'd been kissed by a nameless burglar. And enjoyed it! She'd definitely lost her mind.

Oh God, he'd taken Tavish's treasures! The items she was pledged to protect.

Swearing at her stupidity, she ran into the apartment, grabbed her cell phone off the coffee table and punched in 911.

"*911. Where are you located?*"

"210—" Claire cleared her throat. "210 Dartmouth, third floor. A man broke in and stole a broad—"

Oh crap! Her front door was still deadbolted and she had the only key. Upstairs.

"*Ma'am?*" the nasal voice asked, "*Your name?*"

Claire snatched the keys off the table and raced for the stairs, praying her intruder had seen the loading dock door. It was only secured by a steel bolt. "Claire MacGregor," she told the operator.

"*Ma'am, are you in danger?*"

Panting, Claire hit the second floor landing at a run. "Not now, he's leaving, but he took the swords and brooch."

"*Swords?*"

"Yes! Hurry!"

Claire stumbled into the storage room, saw that the loading dock door was still securely locked and shouted, "Wait!"

The sound of breaking glass reverberated throughout the first floor and was quickly followed by the screams of her security system alarms.

The dispatch officer forgotten, Claire ran into the Velvet Pumpkin.

Her beautiful glass doors were again in shards.

"Shit! Shit, shit, shit!"

Where in hell am I?

Cameron's head and stomach reeled, much as they had when he'd been a bairn and gone over a burn in a stolen ale cask. He pressed into a shallow doorway and watched in disbelief as a huge horseless coach with glowing lamps and a plow before it ground past on fat, chain-coated wheels.

The houses he'd run past were much like those in Edinburgh, closely packed and multistoried, but he wasna in Edinburgh. Of that he was certain. The signposts and those plastered to shop fronts were in English, though what most said was beyond his ken. As if to drive the point home, the shop across the wide thoroughfare suddenly lit from within and a glowing orange sign blinked to life in the window. *Open*, it read. The shop to the right touting Copy Central remained in the dark, as did the one on the left.

Not a public house, surely. And how did the signage glow so? Claymore in hand, his heart beating a furious tattoo against his sweating chest, he panted, sending white clouds into the air.

Nothing appeared real, much less familiar. Worse, he recalled naught prior to finding himself standing in Claire MacGregor's bedchamber.

Catching movement out the corner of his eye, he glanced left. A hunched man dressed in a heavily padded jacket was making crunching progress toward him. Before he came close enough for Cameron to grab and question, the man vaulted the banked snow and crossed the roadway to the open shop and disappeared.

God's teeth! Where the hell had he left his boots? His horse? He took a deep breath in an effort to steady his galloping heart and caught a whiff of salt-water under the crisp scent of new snow. Ah ha! The sea was close by, but where? Like a wolf on the hunt, he turned his head trying to catch the scent again. Damn. Nothing.

He needed a safe place to think.

Spying a dark cave to the right, he edged closer. From there, he could wait and watch.

Just yards from his goal, a distant keening caught his attention. His steps faltered. A brilliant light suddenly flooded the entrance. Cursing, he backpedaled on frozen feet. The screeching, much akin to a blade on a smithy's wheel, only louder, grew to an ear-shattering din. Then to his horror, a monstrous metal beast erupted from the hole, its singular lamp high and centered, like the eye of a Cyclops. As he scrambled over the nearest snow bank, one horseless coach after another screamed past on metal wheels, sparks flying.

Christ's blood! What manner of hell was this?

Heart nearly breaking his ribs, his breath catching, he peered over the mounded snow to watch the snaking coaches come to a hissing stop a short distance ahead, watched the doors swing wide without help, a few faceless figures shift within the lit interior before the doors hissed shut. None too soon, the snakelike coaches began to roll again.

Praise the saints.

As if the fates feared he'd grow complacent, all the lanterns casting blue-white arcs high above the street suddenly went out. He rolled, expecting an army of lamplighters at his back only to find the street deserted.

And Minnie? He could see her beautiful face, her creased cheeks, and prayed she was safe, that whatever had befallen him she had been spared. He started to rise only to duck down as a rolling beast with flashing blue and red lights careened around a distant corner.

A moment later, another horseless coach—this one tall and square with the words *The Boston Globe* on the side—rolled to a halt directly before him. He held his breath, mindful that the white puffs he emitted into the frigid air could disclose his presence.

A door opened and Cameron tightened his grip on his claymore as a man dressed much like the other jumped out and jogged to the back of the coach, where he lifted a great rolling door with a clatter and reached in. With a grunt, he tossed a gray block onto the snow to Cameron's right, and then scrambled back inside and drove away.

Cameron waited for the coach to travel a good distance before racing to the block the man had tossed away. Paper!

Prize in hand, he ran the length of the buildings and ducked into a mews. He hunkered down behind a high drift only to notice that his footprints were the only marks on the perfect white blanket before him. Clear as day, they'd lead anyone straight to him, but he hadna time to fash about it.

Teeth chattering, he sliced through the string making two equal lengths, then quickly secured two thick wads of paper around his near-frozen feet. Ack! He'd grown soft in Rubha. Time was he could have run naked through snow and not minded in the least.

He waggled a foot. 'Twould do until he could steal a pair of boots. As he began to rise, he looked down at the bold print on the remaining broad sheets. *Embassy Blast Kills Three*. Below it—in unbelievable clarity— he found an image of the destruction. In more bold print, he read BIRD FLU DECLINES. Humph. How could birds not fly? SECOND WALK ON MOON RESCHEDULED.

Huh?

He held the page to the light, sure he'd misread. Aye, 'twas what it said. He tossed it aside and reached for the next, which read the same. As he tried to make sense of the fine, oddly phrased print, a brightly lit coach rolled past. A dog barked in the distance and then from above a bright splash of light illuminated the snow before him.

God's teeth! Those around him were waking. He could ponder the insanity of men on the moon and flightless birds another time. He needed a place to hide, needed a cloak, boots, and food. Once he'd acquired those, he could better reason, for surely there had to be a logical explanation for all he was seeing.

And there was only one who could fulfill his needs. Claire MacGregor.

Finding his way back to the lass with stormy green eyes and decidedly fine hurdies proved easy enough. Where he'd left no footprints—where he'd run along snow-packed roadways—he watched for familiar sign posts. Ah, there. Dartmouth.

Around the corner, he slowed, finding men standing before her home and next to them a flashing white and black mechanical beast. He ducked into a cellar stairway as one man pointed at the snow, no doubt to his tracks. The other nodded and with a hand on his hip, took off at a trot. Praise the saints, he'd used the roadways more often than not.

The remaining man climbed into his coach. With steam belching from its ass, it rolled past, its chain-coated wheels crunching and clinking.

Cameron glanced back at the house. Claire's door had been covered with sheeting. Aye, now was the time. Before someone spotted him lurking and summoned the men again.

He straightened, readying to cross the roadway.

WHUUPP WHUUPPP WHUUPPP WHUUPPP

The sound from above vibrated against his chest and caused the hairs on his arms and neck to rise. Instinctively, he reached for his claymore.

"Merciful mother of Christ!"

A monstrous mechanical dragonfly—its wings whirling sideways like a tipped windmill, its red and white eyes gleaming—suddenly whipped overhead at unimaginable speed. A few stuttering heartbeats later, it disappeared into the dawn, its *whuup whuup whupp* growing fainter with each breath Cameron managed to draw.

Ack! The size of the beast! But for the grace of God and Saint Bridie he'd be dead.

That's it. He'd had enough.

Muscles tense, his gut rumbling with fear, he sheathed the claymore with a shaking hand and strode purposely toward Claire's front door. Anyone who watched through their windows—another oddity, all this glass—would assume him to be a man on a mission. There was naught else to take note of, save for his odd footwear. He hoped.

At her door, he pressed a hand to the opaque bubbles stretched over the frame. Humph! Pliable and far too easy to breach, which he promptly did. He must speak to Claire about installing a stout door as soon as he had his bearings and something warm in his belly.

Inside, the air felt blessedly warm and smelled of flowers and baking. Having focused only on a means of escape when he'd initially run through, he examined the quantity and quality of furniture crowding the room. He gave the multiple candelabras hanging from the ceiling a cursory glance, then shifted his attention to the books, dishes, and glassware crowding every surface. "Humph. Claire MacGregor is apparently a verra wealthy woman."

Passing a chest, he caught the scent of cinnamon and slowed. Ah, buns, piled nice as ye please on a platter. His stomach rumbled as he snatched one from the pile. He took a bite as he stared at the tree festooned with hundreds of glass balls.

"*Acck!*"

He spat and wiped the back of his hand across his mouth and dropped what remained of the bun on the chest. Good God. Claire MacGregor might have many a talent but cooking wasna one of them. And where might she be?

As if hearing his thoughts, wood clattered and the lady in question yelped, then issued a string of decidedly unladylike curses. Ah, 'twas Claire of the fine hurdies. He'd recognize that snarl anywhere.

Mindful of his backsword and the breadth of his shoulders, he eased sideways through the clutter and made his way toward the back room, where he found Claire, her back to him, dressed in breeches and a woolen tunic, her chestnut curls tied loosely atop her head, tugging on boards.

Seeing she was alone, he leaned against the door frame and folded his arms across his chest, feigning a calmness he dinna feel in the least. "May I help ye with that?"

Chapter Four

"*Augh!*" Claire leaped a good foot, her hammer dropping to the floor. Oh, God, not again. "What in hell are you doing back here?"

Her intruder straightened, and she stumbled backward, tripping over the pile of wood at her feet.

"Be at ye ease, lass, I mean ye na harm. Truly. I return in hopes that I might find something warmer to wear." He waggled a soggy, newspaper-encased foot at her. "Hoped ye might also find it in ye heart to offer me a wee bit of food and then kindly explain where I will find a horse, so I might escape this ungodly place."

"Go away or I'll call the police!"

Looking bemused, he relaxed against the door frame again, this time his hands loose at his sides. "Naught is as it should be, mistress. Worse, I dinna ken how I came to be here." He heaved a sigh. "Or for that matter, where *here* is."

Claire groped behind her for something—anything—to use as a weapon. "Are you on medication?"

"Medikay—?" He huffed in apparent exasperation. "Lass, I awoke in yer bedchamber. How I came to be there is beyond my ken. Last I recall, I was preparing for war. We were to leave at dawn. Then . . . naught."

"War?" Claire gaped at him. "Oh, you poor thing."

He was a soldier . . . one apparently suffering from posttraumatic stress syndrome. Great, just what she needed. "Well, we have to find out where you belong. Do you have any ID on you? Know where you're stationed?"

His eyes narrowed. "Lass, I dinna ken yer meaning."

She held up a hand, fearing she'd agitate him further. "Not to worry. We'll find out. Somehow."

He was obviously Scot, which meant he'd probably wandered off a British battleship stationed in the naval yard. It shouldn't be too hard to find. She smiled in hopes of appearing nonthreatening, friendly, in fact. "Do you know your name?"

Obviously affronted, he straightened. "Aye. Sir Cameron MacLeod, third son of John MacLeod, laird of Rubha and the clan MacLeod."

As the words tripped from his lips, blood drained from Claire's head. The name on the hilt of the backsword; the one he'd stolen and now wore, had claimed as his and so easily wielded. This wasn't possible. "Did you say MacLeod? Sir Cameron MacLeod?"

"Aye, I did."

Dare I ask? "And your mother's name?"

"Elizabeth MacLeod."

Ah, good. Not the same. He'd somehow managed to read the name engraved on the sword's hilt. Although how he'd managed to do so without a magnifying—

"She died birthing me. I was raised by my aunt, Mhairie Stewart."

"Mhairie . . ." Black spots began dancing before Claire's eyes. Blinking, she reached for one of Tavish's kitchen chairs and dropped onto it. "Mhairie Stewart. Your aunt."

"Aye." He took a step toward her. "Are ye all right, lass? Ye appear a wee bit green."

She held a hand up, warning him to keep his distance. "I'm fine. I just need to think."

He nodded. "Dinna we all."

Her hands shaking, wishing with all her heart that Tavish was at her side, she asked, "What day is this?"

The handsome man before her shrugged. "Sunday. Mayhap Monday. I dinna ken for certain."

Hating to badger someone who was obviously stressed but needing to know, she asked, "And the year?"

His beautiful cobalt eyes narrowed. "The year of our Lord, 1745. Or so it was before all went withershins."

Oh God, this isn't happening.

His height impressive, his formidable legs braced and well apart, he glared down at her. "Naught as it should be, lass. Naught!"

Oh, he had that right. Could he be . . . ? No. If not, then how . . .

"How did you get into my apartment?" Her security system had been armed. And no way had he come into the shop earlier in the day and simply hidden until she'd closed. She'd spent the entire day in the front of the store, robbing from one account to fill another, trying to balance her books. At six and a half feet, he was far too large for her to have *not* noticed his arrival.

He threw out his arms. "That, lass, is the verra point I've been trying to make. The last I recall I was in Rubha's great hall. The tables were bowing beneath the weight of the feast before us. Wine and ale flowed as if from a burn. All kenned the feast might be our last for a good many months, mayhap a year. Mayhap, ever. Then . . . there ye were, half-naked before me and screeching to wake the dead."

"Augh! Need I remind you that I was the one with a naked stranger twice my size in my room?"

He heaved a sigh, his expression nonplus. "I humbly beg ye pardon, mistress."

Oh God. If his being here had anything to do with the box she'd opened . . .

"Mr. MacLeod, it's the year 2007."

He blanched. "That canna be."

"I assure you that it is. And you're in America. In Boston, to be exact. And this is my home." Her head pounding, Claire looked at her watch. Almost seven o'clock and she'd yet to get the crating out to the dumpster or shovel the steps.

"Look, I have a lot—hey!" Claire slapped at the hand encircling her wrist like a steel manacle. "You're hurting me!"

Her intruder pulled her up against his chest, and loomed over her. "Speak the truth."

"I am. Look at the calendar. In there."

"Humph!" Muttering under his breath, he hauled her at breakneck speed into the shop, where he brushed up against the bentwood coatrack, sending it toppling to the right, where it crashed into the mahogany cart, sending the silver tea set crashing to the floor.

"Damn it, slow down before you wreck the place!" Panting, she pointed to the left. "Over there, by the large mirror."

MacLeod came to a halt before her desk. "The calendar."

"I'm getting it." She reached down, jerked open the buffet's top drawer with a shaking hand and pull out her calendar. As she handed it over, she saw on December 24th *12:30 PM, Lunch with Tavish.* God. "Look at the top. See? Right there, December 2007. And look." She hit the power on her computer and it sprang to life, clicking and grinding. When the monitor lit up, she heard MacLeod gasp then curse. "Wait. Just wait."

She pulled up CNN and turned the monitor so he could see it more clearly. "See, December 2, 2007, right there. Now watch."

She clicked on the weather link, bringing up the national forecast map. "See right here? This is America, and this," she moved the cursor to Massachusetts, "is where you are now."

Ghastly pale, he pointed to the screen. "This cannot be." Color then flooded his cheeks and the blood vessels at his temples throbbed.

Deep breath, Claire. Stay calm. If he is who you think he is—no, who you fear he is—he'll likely kill you as look at you.

"What manner of witchcraft is this?"

Oh shit! "Please, try to stay calm and listen. I'm telling you the truth. Tavish MacLean willed me this box with your sword and stuff in it. It came with a scroll and. . . . Never mind. Let me show it to you."

"Do so."

She nodded like a bobble-headed doll. "No problem, but please, can you let go of my arm?" Her fingers were numb.

He grunted and released her. "Which way?"

Claire eased out from behind the desk and reluctantly led him back to the storage room. Before the large elaborate box that had once been secured in bubble wrap, she stopped and pointed. "There."

He squat before the box and ran his hand over the hieroglyphs. As if to himself he mumbled, "I ken this, but how?"

"Do you know what the symbols mean?"

"Aye, they're celestial symbols, verra auld." He rocked back on his haunches. "This was given to ye by a MacLean?"

"Yes. There's more. Another box and a scroll written in Gael. They're upstairs."

He rose and held out a massive paw. "After ye."

"I'll bring them down—"

He palmed the short blade as his gaze shifted around the room. "Nay, ye lead the way and I shall follow."

And follow he did. So close on her heels she could feel the heat emanating from him, caught the scent of him again.

As they stepped onto the second-floor landing, her

tenant's door suddenly opened. Before Claire could cry out in warning, she found herself being hauled backward and up against her intruder's side.

"Claire, I just baked—Oh my, who's this?"

Her white hair still encased in pink foam rollers, a crumb cake in her hands, Mrs. Grouse eyed the Highlander approvingly, then frowned, looking at Claire. "Should I call the police, dear?"

"No! No, no, that won't be necessary, Mrs. Grouse."

The last thing she needed was the police. The Highlander, already agitated and confused, would likely hold her hostage. As much to free herself as to reassure Mrs. Grouse that all was well, Claire elbowed the Highlander in the ribs. His grasp on her waist loosened, and she jerked away only to stumble. When his hand shot out to steady her, she knocked it away. "Mrs. Grouse, this is Cameron MacLeod, a . . . friend, who'll be leaving. Soon."

"Oh." Mrs. Grouse's bright blue gaze wandered over the Highlander again before settling on his feet. "Have you no boots, young man?"

MacLeod eyed Claire in accusing fashion. "Nay, mistress. 'Twould appear I've lost them."

"Oh. That will never do. Wait right there." Before Claire could protest, her renter shoved the cake into MacLeod's hands and disappeared.

Glaring up at him, Claire hissed, "Don't even *think* about harming her. She has nothing to do with this."

MacLeod grunted and poked a finger into the cake as one might poke a carcass, then sniffed it. "I hadnae intention of doing so."

Right. "Like you had no intention of hurting me."

She pushed up a sleeve and displayed the bruise he'd inflicted on her right wrist just hours ago. "I'm serious. I'll—"

"Here you go, young man." Mrs. Grouse stood in the doorway holding out a pair of glossy black galoshes decorated with a line of equally glossy metal buckles, white socks poking out of the tops. "They should fit. My Henry had the feet and hands of a man twice his size." She winked at Claire. "Was one of the reasons I married him, if you get my drift."

"Ah." Never having thought to imagine the recently departed Mr. Grouse's genitals but doing so now, Claire shuddered, grabbed the boots then took hold of the wide belt encircling the Highlander's waist and tugged. "Thanks for the boots and cake, Mrs. Grouse. You're the best."

To her annoyance, MacLeod remained rooted in place. "Mistress, my humble thanks."

Mrs. Grouse, her hands over her heart, beamed up at him. "Such a nice young man."

Not.

Claire tugged on his belt again in hopes of moving him toward the stairs. "We really need to go."

Instead of taking the hint, Cameron took one of Mrs. Grouse's hands in his and kissed her knuckles as he bowed. "Good day to ye, mistress. And my thanks again."

Claire pointed up the stairs and growled, "Now, MacLeod."

Halfway up the last flight, he said, "Lovely auld lass, but the worms do naught for her countenance."

Worms? Oh. "They're curlers."

"Curlers. Humph. I dinna like them."

"No one said you were supposed to."

Claire heaved a sigh the moment they entered her apartment. Cameron did as well, then bolted the door, grabbed Claire by the arm and ignoring her squawk of outrage, strode to the window and peered out. Finding the street blessedly empty, he let go of her arm and then turned his attention to the delicious-smelling cake in his hand. He broke off a hunk and popped it in his mouth. Ah, heaven. He broke off another piece. "The box and scroll, if you please."

The lass dropped the odd boots the auld woman had so graciously given him onto a chair and pointed with a shaking hand to her bedchamber. "In there."

He put down the cake and waved her ahead of him, anxious to get to the bottom of this insanity and get back to Rubha.

In her bedchamber, Claire lined the objects she'd spoken of across her bed covering.

He picked up the box. Naught about it looked familiar but something rattled within. He tried to open it, and failing, put it down and picked up the scroll. As it unrolled, he recognized Minnie's hand, a tight script done in a backward slant. Only she made the letter B just so. More unsettling, the verse held no meaning for him.

"Here's Tavish's letter. It may help."

He looked up to find Claire holding out a bright white piece of paper. Finding only her name on the front, he flipped it over and saw another piece of paper cleverly secured within the outer sheet. He pulled the second out. As he read, blood thudded in his ears and with the thudding came images of Tall Thomas's seaside croft, of candles and fire, of drinking wine and then . . . naught.

"Damn the woman!"

At his side, Claire MacGregor jumped a foot.

His mother had lulled him with a bloody lie! Had told him she was merely casting a spell of protection. How could she have done this to him? And why?

He tossed the missive onto the bed and glared at Claire. "Send me back."

How much time had he lost? Four centuries couldna have possibly passed. More important, had the battles already begun? Had the clan joined the Stuarts?

Claire scampered backward, her hands before her. "I don't know how to send you back. I just opened the box and then . . . there you were."

Ha! A witch, then. Two of a kind, his Minnie and this Claire. When he found his way home, Mhairie Elizabeth Stewart would rue the day she ever drew breath.

"Woman, undo that which ye've done!"

"But I didn't *do* anything . . . other than open the box." The lass, her eyes bright with unshed tears, began edging toward the doorway, escape doubtless on her mind.

He sidestepped, blocking her path. Placing his hands on his hips, he puffed out his chest and glowered, giving her the look that had loosened many a strong man's bowels and tongue.

He waited. And waited.

Ack. He leaned over her, bringing his nose close to

hers and caught the scent of vanilla and lavender. It suited her, petite as she was, like purple on heather, and did naught to mask the scent of frightened woman about her.

"Lass, do it."

She tottered backward, tripped, and landed with a thump on a wooden chest. She took a shuddering breath. "Trust me, I would if I could, just to be rid of you, but I *don't . . . know . . . how.*"

He picked up the small box and dropped it into her lap. "Open it again."

"I need a pin to do it."

He backed a step, and she reached for the wicker basket she'd stumbled over. After removing a needle, the thinnest he'd ever seen, she turned the box in her hands, poking here and there, in an order apparently known only to her if Tavish MacLean's missive was to be believed.

One side popped up and he snatched it from her hands.

With breath caught, his muscles taught, braced and ready for whatever might happen, he pulled the raised side.

To his raging disappointment, naught changed save for his having an acorn in his hand.

Christ's blood. And he kenned this acorn. Minnie. She'd placed this about his neck. Aye, only hours before summoning him to Tall Thomas's croft. But there hadna been words inscribed on the acorn then. Only a few small spirals.

He read the inscription aloud.

From the chest, Claire MacGregor asked, "What does it mean?"

"*Breathe, my heart.*"

Claire sniffed. "Well, you certainly did."

He looked at her, the fine hairs on his arms rising. "Ye said these words?"

Claire nodded, her finely arched brows tenting above her aquiline nose. "I'm sorry."

Aye. And would be more so if she didna reverse this spell. But how to convince her to do so without incapacitating her? Ah, his fief for a rack. The mere sight of one would surely turn her tongue loose and have her do his bidding.

"Mister, I've got a bear of a headache. I need food and more important, I need coffee. Would you mind? Eating, I mean, before we worry any more about getting you back to where you belong? Wherever the hell that might be."

Not waiting for an answer, the witch sidled past him, muttering, "I could skin you, Tavish MacLean. I swear to God I could."

Claire pulled eggs, coffee, and bacon from the refrigerator and utensils from drawers, keeping a watchful eye on the Highlander while he sliced through the string securing the newspaper to his feet.

God, he was huge, even kneeling.

His stomach suddenly rumbled, the sound making him seem more human. Claire pointed to a white container. "Throw the papers in there, then take a seat while I make something to eat."

"The cake will do."

"I seriously doubt it."

Having been responsible for her family's supper since her early teens, she slung bowls and skillets about with practiced ease while he stood, tall and silent, tracking her every move. Did he honestly think she'd be stupid enough to lunge at him with a paring knife? He'd have it out of her hand and her wrist broken in a heartbeat.

It took several minutes of her ignoring him, but finally he rolled his shoulders and sat where she'd indicated.

Feeling more relaxed now that he was and soothed by mundane routine, she turned on the stove. When the perfect blue flame licked the bottom of the skillet, she heard him gasp, looked over her shoulder and found him scowling.

"It's a gas stove. Turn a knob and instant fire. Everyone has one. It's nothing special."

"Humph."

The thick, apple-smoked bacon she purchased in a Faneuil Hall Marketplace began sputtering, filling the room with its mouthwatering scent. "How do you like your eggs?"

"Cooked."

She heaved a sigh. "Scrambled it is."

A few minutes later, she placed their breakfast on the table, handed him some cutlery and took the seat opposite him. "Dig in."

She swallowed a second mouthful and looked up, surprised to see Cameron watching her, his hands still in his lap. "You don't like bacon and eggs?"

"Aye, I do." He glanced down, murmured something in Gael, picked up his fork, examined it front and back, then began to eat in a quick and efficient manner. Hmm, table manners. A moment later, he murmured, "'Tis verra good."

"Thank you. You were worried that I'd poison you, huh?"

He fought a grin. "Never entered my thoughts."

"Ya." She grinned for the first time in what felt like days.

Having come to a truce of sorts, they ate in companionable silence.

When their plates were empty, she rose, refilled their mugs with coffee and resumed her seat and stared at him.

The man had to have the most attractive eyes she'd ever seen. Framed by thick, sweeping lashes, they were the color of Flow Blue china. Deep blue with flecks of silvery white. And that square jaw and chin . . . movie idol material. The muscles of his shoulders and arms rolled as he brought the coffee to his finely crafted lips and something warm flashed in her middle. Yup, this man sitting across from her was definitely the stuff of dreams.

Without looking up from his plate, he said, "Ye look at me as if ye've never seen a man before, lass."

"That's because I've never seen a man quite like you before."

"Humph. Highlanders are scarce in these parts?"

"Yes." Of your kind, at any rate.

He appeared to give that some thought, then asked, "Where is yer husband?"

She straightened, his comment tossing ice water on her daydreaming with the reminder that she lived alone and was vulnerable.

Dare she lie? Say that her dear hubby was traveling and would return today? The Highlander had likely noted there wasn't a hint of a man within her apartment—no clothing, no shaving gear. "I don't have one."

"My sympathies on yer loss, mistress."

"Please call me Claire, and thank you, but I've never been married."

He glanced at her hands and the modest pearl ring she wore, a sweet-sixteen birthday gift from her mother. "Engaged then?"

She shook her head. "No. I've never been engaged either."

"Humph. 'Tis because ye're a witch?"

Her laugh was more of a bark. "No, I'm not a witch, although a few of my customers might tell you otherwise when I won't negotiate my prices."

His eyes narrowed as he tipped his head to study her, his gaze finally settling on her breasts. "So when do ye expect yer patron to call?"

"My patron?" Oh good Lord! He thought she was a kept woman. "I'm *not* a mistress. I'm an antique dealer. Downstairs . . . that's my shop. The Velvet Pumpkin. I buy and sell furniture, china, and the like." She shook her head.

Looking aghast, he grumbled, "I humbly beg yer pardon. I've inadvertently insulted ye, lass, but given yer wealth and bonnie green eyes and . . . other parts, I'd just assumed . . ."

She had bonnie green eyes and other parts? Who

knew? "There's no need to apologize." Truth to tell, she'd been flattered that he thought her attractive enough to be *maintained*. Tracy, ya. Claire MacGregor, never.

Wanting to know more about him, she said, "Tell me about your home, where you once lived."

"Live, lass." He looked toward the window. "It had snowed there during the night as well, but gently. The parapets are crowned with only a hand's width of white; the scent of peat smoke and sea hangs in the air. The cattle, down from the high pasture and growing round in the fold, can be heard for miles at gloaming when the winds turned seaward."

When he grew silent, Claire, longing to hear his deep-timbered burr again, prodded, "And your family?"

"Da is a chieftain, laird of our clan and of Rubha. I've two half-brothers. Robbie, the eldest, is our steward and John," he grinned, flashing great dimples at her, "is the wit. Both are married and have bairns."

"You miss them."

"Aye, I do, but more I fash over them." He was silent for another moment, then asked, "The map below . . . is it true?"

Map? Oh, the one she'd showed him on the computer. "Yes."

"I've seen maps of the colonies before, kenned the West Indies isles as well, but hadna realized this place was so vast." After a moment he asked, "And your king? Is he of the Stuart line?"

Oh crap. Here goes our peaceful interlude. Now he'll ask about Scotland and grow agitated again.

"We no longer have kings. Haven't had one since

the Revolutionary War in 1776 when we defeated the British."

"Truly?" He grinned, the news apparently pleasing him.

"Truly. We're a democratic republic with elected presidents. One citizen, one vote. The candidate with the greatest number of votes wins." There was no point in going into the electoral college.

"As in Roman times. Interesting. So how did we fare in our uprising? Did Prince Charles become king?"

Oh God, dare she tell him? If she couldn't return him to his own place and time, he'd learn the truth anyway. "I'm sorry, but the Jacobite uprising was . . . a monumental failure and was the last of its kind. The Scots have been ruled, have been English citizens for centuries."

He rose abruptly, the chair crashing behind him, his face a livid red, his fists balled as he loomed over her. "Nay!"

Chapter Five

"Ye lie!" Had the Highlanders lost a battle they'd have withdrawn and regrouped as they always did, but never would they have rolled over like lapdogs. And what of the French? Surely they would have come to Scotland's aid. Eventually sent troops, if not an armada.

He strode toward Claire, ashen and shaking, backed up against the wall. "Tell me all ye ken, lass."

The more he knew, could take back with him, the more likely he could turn the tide of battle.

She swallowed convulsively, her hands out. "I don't know all that much."

Intent on frightening the truth out of her, he growled deep in his throat.

In response she sputtered, "The death toll among the Jacobite forces, mostly Highlanders, was horrendous. They were tired, hungry, poorly equipped and badly outnumbered by the time they reached Culloden. Sometime during the battle—when it became apparent the cause was lost—Prince Charlie told the chiefs it was over and ran. He escaped to the Isle of

Skye dressed as a lady's maid with the help of a woman named Flora MacDonald, never to return. He died in exile. I don't recall the year."

Friggin' bloody bastard! To call his subjects to arms and then run. The cowardly French prick.

Hard pressed not to slam his fists into the wall, he growled, "And what of those he left behind?" What had happened to his clan? To the neighboring clans?

Claire shook her head. "The British general—I forget his name—went down in history as the 'Butcher.' All the Highlanders on the battlefield were killed. After that, the British hanged or deported many men, leaving the women and children to fend for themselves. What chiefs remained lost their power to govern. The history books call the postwar period The Clearance."

"A fucking *Clearance*?"

Imagining the murder, rape, and pillage an unchecked English army would do storming through his homeland, fury the likes of which he'd never experienced bloomed in his chest. Turned his blood molten. His fists hit the wall, rattling the windows, sinking deep into the plaster and slats of wood beneath. Between his outstretched arms, Claire shrieked.

Christ's blood.

With tears burning at the back of his throat and eyes, blood roaring in his ears, he backed away, needing air.

He strode to the parlor and Claire ran after him. "Where are you going?"

"*Out*."

Where didna matter. He just needed space, a place to think, to breathe.

"At least put these on." Claire stood with the odd boots in her hands. "Here. Please? You'll catch your death."

He snatched them from her hands and jerked open the door. Halfway down the stairs he met Mrs. Grouse, her expression worried.

Without slowing, he jerked his head toward Claire's apartment. "She's unharmed."

Mrs. Grouse, her back pressed to the wall, eyed him warily as he thundered past.

Two hours later, Cameron sat on a long pier staring at vessels the likes of which he'd never imagined. They made slow progress without benefit of sail through the choppy gray channel before him. Towering ships of iron crewed by nary a man, accompanied by a few soaring gulls.

Huddled against a biting wind, he pulled the cloak he'd taken from the pile of garments he'd found on Claire's storage room floor tighter about him and brushed the errant tears from his cheeks.

Aye, he was in the year two thousand and seven as Claire had said, for all about him was too bizarre to be simply foreign. But there wasna a way in hell he'd slept for four hundred years. No man could live so long no matter what Claire MacGregor claimed. He'd be dead. Mummified. 'Twas magic, pure and simple, that had pulled him through time, and by God that same magic would return him to his home and clan.

He simply had to wait Claire MacGregor out.

And he'd take all the knowledge he could garner from this age with him back to his people. If he had to talk himself blue in the face he would make Da and the rest listen to reason for 'twould be the only way to prevent the defeat of his clan and *The Clearance*.

The word alone turned his gut to fire, bringing fresh tears.

Worse, he didna need history texts to ken that the horde of Sassenach, their blood hot after battle, wouldna have simply confiscated the Highlanders' cattle and flocks, but would have decimated their winter stores, then torched as many keeps as possible. Minnie, frail as she was, wouldna have been able to run. Nor would she have survived a blow, much less starvation. And his sisters by marriage, young and bonnie, would have been raped if caught. The bairns . . . he shuddered to think of what the wee ones had witnessed, had any survived.

Please God, let some have survived.

His clan had nearly been decimated in '51, had never fully recouped, and was now a sept under the protection of the MacDonald. Had those who remained of his kin been killed?

Thunk, thunk.

Cameron looked over his shoulder and found two men—one nearly as tall as he, the other shorter but burly—dressed in like livery of dark blue coming toward him. Behind them on the carriageway sat a black and white horseless carriage with flashing lights identical to the one he'd seen in front of Claire's home. The authorities.

"Sir," the tallest of the two shouted, "can't you read? The sign says no loitering."

Cameron turned his back to the pair. He wasna loitering but thinking.

"Hey, I'm talking to you, big guy."

Cameron blew through his teeth and rose to find the men, knee deep in snow, only yards from him. "What ails ye? I'm doing nae harm to anyone or anything."

"On his back," the burly fellow mumbled.

The taller pointed at him. "Sir, is that sword real?"

"Aye. What else would it be?"

"Sir, it's against the law to carry a concealed weapon."

Were they daft? "Ye see the sword, so there isna a thing concealed about it."

"You're going to have to hand it over."

"Nay. 'Tis mine."

The shorter of the two reached for the small black box resting on his shoulder. "Echo 12. We need backup."

As he continued to mutter, the taller man pulled a long black box from his belt. "Look, mister, we don't want any trouble. Just hand over the sword and your ID."

Eye-dee. Claire had used the word but he still had no idea what it meant. He huffed, too cold and emotionally drained to argue. If they wanted him gone, so be it. "Step aside and I'll take my leave."

The shorter of the two mumbled to his friend, "Backup's on the way." To Cameron he said, "No one's going anywhere, sir, until we see some ID and you hand over that sword."

Were they friggin' deaf? "I'll hand over naught."

Cam shrugged and his borrowed cloak fell to the snow, leaving his bare arms free and his sword at the ready. They wanted trouble? Trouble they'd have. Perhaps a fight would rid him of his pent-up fury.

In a voice one might use when speaking to a bairn, the shorter one said, "Look, buddy, all we want is a name."

"The name is Cameron MacLeod of Rubha."

"Okay, Cameron MacLeod of Rubha, why are you standing out here half-naked looking like an escapee from *Macbeth*?"

Macbeth? Cameron glanced left and right and seeing only a lone seagull squatting on a piling, humphed. Ah, the man was taunting him with Shakespeare. Not a good thing given his current frame of mind. "Leave me be and I'll go."

"Put your hands over your head," the taller of the two ordered as he aimed the black box at Cameron's chest.

Fine with him. Cameron raised his arms, elbows bent, his right hand grabbing his backsword's hilt. The squatter man—now holding what appeared to be some form of pistol—shouted, "Knife! Left arm."

Christ's blood! He pulled his backsword free and metal struck his chest. What . . . ?

Searing pain, hot and vicious, raced through his trunk and limbs. As his knees inexplicably buckled and the world went black, he heard the unmistakable clatter of metal on stone. He'd dropped his sword. Something he hadna done since being a bairn.

Chapter Six

"Come on, Sleeping Beauty, move!"

Someone grabbed Cameron's arms, sending pain radiating across his chest. He opened his eyes and discovered he was on his back on a bench in a small, strange compartment. What the hell—?

"I said move it."

Not liking the man's tone, Cameron made an effort to swing a fist only to realize his hands were bound behind him. Blood surged into trapped muscles as his alarm grew.

The man pulled him backward out of the coach. When his feet hit the ground, Cameron looked around and recognized the two men as those who had challenged him at the sea wall, who'd fired the painful metal darts at his chest. The shorter of the two took hold of his left arm while the taller took hold of his right.

"Come on, Macbeth. The stun gun didn't do that much damage."

Not about to be dragged anywhere by anyone, least

of all by those who'd disarmed him so easily, Cameron fell backward, kicking, and connected with the shorter man's face.

"God damn it!"

Cameron's satisfaction in landing the blow was short lived, thanks to something hard and thick catching him in the ribs. Before he could regain his breath—or his feet—another blow landed in his middle. He was rolled and a knee landed in the middle of his back. Strong hands gripped his neck and hair, forcing the right side of his face onto the rough pavement. He then felt a pistol press his temple.

"Move and I'll blow your fucking brains all over the sidewalk. Got it?"

Not doubting the man would, given Cameron had spread his friend's nose all over his face, he ceased struggling.

"Get the damn cuffs on his ankles," the man sitting on his back shouted.

Once they had him shackled hand and foot, they hauled him to his feet, and grabbing him from either side, marched him up the icy steps and into the red brick building.

Cameron squinted against the glare of the overhead lamps in the hot building where he was led past an open window and into a large room where they shoved him toward a chair.

The men arresting him separated and the tall man ordered, "Sit."

Having no choice, Cameron sat.

The taller shrugged out of his coat, threw it onto the back of his chair, and took a seat. He then said, "Name."

Looking about, wondering why bells were ringing, he said, "MacLeod. Sir Cameron MacLeod."

The man banged on a glossy black pallet covered in buttons, a thing much like the one Claire MacGregor had. "Address."

Someone shouted and Cameron looked over his shoulder. Another official was hauling in a skinny man, his skin the color of burnt wood. Having heard there were such dark-skinned people but never having seen one, Cameron followed the man's jerky progress across the room to another desk. Behind him came two women with the gaudiest hair—one purple, the other silver—he'd ever seen. The purple-headed woman, noticing his stare, elbowed her friend. "Hey, Shelley, check out Braveheart."

"MacLeod! Pay attention. We haven't got all night."

Cameron turned his attention back to the man interrogating him. "What?"

"Address?"

"Castle Rubha."

The man leaned forward and glared at him. "Look, shithead, we can do this the hard way or we can do it the easy way. What will it be?"

Given the shackles and the condition of his ribs—the man had managed to land three more blows on the way up the stairs—Cameron growled, "The easy."

"Good." The sheriff placed his hands back on the buttons and said, "Address."

"Castle Rubha, Rubha, Scotland."

The man glared at him again. "Here, in Boston."

Since he wasn't staying anywhere, Cameron gave him Claire's shop name and street.

"Got a house number?"

Cameron shook his head.

"Date of birth."

"Hogmanay, the year of our Lord, 1716."

"*What?*"

Cam blew through his teeth. His English wasna apparently as good as he'd thought. That or this man—Joe O'Brian, according to his badge—was as deaf as a stone. Enunciating clearly and slowly, he repeated, "On Hogmanay, the last day of each year. In 1716."

Banging on the buttons, Joe O'Brian muttered, "Why am I always the one stuck doing the paperwork on the space cadets?" He then asked, "Occupation?"

"Sitting . . . in shackles." Ye friggin' cattle shit.

O'Brian gave him a baleful look. "What do you do for a living?"

"I'm a soldier." Leastwise he was before he awoke in this God-forsaken place.

"Oooh-kay." O'Brian banged on the buttons for a moment, then asked, "Next of kin in case of emergency?"

Wondering what constituted an emergency if being shackled and beaten did not, Cameron said, "I have none."

"Look, I need a name, someone we can notify should you keel over dead."

A lovely thought. But should he die, he'd be taking one of these bastards with him. But then, should something worse await him in this building, who'd bury him? He kenned only one person here. "Claire MacGregor."

He gave O'Brian the rest of the information he requested. He was told to stand and was hauled into another room where they placed him against a wall and gave him a plaque to hold. Bright lights flashed in his eyes.

"Face left," the woman said. The lights flashed again. Not a minute later his hands were coated in ink and pressed onto paper.

They then marched him into a white tiled room where O'Brian said to another man, "He's gotta be on something. Do a cavity search."

O'Brian left grinning.

The new man—squat, about fifty, and also in livery—tossed a white crate onto the table before Cameron. "Put all your personal possessions in the box. Jewelry, belt, all of it."

Cameron held out his shackled wrists. "I canna get the cuff or brooch off with my hands like this."

"Fine." The man undid the brooch and lifted the brass cuff from his wrist and put them in the box. He then pulled the belt from Cameron's waist and his breachen feile fell away.

The man grinned. "Well, that certainly answers an age-old question about what you guys wear under a kilt."

Bastard. Not that Cameron had anything to be ashamed of.

The man tossed his plaid into the basket and told Cameron to take off his boots. As Cameron dropped them into the box, the man pulled on thin, white gloves.

After running his hands through the back of Cameron's hair, he said, "Open your mouth and lift your tongue."

Not liking it one bit for his teeth were sound as any man's, Cameron did, and the man looked inside.

"Okay, turn around."

Huffing, Cameron turned.

"Now bend over and spread your legs."

"*Bugger that!*" Cameron rolled and this time kicked with both feet.

Claire ran her hand over the new glass in the Velvet Pumpkin's front door. "At least it was only one pane this time."

"Ya." The glazier closed his toolbox and pulled out a receipt book. "Here you go."

Claire took the bill from his outstretched hand. "Four hundred? But you only charged me three-fifty last time."

"Sorry, but it's Sunday. Overtime."

Cursing under her breath, Claire wrote out the check.

The man gone and the alarms on, she continued grumbling as she climbed the back staircase to her apartment, where Mrs. Grouse patiently waited, the floor swept, and fresh coffee was brewing.

As she tossed the bill into her mounting stack of to-be-filed-in-this-lifetime, Mrs. Grouse said, "Here you go, dear."

Claire caught the unmistakable scent of anisette as her hands wrapped around a warm coffee mug Mrs. Grouse held out to her. "Bless you."

"You're welcome. Is the door fixed?"

"Ya." She flopped down onto the kitchen chair

Cameron MacLeod had sat on only hours earlier, and Mrs. Grouse settled across from her. "Will you look at my wall? I just finished painting the damn thing. When his fists flew past my ears, I thought . . . God, I don't know what I thought, but I've never been so frightened in my life."

Mrs. Grouse clucked as she, too, examined the craters MacLeod had left in the plaster. "Well, at least it's fixable."

"Ya, but this situation isn't. He's out there, confused, furious, and no doubt running amok."

"I doubt it, dear. If he is who you fear he is—and I must tell you your tale stretches the bounds of belief even for me—then he's developing a plan of escape, a means of returning to his own time and place. He's a warrior, and from what you've told me, lives depend on his doing so."

Claire nodded. "Precisely, which will make him desperate."

Mrs. Grouse tapped her fingers on the table for a moment. "You have no idea where he might have gone?"

"None." Claire looked at the clock again. Seven hours. She never should have told him about The Clearances. Should have lied or at least waited until—

Brrrrring

Claire lunged for the phone hanging by the refrigerator. "Hello?"

A gruff baritone said, "Ms. Claire MacGregor, please."

"This is she."

"This is Sergeant Tillis at the 23rd Precinct. Do you know a Cameron MacLeod?"

Oh no. "Yes. Is he all right?"

"He's been arrested and charged with carrying a concealed weapon and resisting arrest. Would you like to come down and bail him out? He's combative and . . . confused."

She could well imagine. "I'll be right there."

Given what he was likely telling the police, if she didn't get him out of there, they'd ship him off to Bridgewater and throw away the keys.

After scribbling down the directions to the station house, Claire hung up. "He's in jail."

Her tenant tsked. "So I gathered. Now what?"

"I have to bail him out." For how much, she hadn't a clue. She'd forgotten to ask.

Tavish, if you were here . . .

Claire picked up the phone again, called for a taxi, then ran into the living room, where she pulled her coat from the closet and picked up her purse. "Do you think they take credit cards?"

Mrs. Grouse grinned. "I'm sure they do, but if you need cash, I have some stashed in my sugar bowl."

Doubting they had enough cash between them to pay for the taxi, much less bail, Claire gave Mrs. Grouse a hug. "Thanks, but I have some. I'll be back . . . sometime."

"Just go. I'll have supper waiting for you when you get back."

Claire nodded, the knot in her stomach tightening at the very thought of food.

When the taxi arrived, she scrambled inside and

was immediately assaulted by the stench of curry and garlic, made worse by the taxi's heater set on high.

"Where to?" Her turban-headed driver studied her through black, soulful eyes in the rearview mirror.

Wondering if the man had ever seen snow—much less had experience driving in it before today—she gave him directions and searched between the seat cushions for the seatbelt as they fishtailed away from the curb.

Why couldn't you have sent me a Russian?

Thirty minutes later, they pulled up before the precinct station house and Claire handed over her fare. "Next time you spin out, take your foot off the brake and steer into the slide, okay?"

But for a well-placed snowbank and mailbox, they'd have landed in a Macy's display window.

The taxi driver grinned as he took the cash from her hand. "Yes, I shall, but you must admit it was rather exciting for a moment, was it not?"

Not.

Her legs still shaking from her near brush with death, Claire climbed the salt-coated precinct house stairs. Inside, she stopped before a glass-fronted cubicle that bore the sign *Check In.* "Excuse me."

A thick-necked officer of about fifty looked up from his paperwork and leaned toward his microphone. "May I help you?"

"I'm Claire MacGregor, here to bail out Cameron MacLeod." Good God, never in her life had she ever imagined herself bailing out anybody. Well, maybe Tracy . . .

"One moment." He rifled through a vertical file,

then picked up the phone. A moment later, he hung up and pointed to a long wooden bench that was bolted to the floor and above which hung a No Smoking sign. But the place reeked of smoke. "Wait over there. Someone will be with you in a minute."

A minute turned out to be thirty as she watched one unhappy perp after another being led in by red-faced officers and then hauled away.

"Claire MacGregor?"

Claire jerked and found a middle-aged woman in a gray pantsuit standing in an open doorway to her left. "Yes?"

"This way, please."

Claire followed the woman down an industrial green hallway, where she stopped before an open window and slid the manila folder she'd been carrying onto the counter. "This officer will help you."

Sgt. Babcock, a young officer, opened the file, then studied her for a moment. "Are you here to bail out Cameron MacLeod?"

"Yes." She hoped. It all depended on how much they'd charge for the dubious privilege.

"Are you a relative?"

"No, just a friend." *Sort of.*

He turned the paperwork around so she could read it. "It says here that he's been charged with loitering, carrying a concealed weapon, refusal to show proper identification, resisting arrest, and three counts of assaulting an officer."

Three?

"After his arraignment," the officer continued, "bail was—"

"Wait. He's been arraigned? But what about a lawyer?"

"He had a court-appointed attorney present." He flipped a page and used his pen as a pointer. "Says here his court date has been set for March 4, 2008. Have him at the county court house by 8:00 A.M. Here's the address and a map. His bail has been set at $5,000."

Oh. My. God. Totally out of her element, she asked, "Do you take credit cards?"

"Yes, ma'am, we do, but if it's a hardship, I can provide you with a list of bail bondsmen."

Picturing a shabby office stinking of cigar smoke, filled with sweaty, drugged-out felons and wanted posters, Claire shook her head, pulled out her wallet and held out her business credit card. "Here."

As he ran her card through the machine, the door to her left opened and Cameron MacLeod came through, looking none the better for his brush with the law.

Dressed in a too-small yellow jumpsuit and paper slippers, his hair disheveled, his thick wrists bound in handcuffs, her warrior looked like hell as he shuffled toward her.

Seeing a large abrasion on his left cheek and bruises on his neck as he drew near, Claire's heart constricted despite all he'd put her through. She reached up and touched his cheek. "Are you all right?"

He cast a scathing glance toward the tall, barrel-chested officer at his side. "Aye." He then shifted his attention back to her. "I'm surprised you've come."

She sighed. "So am I." Taking in his ill-fitting jump-suit, she asked, "Where are your clothes?"

"They took them."

The officer at his side pulled a set of keys from his belt and reached for Cameron's shackled wrists. "They're at the desk."

Cameron scowled. "My breachen feile wouldna stay put without the belt and well they kenned it, but they took it anyway."

"Ms. MacGregor?" She looked over her shoulder. The sergeant was waving her back to the window. Cameron and the officer followed.

The sergeant pushed her credit card receipt, and another form toward her. "Sign there and there, af-firming that you're taking custody of the defendant and offering assurances that he'll show up for his court date. If he doesn't, you forfeit your $5,000."

Cameron, rubbing the red marks on his freed wrists, leaned over her shoulder to scan the form. "How much is this in pounds?"

Claire signed on the dotted lines. "I'm not sure. Maybe three thousand."

To his credit, Cameron looked horrified. "Ye're jest-ing, surely?"

"I wish I were." She slid the completed form toward the officer.

He then passed a pen and a stack of papers toward Cameron. After explaining each form, he said, "Sir, look these over and sign at the bottom."

Cameron picked up the pen, examined it from every angle, clicked it innumerable times, then scrawled his name in handsome cursive across the bottom of the page—without reading a word.

The man was a menace to himself.

Apparently thinking the same, the sergeant rolled his eyes and placed a large plastic crate on the counter. "These are your possessions, Mr. MacLeod. Check to be sure nothing is missing and sign this form."

"Where's my sword?" MacLeod rifled through the contents of the crate, then tore open a small paper bag he found in the crate, dumping his brooch and brass cuff onto the counter. "And my sgian duhb?"

"Your what?"

"The short blade, man."

"Ah. The evidence. They'll remain in the Property Room until after the trial."

To her alarm, Cameron's jaw muscles began twitching and his already impressive chest suddenly puffed, straining the seams of the bright yellow garment he was crammed into. "Evidence of *what*?" he demanded. He then turned to her, his indignation and ire obviously on the rise. "I swear I didna do anything to warrant—"

Claire gripped his arm. "Cameron, honey, listen to me. This nice man is letting us *go*. Let's not cause any more trouble. You'll get your sword and blade back later." She shoved the form toward him. "Just sign this and let's get out of here."

Claire held her breath when Cameron closed his eyes, his thick black lashes lying like fans across high cheekbones. When the thick muscles of his forearm began to relax beneath her hand, she dared to exhale. He finally opened his eyes and nodded. "Aye, later."

Thank God! Now to get him dressed and out of here. To the officer at his side, she said, "Where can he change?" She could worry about hiring a lawyer later.

"Over there."

When Cameron, crate in hand, disappeared into the men's room, the officer asked, "Is he mentally ill?"

"Uhmm . . . no. I mean not really." Think, Claire! "He worked construction, fell from scaffolding. He hasn't been right in the head since. Last week, he was the President. This week he's Robert the Bruce. But he's harmless, really."

The officer grunted. "Tell that to my partner. He's at Mass General, nursing a broken nose."

Oh shit, not good. "I'm *so* sorry."

The officer snorted derisively. "Not as sorry as your friend is, trust me."

"What do you mean by—"

"I'm ready."

At the sound of Cameron's voice, Claire spun and found him scowling, dressed as well as could be expected in a few yards of plaid, unbuckled galoshes, and a too-small trench coat hanging from his massive shoulders.

One more thing for her to-do list: Get him into some real clothes.

Without a word, she took him by the arm and headed out the door.

* * *

Cameron shook his head. "Nay, I shall walk."

No way would he be getting into the mechanical beast Claire had summoned with a wave of her hand and a shriek of a whistle.

From inside the yellow machine, Claire growled, "Cameron, it's been a long day. Get in."

"Nay." The last time he'd found himself in such a contraption, he'd been shackled, beaten, and then finger-buggered. He'd tolerated quite enough abuse for one day, thank ye verra much!

"Cameron, we're *not* walking home in the dark. Besides, it's getting colder and you're not dressed for it."

What dark? There were brilliant lights of every imaginable color glowing in every direction. And cold had never proved a problem for him. "You go on. I can find my way."

Claire huffed. "Did I or did I not just bail you out of jail?"

"Aye, ye did, and grateful I am." And he'd pay her back . . . somehow. Christ's blood, they'd charged her a king's ransom.

"To get you out, I swore that you'd follow the letter of the law until your court date. And by God I take my responsibilities seriously—particularly when I have $5,000 at stake, so please, pretty please, get in the damn taxi."

"But I havena intention of breaking any of yer laws."

"Ya, just like you had no intentions of breaking the law this afternoon."

He bristled—naught that had happened was in any way *his* fault—and she held up a hand. "Look, Cameron, I don't blame you. You didn't know the rules, so it's completely understandable that you got into trouble. If you come home with me now, I promise to teach you all you'll need to know."

All? "Are ye a woman of yer word, lass?"

"Yes . . . I *promise*."

He huffed and examined the latch on the door. After giving it a jiggle and satisfying himself that it would open from within, he climbed into the tight compartment.

Claire said to the driver, "Macy's, please."

With one knee pressed against the seat before him and the other cocked and pressed against Claire's slender thigh, he asked, "Are all coaches called taxis?"

She sighed as they started to roll down the snow-packed carriageway. "Only the yellow ones. See that line of black and white vehicles with the red and blue lights on top over there? Those are called squad cars. They belong to the police and are to be avoided at all costs."

"Aye." And well he kenned it. They didna have latches on the inside so one might escape.

"The rest," she said, "like that red one coming toward us, are privately owned. We just call them cars."

"Cars. Do ye ken how to maneuver such?" He had to learn if he was trapped in this place for any length of time.

"Yes, I have a license to drive, but can't afford to own one. I use the MTA—our mass transportation system—or taxis."

Ack, this place was a confusion.

As they turned left onto a main thoroughfare, his breath caught gazing up at dozens of brightly lit buildings that he'd seen only from afar, all so high and closely packed they appeared to be mountains.

At his side, Claire murmured, "We call them skyscrapers. This is the financial district. Most of these buildings house businesses that deal with the stock exchange, insurance, or banking."

Ah, they had such business in Edinburgh. "Most impressive." How men built so high, however, was beyond kenning.

"We're coming up on the retail—ah, market—district."

Staring at the brightly lit, expansive windows, he shook his head in wonder, never having imagined anything so fanciful. Their driver suddenly swore and Cameron shifted his attention to their driver. Steering this machine certainly appeared easy enough. He leaned forward and saw that the driver pushed pedals much like those on a loom. Humph. Right pedal, go. Left pedal, brake, much like a hand brake on a wagon. Verra good. He could do this should the need arise.

As they passed yet another bearded man dressed in brilliant red ringing a bell, he murmured, "Ye seem to have an inordinate number of bishops about."

Claire's brow furrowed and she leaned toward him to look out the window. As her hair brushed his chin, he again caught the scent of lavender.

"Oh, those aren't bishops. They're volunteers dressed as Santa Claus—St. Nicholas. They work for the Salvation Army. See that bucket? People put money in it as they pass to help feed and house the homeless."

"Ah, 'tis an interesting method for collecting alms."

But an odd appearing saint to be sure. "Do ye pay taxes in the same fashion?" 'Twould be a far fairer system than the dictated—and often crippling—tithing his people endured.

Grinning, she straightened, taking her warmth and delicious scent with her. "No. I wish we did."

They came to a stop and Claire passed several green paper notes to the driver. "We get out here."

He lifted the latch, happy to unfold and stand on firm ground even if it be covered in slush, and offered Claire his hand. "My lady."

Looking somewhat surprised, she took it. "Thank you."

"Humph." *He* should be thanking her. And paying their fare.

She led him past two doorways and stopped at the third. Anxious to have a word in private with her, he placed a hand at the small of her back and guided her into the shop's alcove, out of the wind and away from the harried patrons going in and out. "Mistress, a word if ye please before we go in."

"Yes?"

God, he hated swallowing his pride, but it needed doing for if it were not for her . . .

"I didna ask the authorities to summon ye." He'd have rotted in that hell before stooping so low. "They did so of their own accord. But I do thank ye most humbly for coming and I promise to repay my outrageous ransom as soon as I'm able." Ack, he still couldna believe the amount the bloody buggering cattle shits had charged her for his release. Ye'd have thought he was blood royal.

She studied him for a moment, her head cocked to the side. "Really?"

"Aye, I most certainly will."

"All right, and given what we're going through I do wish you'd call me Claire instead of mistress."

She smiled then, the light in her eyes reflecting a compassion he didna deserve, but found warming none the less. More disturbing was realizing she was far too trusting and naïve for her own good. "Aye, but on the condition ye call me Cam."

"Cam it is. But we can talk more later. Right now we need to get you some clothes before you're arrested for indecent exposure."

Inside Macy's, Claire felt like a fox with a turkey stuck in its teeth as she hauled MacLeod . . . er, Cam—that would take a while to get used to—through the crowded racks, while other shoppers stopped to gawk at them. Accustomed to going unnoticed, the attention was unsettling and she tried to quicken her pace. MacLeod—Cam, on the other hand, apparently un-mindful of the stares he was generating, slowed to touch or gawk at everything they passed. Finally, she got to the wall of jeans. "You don't happen to know what size your waist is, do you?"

"Large?"

She rolled her eyes, then looked about. "Why is it you can never find a sales guy when you need one?"

She started rifling through the stacks. Thirty-three inseam? No, better go with the longest. Thirty-seven inches. Now for the waist. Finding a pair she thought might fit, she held them out. "These might work. What do you think?"

When she got no response she turned and found she'd been talking to air. "Cam? Cam!"

Where the hell had he gone?

She took off at a jog down the nearest aisle, her head swiveling like an oscillating fan on speed.

I'm gonna kill him if he's taken off on me. I swear to God I will!

"MacLeod!" Seeing a polished salesman fussing with the merchandise behind the tie counter, she shouted, "Have you see a tall guy in a kilt go by?"

"A striking man with long hair?"

"Ya." How many guys in plaid were there running around the store?

He grinned and pointed to his right. Claire immediately changed course. A moment later she came to a screeching halt behind a buzzing crowd standing at the foot of the escalators.

"Who do you think he is?" a woman asked.

Another grinned. "I don't know, but he can put those galoshes under my bed any day."

Muttering "Excuse me," Claire elbowed her way to the front and found Cam MacLeod loping up the escalator stairs, taking them three at a time.

What the hell was he doing?

When he hit the top, she shouted, "MacLeod!"

He turned and broke into a great grin, his fantastic dimples evident as he caught sight of her. "Claire!"

"Will you please get down here?"

"'Twill be right there." To her horror he leaped, his flying kilt giving every woman at the bottom an eyeful, caught the handrail on a hip and slid at lightning speed toward her.

As his feet hit the floor, he laughed and several people clapped. When he made a quick bow, the woman at her side heaved what could only be described as a wistful, *do-me-now* groan.

Good God, the man will be the death of me.

Grinning, he made his way toward her, his chest puffed, his arms held out like some conquering hero. "Have ye tried them, lass? They're bloody fantastic. Go all the way to the top."

Grinding her teeth, Claire latched onto his arm and hauled him back toward the dressing room. "Come on. We have to get you clothes before the store closes."

She snatched several sweaters from a rack and picked up the jeans she'd thrown on the display table when she'd realized he'd disappeared. "Here, take these and go in there and try them on."

Still grinning, he clucked her under the chin. "As ye lust."

Fighting a grin—he did look like a kid in his first candy store—she rolled her eyes. "Just do it."

Five minutes later he bellowed, "Claire!"

"What?"

"The trews dinna fit."

She stuck her head in the dressing room doorway. "What doesn't fit?"

"The bloody breeches!"

A deep voice behind her asked, "May I help you?"

Claire jerked around and found the impeccably dressed salesman who'd been straightening the tie display. "Yes. Would you mind going in there and finding out what he's complaining about?"

"I'd be delighted to."

"Thank you."

A moment later he heard Cam curse in three languages, then the salesman came out. Grinning, a tape measure strung around his neck, he told her, "The gentleman needs a relaxed fit. Those massive thighs, you know. I'll be back in a minute."

"Oh . . . thank you." Hell, what did she know about men's fashion?

The salesman returned, his arms loaded with what appeared to be half the garments in the men's department, and her heart sank. Picturing the damage Levi and Lauren were about to do to her credit card, she remained mute as the salesman waggled a package of black briefs at her, winked, then disappeared into the dressing room. A minute later he walked out. "I'll be at the cash register when you're ready to check out."

I bet you will. "Thank you."

"The pleasure was mine. It's not often I get to see that much man in the buff."

Augh, no wonder MacLeod was cursing.

She didn't have long to wait before Cam walked out, scowling and dressed in his plaid, a few garments draped over his arm. "These shall do."

"You all right?"

He nodded. "Ye live in a strange place, Claire. Verra strange."

Not wanting to know, she said, "Let's find you some shoes."

The task proved easier than she expected. He wore

a size thirteen and liked sneakers. But when he tried to put them into the galoshes, they just wouldn't go. She picked one up and looked inside. "No wonder. They're two sizes too small."

He grimaced as he looked at his feet. "That I did ken."

"Right." She forced a smile as she asked their hovering salesman, "May we see some boots?"

Outside, a package dangling from each wrist, Claire MacGregor pointed to her right. "The tall men's shop is down there. They should have a coat that fits you."

"Claire, I dinna need a coat. 'Tis not so cold and you've spent enough of yer coins already."

Dodging other shoppers, Claire yelled over the strains of "What Child Is This" coming from where he didna ken, "Trust me, you'll need one."

Cam grunted, his attention drawn to a shop window with more glossy mechanical devices than he'd seen in his lifetime. "Claire, is this—" he pointed to the shiny silver and black tube on a stand, "truly a telescope?" His father had one but this was like nothing he'd ever seen before.

She peered at the item he pointed to. "Yes, it's a high-powered one you can hook up to your computer."

He pointed to the odd chair. "And that?"

"It's a vibrating massage chair. This shop—Sharper Image—specializes in all sorts of things men want but don't need. Come on."

A moment later, he came to a stunned halt before

a gaily decorated window filled with beautiful man-nequins with huge white wings. "Claire!"

Several yards ahead of him, she looked back and then to the window where he, his jaw slack, pointed to the skimpy bits of scarlet lace strategically draped on the mannequins.

"What manner of shop is this?"

One corner of her lush lips quirked up. "The shop's called Victoria's Secret, and the garments are lingerie. What women with great bodies and lots of money wear under their clothes to entice the men in their lives. Now come on."

Hmm. He eyed Claire as she strode ahead of him, picturing her lovely hurdies in red. Aye, 'twould be a delight to see.

His grin vanished when his attention shifted to the two men with black hair and pierced countenances, who eyed him in much the same fashion as he eyed them. Was their sickly pallor and gaunt state due to a lack of nourishment? Or disease?

As they drew abreast, Cam slipped an arm about Claire and eased her closer to the building. The shorter of the two men hissed and the man sporting a steel loop through his nose like a prize bull laughed, displaying the longest eyeteeth Cam had ever seen in his life. Cursing his lack of a weapon, Cam growled loud enough for both to hear.

At his side, Claire looked up. "Did you say something?"

Cam glanced over his shoulder at the retreating pair. "Nay."

"Oh. It's closed."

They'd stopped before another shop, this one with

a dark interior. Verra good. She'd spent far too much already, he was famished and his head ached. "May we go home now?"

"I suppose."

They walked to the corner where Claire waved and another taxi came to a stop.

As they rolled away, Cam calculated the amount he now owed. After adding another twenty pounds for the glass door he'd broken, he decided he'd be hard pressed to repay Claire in this or any other lifetime. A depressing thought if ever there was one.

Worse, he'd yet to consider the cost of hiring a barrister.

"That's the Boston Common." Claire pointed to a wooded area decorated by too many white lights to count. "Isn't it lovely?"

"Aye." Ahead and to his right sat a large, lit crèche with statuary depicting Christ's birth. 'Twas odd to see such outside but good to ken that people here believed.

"Oh, look, people are skating. Once, when I was very young, my father rented one of those paddle boats over there." She pointed to a line of docked boats shaped and painted to look like giant swans. "We paddled all over this lake." She sighed. "I pretended we lived up there," she pointed toward a large gold domed building at the far end of the park, "on Beacon Hill."

Assuming her president lived beneath the gold dome, he said, "Where did ye live?"

"In a poorer part of the city, in a third-story flat—apartment—with a sagging back porch you didn't dare step out onto for fear of it crashing to the ground. Worse, the building backed up to the MTA tracks." She grinned. "Every thirty minutes the MTA would scream past, rattling the doors and windows and Mom would lunge for whatever glassware might be sitting on the table."

Falling porches and *empty-ays*. What a strange world for a bairn to grow up in. "And where are yer parents now?"

She looked away. "Mom died a while back and my father . . . let's just say the less I see of him, the better."

Humph. 'Twas often the case in his world as well. He'd been one of the fortunate. "Have ye brothers or sisters?"

"No." She tapped the glass. "That's the library."

Cam looked right and found an impressive building of gray stone fronted by multiple wide steps leading to huge columns. "Whom does one query to gain entrance?"

"No one. It's free and open to the public."

Would wonders never cease?

A wee bit later, a long impressive building of light stone with huge banners hanging before it came into view. "And that building?"

"That's the Museum of Fine Arts. They have a very nice collection of Impression—"

"Asshole!" Their driver shouted another obscenity as they jolted forward, their view out the forward window obscured by a huge yellow coach with flashing red lights that hadna been there a breath before.

Instinctively, Cam braced for impact, pulling Claire into his side. They spun in dizzying fashion for several heartbeats, then slammed front first into a head-high mound of snow.

The driver, pale as a ghost, shouted through the glass partition, "Are you folks all right?"

Cam pushed the hair out of Claire's eyes. "Are ye injured, lass?"

"No, I'm fine."

Cam flung open the door and carefully pulled Claire out to better examine her in the light. Once satisfied she'd told the truth, he asked, "Was that an *empty-ay* that jumped before us?"

"A bus."

Humph! It was all too much for a man to fathom on an empty stomach. He strode toward their coachman, a skinny man of perhaps twenty years, who now stood shivering with one hand shoved in a pocket, the other pointing to the front of their vehicle, most of which was buried in snow. "Look at that wheel. I'm going to have to call for a goddamn tow."

Cam ran a hand over the twisted metal above the wheel, then tapped it. 'Twas far too thin to be racing about at such speeds. "We need push the taxi free of the snow so we can better look at the wheel. Mayhap we can free it."

The man grunted, reached into the taxi, pushed a lever, and directed Cam take hold of the door. "On the count of three. One. Two. Three!"

Cam heaved and the taxi rolled back smartly, apparently taking the driver by surprise. He fell.

"Shit, man." After a bit of slipping and sliding, the driver finally made it to his feet and came to Cam's side where they crouched before the crumpled metal. "I'll get the tire iron."

Claire, who'd been eyeing them, asked, "Is the axle broken?"

Cam shook his head. "Not that I can see." There were more bloody parts beneath their taxi than could be found in a king's clock. "I believe 'tis just this piece of metal," he rapped on the offending plate, "keeping the wheel at an odd angle." Which shouldn't prove a problem. He'd straightened out thicker, more crumpled armor many a time.

Their driver returned with a short steel shaft, jammed it into a wee space before the wheel and pulled. When the twisted metal remained as it was, he threw the rod to the ground. "Damn it. I guess I'm gonna be docked for damage *and* a tow."

Ack, the man was totally incompetent. "Go help the lady with her packages, will ye?" Cam picked up the rod and eased it under a crumpled edge, pulled, moved the rod, pulled again, and the wheel was free. Straightening, he said, "'Tis done."

"You're kidding." The driver made his way back to Cam. As he bent to examine the repair, Cam tucked the steel bar into his breachen feile.

"Wow, man, you just saved me fifty bucks."

Ah, stags were also currency—he'd seen Claire pay with only cards and bank notes. At least now he kenned why there were so many images of deer in shop windows.

Now once again armed, albeit poorly, Cam grinned. "Ye're most welcome. Consider it fair exchange for the fare."

"Ya, sure." The man straightened and held out his hand. "I'm Eddy, by the way."

"MacLeod." Cam shook Eddy's hand and found it as smooth as a lass's. Humph! No wonder he'd needed assistance.

Cam looked about and recognizing a street sign—Huntington Ave—turned to Claire only to find her staring at him, her arms loaded with packages, her mouth agape. "We're close to home, aye?"

Her eyes narrowed as her gaze shifted to where he'd secreted the steel rod. "Yes, but—"

"Grand." He took the packages from her and threaded his free arm through hers and started walking.

"But you can't take—"

Ack, in typical female fashion she was about to rail over his wee bit of prudent reiving. Silly lass. He lengthened his stride pulling her along. "Claire, *honey*, the nice man said we're even, so come along."

Claire shoved her key into the lock of her newly glazed front door. "I still can't believe you stole that man's tire iron!"

She'd just bailed him out of jail and here he was committing another felony. Well, maybe not a felony . . .

"Claire, dinna fash. I've promised to return it, have I not?"

"Augh!" The sooner she called Mr. Brindle the better. Totally exasperated, she strode to her security alarm. "See this beeping box? It's the security alarm. When you open that door from the outside you have exactly forty-five seconds to punch five, five, five." She hit the keys. "If I'm not here and you wish to leave, you have to punch five, five, five before opening the door. Do you understand?"

She couldn't afford to keep replacing glass. Particularly after laying out five grand in bail.

Grinning, he said, "Aye, I push five three times whether coming or going, but I dinna have a key."

Right. Because she'd not given a moment's thought to where he'd be staying. Not one.

She could put him up at a hotel or the YMCA but that would be expensive and he'd already proved he was a menace to himself and society. She had to keep an eye on him until she could get her five thousand back.

And what if he disappeared as suddenly as he'd come? Would the court believe her? Give her back her money?

Augh! I am sooo not happy.

"Come on. You need to get cleaned up."

Upstairs, she shrugged out of her coat, pulled his new clothes from the bags and led him into the bathroom. After pulling fresh towels from the cupboard, she turned on the shower. "Don't take too long. Mrs. Grouse is holding supper for us."

Cam stuck his hand in the spray. "'Tis warm."

"Yes, but it won't be for long, so you better hurry. The soap and all are sitting on the ledge. You can use my razor."

"Thank ye."

"You're welcome."

Grinning, he slipped the infamous jack handle from his kilt, placed it on the toilet seat, and unclipped his brooch. Realizing he was about to strip right there in front of her, Claire turned toward the door.

"What, lass, is this?"

She turned and found him, bare to the waist, holding out her purple Lavender Fields. "Shampoo. You wash your hair with it. And what in God's name happened to your chest?"

Bare-assed when he arrived, she knew for a fact that there hadn't been a mark on him and now he was sporting several huge bruises and two scarlet welts.

"'Tis naught to fash about." He reached for his belt.

"Wait just a minute." She stepped closer and placed a tentative finger on one of the marks above his heart. "My God, they're burns. How did you get these?"

He looked down and color rose in his cheeks. "I dinna ken what they call it, but the shock brought me to my knees."

Sweet mother of God. "They used a *stun gun* on you?"

He shrugged and reached for his belt again. "The warm water is wasting, Claire," he wiggled an eyebrow at her, "unless ye'd care to join me?"

"I'm going." She'd dress his wounds later. After she gave Mr. Brindle, attorney at law, an earful about the Boston police.

Never having expected to need it, it took her a minute to find the attorney's phone numbers. As she dialed his home—the number to be used only in emergencies—she pictured Cam's wounds. He'd taken a beating. Of that she was certain.

On the fourth ring, a deep voice said, "Hello?"

"Mr. Brindle?"

"Yes?"

"This is Claire MacGregor. We spoke yesterday. I'm Tavish MacLean's—"

"Yes, Ms. MacGregor, I remember who you are. How may I be of help?"

"I'm sorry to disturb you at home, but you know that stuff Tavish willed me? In one of the crates, there was this big box . . ."

She rattled on, bringing Mr. Brindle up to date on her hellacious day, knowing all the while she sounded like a raving lunatic, but there was no help for it.

She'd just gotten to her using a credit card to bail Cam out when Mr. Brindle said, "Ms. MacGregor, I hate to interrupt this . . . unusual story, but what's all that racket in the background?"

"Oh, that's just Sir Cameron MacLeod in my shower singing 'You Take the High Road.'"

"You're not serious."

"Oh, but I am. That's what I've been trying to tell you for the last fifteen minutes." There was dead silence on the line for several seconds. "Mr. Brindle?"

"I'm sorry. I can be there in two hours if that's not too late. You can finish telling me the story then."

Thank God. "Thank you. Just ring the bell when you get here."

She closed her cell phone, looked up, and found Cameron MacLeod standing barefoot in her bedroom doorway, his wet hair raked off his freshly shaven face and curling about his shoulders, his chest bare, and his narrow hips and powerful legs encased in skin tight—albeit relaxed fit—jeans. Good God, he was simply magnificent.

About to sigh at the heart-tripping sight, she spotted

the jack handle poking out from MacLeod's rear pocket and groaned instead, then flipped opened her cell phone and added Mr. Brindle's phone numbers to her speed dial, something telling her she'd be needing them again.

"Have some more, dear."

Cam patted his middle. "I canna, Mrs. Grouse. I'll explode like a cannon should I try. But I thank ye."

"No need. It's been a pleasure cooking for a man again, watching him eat like there's no tomorrow."

She rose and started clearing the table. He came to his feet to help. "Have ye been widowed long?"

"A year."

"My deepest sympathy."

"Thank you. Henry was a good man and I miss him. Sometimes it feels like forever since we've spoken and other times it feels like just yesterday that we were arguing about where to set up the Christmas tree. He always wanted it there before the window and I liked it tucked in the corner to the right, so he wouldn't keep knocking the needles off . . . making a mess." Her pale blue eyes grew glassy. "What I wouldn't give now to see him make a mess."

Ack, the poor wee woman.

When his Margie had died of influenza, he, too, had wept and despite their being poorly matched. He couldna imagine the pain one might feel losing a mate one had loved for a lifetime.

Hoping to distract Mrs. Grouse from her grief, he

asked, "Could ye kindly explain why ye have all these glittering trees about?" They were everywhere.

"They're how we celebrate Christmas. Right after Thanksgiving—our national day of thanks—we buy trees, decorate them, and put gifts underneath. On Christmas morning, we gather around the tree and open the presents."

Aha. His people exchanged gifts only at Hogmanay. Christmas Day was a day of repentance, when one went about asking people to call them by their most grievous fault. He'd been addressed as Sir Vain on more occasions than he'd care to remember.

He peered beneath Mrs. Grouse's tree and found three gaily wrapped packages. "Are those for your bairns—children?"

"No. They're from my daughter. She lives in California . . . on the west coast. I was hoping she'd come home for Christmas this year, but she couldn't take time off from work. She works for a set designer, a man who decorates stages and theaters with furniture, lamps, and such."

Humph. The daughter should be here, caring for her aged mother, not traipsing after some troubadour.

And speaking of women . . .

He followed Mrs. Grouse into the cramped kitchen. "Do you think Claire will be much longer?"

When the barrister had arrived she'd excused herself, saying she needed to speak with the man in private. Which was all well and good, but she'd been gone an hour according to Mrs. Grouse's authentic Black Forest cuckoo clock, a most peculiar timepiece if ever there was one. An hour was more than ample time for any man to initiate mischief were he of a mind.

"I shouldn't imagine they'll be much longer. Why don't we sit in the living room and watch TV. Do you like TV? Oh, of course, you don't know if you like it or not, do you?"

He shrugged, kenning naught of teevee, his thoughts still consumed with the vulnerability of the young woman one story above. "Why is Claire not married?"

She should have a husband, someone to protect and provide for her.

Mrs. Grouse motioned for him to follow and waddled into her parlor. As she settled into her padded chair and he took a seat on her sofa, she said, "In part because no one has asked her."

Were the men of this century daft? Although Claire wasna what one might call fair and fulsome, for her nose was too sharp and her countenance more heart-shaped than oval, she was most certainly attractive, compassionate, wealthy, and had without doubt the finest hurdies he'd seen in many a season. And he'd seen his fair share. "And the other part?"

"She's never fallen in love."

"Ah." *Love.*

At its best, love was simply exalted lust. At its worst, love was merely a word cloaking selfishness, an ambitious man's avarice for land and power or a woman's lust for security. Aye, and he didna doubt for a moment that Minnie would claim she'd placed him in this hell because she loved him. He shuddered.

Mrs. Grouse picked up a thin, black box and waving

it in his general direction, asked, "Do you find Claire attractive?"

Ack! Having come away the worse after his last brush with a wee black box, he eyed the auld woman warily. "Aye, verra."

"I'm so pleased."

Much to his relief, she shifted her aim from his chest to a large glass-fronted chest, which suddenly came to life with moving portraits speaking to him in a clipped fashion.

Astounded, Cam came to his feet. As he eased closer, the scene changed to a picture of massive devastation, then a woman appeared, telling him an earthquake destroyed hundreds of homes in Turkey. Amazing. He touched the glass with a tentative finger, then peered behind the box. He'd heard tell the French had revolving theaters, music boxes with mechanical puppets, but had been under the impression that they operated much like a clock. One had to wind the mechanism with a key or handle. Not so this theater.

Behind him, Mrs. Grouse said, "I don't know how it works, but it's entertaining. Watch this."

Suddenly a goose was chasing a huge black dog around a fenced yard.

"That" she told him, "is the *World's Funniest Animals.*"

Speaking of animals . . .

"Mrs. Grouse, have ye a game park close at hand?" Should he be trapped here for any length of time, he'd be in sore need of barter. He had much to repay Claire.

"You're a gambler?" Mrs. Grouse heaved a huge sigh. "Claire will be *so* disappointed."

Cam shook his head. "Nay, Mrs. Grouse, I never gamble. Coins are far too hard to come by. I meant a place with elk or deer."

"Oh. We have a zoo."

"Grand." He didn't care what they called the place so long as they had a buck or two worth reiving.

Pointing toward the teevee, she asked, "Would you like to see something else?"

Cam nodded and Mrs. Grouse, grinning, pushed more buttons. A man appeared before a map, much like the one Claire had shown him, telling him more snow was expected in the Great Lakes region.

"That's the weather channel. But it gets better." She clicked again and suddenly a very excited woman with black hair was telling him that for just thirty-nine dollars, he, too, could have skin men love to touch. As he pondered why any man worth the name would want such, the scene changed again and another woman, this one with a wild blond mane, told him he need only make two easy payments of eighteen ninety-nine and he, too, could own the lovely carving knives she held up for Cam to see. "Would you like a credit card?" she asked. Cam nodded. Aye, he most definitely would. He'd seen Claire use hers several times to barter.

"To apply for your home shopping card," the woman told him, "just call the number on your screen and our helpful service representatives will be happy to assist you."

He memorized the address. He would call on this

helpful service representative on the morrow. "Verra good."

"What, dear?"

"'Tis wondrous, Mrs. Grouse. Does Claire have such?"

"A TV?"

"Whatever this is called." He waved toward the theater where the woman now displayed a gleaming array of knives.

"Yes, but Claire's is a newer model. Hers hangs on the wall in her living room."

"Ah, aye." He'd seen it and thought it a black mirror.

He grinned. He'd have no problem waiting Claire MacGregor out now. He was clothed, well fed, and would soon have bucks and a credit card. And with them, weapons.

A strident bell rang and he spun to find Mrs. Grouse lifting a wee white box from the side table at her elbow. Smiling at him, she pressed the wee box to her ear and murmured, "Hello?" She then said, "All right, dear. I'll tell him." She placed the box back on the table and came to her feet. "Claire said to come upstairs."

'Twas about bloody time.

"Thank ye, mistress, for the wonderful supper and the bonnie company." He would ask Mrs. Grouse about the workings of the white box later.

Anxious to learn if the barrister had managed to get the ridiculous charges leveled against him dropped, Cam took the stairs two at a time and found Claire, her arms crossed at her waist, her eyes red rimmed and nose scarlet, standing by the door. "Ack, lass, what has happened?"

When she shook her head, Cam looked about the room and spotted a man's coat tossed on the sofa. About to ask where her visitor was, he heard footsteps, turned toward Claire's bedchamber door and saw a man of about forty years, tall and thin, his shirttails out and cravat askew. More damning, however, was the stain on his damn crotch.

Cam took a deep, calming breath and tipped up Claire's chin with the crook of his finger. Within the sea green depths of her eyes he found grief; more evidence—had he needed it—that the man had taken advantage of his time alone with her. Heart-sick that he hadna ignored her request to meet with the man alone, Cam brushed a tear from her cheek and turned to the man. And let fly a fist.

Chapter Seven

"Cam! What in hell—?"

Claire dropped to her knees beside the man lying on her floor, his eyes crossed and mouth bleeding.

Fists on his hips, Cam loomed over them. "He'll not be taking advantage of ye again, lass."

"I don't believe this." Claire grabbed a cloth from the low table before her sofa and pressed it to the man's face as he struggled to sit. "I'm so sorry, Mr. Brindle. Are you all right?"

"Yes." The man snuffled and waved her away then looked up at Cam. "Mr. MacLeod, I presume?"

For reasons known only to Claire, she glared at him as she said, "Unfortunately. Sir Cam MacLeod, please meet your attorney, Mr. Wesley Brindle. Or he was before you clocked him. And why the hell did you do that?"

"Ye've been greeting, lass, dinna deny it. And 'tis plain as the blood on his face," he pointed at the dull white stain on the man's crotch, "that he's the cause."

"Oh, for God's sake—he dropped a piece of coffee

cake on himself. And I wasn't crying because of something he did but because we were talking about Tavish and this—this ridiculous situation!" She huffed and rose. "Help him up."

"Humph." And how was he to know the man hadna done anything? The barrister's coat was off, his cravat askew. Nay, he couldna be faulted for thinking the worst.

He reached for Mr. Brindle's arm, but the man waved him away. "No. I can manage on my own, thank you."

"As ye lust."

Cam left the man to his own devices and followed Claire into her kitchen where he found her pulling several wee blocks of ice from her cold storage and wrapping them in a cloth.

"Here, give this to Mr. Brindle while I make more coffee."

"Aye, and I apologize to ye, although I must tell ye I'm loath to do so, for there isna a reason for a man to undress in a lone woman's presence unless he—"

She pressed a finger to his lips. "Cam, listen to me. You're in a different place and time now. Customs have changed. If you keep jumping to conclusions you're going to get yourself in a world of hurt that even Mr. Brindle can't get you out of."

Humph! Some things—like keeping one's garments on while in the presence of a lady not of yer personal acquaintance—never changed. "As ye lust."

"I do. Now give the ice to Mr. Brindle and maybe we can get on with the business at hand. Namely, keeping you out of prison."

He found Mr. Brindle sitting on the sofa nursing his split lip. "Here."

Eyeing him warily, the barrister took the ice and pressed it to his lip. After a moment, he asked, "Are you always so violent?"

"Since when is defending a lass's honor considered violence?" He looked at the heavy signet ring on the man's right hand. Ack, a laird. And nae doubt, accustomed to taking as he chose.

The man rolled his eyes and sighed. "Claire has given me her version of events. Now I need to hear yours." He put down the ice, pulled a sheaf of papers closer to him and picked up his writing implement. "Where were you born?"

The saints preserve him. Here we go again. "I was born in Rubha, Scotland, on Hogmanay in the year of our Lord, 1716."

Mr. Brindle grunted as he scribbled and continued to ask about not only Cam's personal life but what he kenned of his ruler, the church, and the townships he visited.

"In how many languages are you fluent?" Brindle asked.

"What does this have to do with my arrest?"

The barrister put down his pen. "Mr. MacLeod, I'm trying to assess the veracity of your story, trying to discover if you are who you claim to be. Trust me. I will be checking every detail you've given me. Now, in how many languages are you fluent? In what languages do you read and write?"

"Ack, I ken the meaning of fluent, and the answer is five. How many do ye speak?"

Ignoring Cam's question, Brindle said, "Please name them."

"Gael, Scots, English, French, and Latin."

The man shoved the shaft of paper and the pen across the table at him. "Prove it."

Glaring, Cam picked up the pen and wrote in five languages, *Ye, sir, are an insufferable ass.*

As he pushed the pen and paper back, Claire came into the room carrying a tray laden with fresh coffee and what remained of Mrs. Grouse's cake. He rose, took the tray from her hands and placed it on the table. Waving her to the chair he'd occupied, he said, "Mr. Brindle thinks me a liar."

Brindle bristled. "I never called you a liar."

"Ye didna have to." Cam settled on the opposite end of the sofa and took up as much space as possible, spreading his arms across the back, taking satisfaction in seeing Brindle edge away while still trying to appear comfortable with Cam sitting so close.

Claire looked at Mr. Brindle. "Did he show you the burns?"

"No, we haven't gotten that far." Brindle picked up his pen and turned his attention to Cam. "Tell me exactly what you did after you left here and what precisely led up to your arrest."

Loathe to relive his humiliating defeat—not to mention the gaolers manhandling him—before Claire, Cam did so, but sparingly.

"Did you strike the police officers first?"

"Nay. Had I, they'd be dead. I just wanted to be left alone, and would have wandered away had they let me."

As he told of his incarceration and subsequent

abuse, Claire's jaw muscles twitched. "Cam, please take off your sweater."

"Me what?"

She pointed to his chest. "Your woolen shirt."

Ack, would his humiliation never end? He jerked the blue jersey over his head and placed it on the sofa arm.

Frowning at Cam's burns and bruises, Brindle murmured, "Would you mind standing and turning around?"

Aye, he minded, but did so, unable to decline the plea in Claire's eyes.

He faced forward and Brindle said, "Mr. MacLeod, it's obvious you've taken a hell of a beating and we need to document this." He then reached into the open leather portmanteau at his feet and pulled out a wee silver box.

Having no notion of the man's intentions, Cam looked to Claire for an explanation and found her glassy-eyed, the knuckles of one hand pressed to her lips.

"Don't worry," she murmured. "It's just a digital camera. You'll see the photos—images of yourself—when he's through."

Cam nodded and gritted his teeth, bracing for whatever would come as Brindle aimed the box at his chest. To his relief, only a bright light flashed repeatedly and he was told to turn right, left, and backward.

A moment later, Brindle said, "Thank you, Mr. MacLeod. You can get dressed now."

Cam donned his jersey—sweater, as Claire called it— and found Brindle holding the silver box out to him.

"Look at the screen."

Brindle pushed a button and Cam was astounded to see himself and his wounds at both a distance and at close quarters. More astounding were the size and number of bruises on his back. Shit, nae wonder he was sore.

"What now?" Claire asked.

"Aye, need I go to court?"

Brindle put his silver box away. "I'll do my utmost to avoid that, but there's the possibility that the police will insist on pressing charges. I'll let you know. Right now, we have to decide where you'll be staying."

Claire folded her hands in her lap. "Cam, Mr. Brindle and I have decided it would be best if you stayed with him."

Cam scowled at the pair. "And where might that be?"

"I live in Topsfield. It's a small community about thirty miles north of here. You'll be safe."

Thirty miles north? Were they both as wode as Tillie's geese? "Nay, I shall stay here." He wasna letting Claire MacGregor out of his sight. She held the key to his returning to his own time and place. And to his garnering the information about the battle he needed to take back with him.

"Mr. MacLeod, you can't stay here. Claire has a business to run. She can't keep an eye on you—keep you out of further trouble—and do what she has to do."

"Brindle, ye ken verra well I have to be here should she figure out how to undo this curse." He turned to Claire. "Lass, I'll not be the least bit of trouble. I can sleep below in yer shop. Ye have naught to fear from me. Besides, having a man about to do a bit of heavy lifting and such could only prove helpful."

Claire heaved a sigh. "Cam, I know you'd do me no harm, but—"

Craaash! Whoop, whoop, whoop!

"What the—?"

"Oh shit!" Claire bolted out of her chair, grabbed the walking cane from the tall bucket by the door and ran out of the apartment. Cam, recognizing the cacophony reverberating throughout the house as one he'd heard when he'd broken out just the day before, ran after her, Brindle fast on his heels. At the second landing, Mrs. Grouse, rolling pin in hand, came through her doorway. "Oh, no, not again!"

"Stay inside!" Cam ordered.

Heart thudding, Claire punched in the buttons on her security box. As the shop fell blessedly quiet Cam ran past and bolted through the fractured door pane.

Realizing his intent, fearing the thugs might be carrying guns or whatever the hell hoodlums carried, she shouted, "No!" But too late.

He was down the steps and racing after the glow of receding taillights.

"Shit!" She craned her neck to look out the door. Seeing the car nearing the end, suspecting Cam had little hope of catching them, and praying that he wouldn't, she watched until they all disappeared around the corner.

From behind her, Brindle asked, "Who'd do this?" He was frowning at the broken glass at her feet. About to tell him, she heard footsteps behind her and found Cam, huffing huge white clouds, coming up the stairs.

"I'm sorry, lass. They got away."

Thank God for small favors. "Thanks for trying."

Claire flipped the light switch and was somewhat comforted by the warm glow from her six, still-intact, and carefully restored chandeliers until she saw what remained of her mahogany breakfront at the center of her shop, sitting next to the mirror. "Oh no!"

Oh God. If whatever they'd thrown had gone a foot to the left she would have lost her most prized possession. The eighteenth-century baroque mirror. After the first attack, she should have moved the mirror and her best pieces back where they'd be safe. But no, she'd rationalized that the best pieces were safe enough being a good thirty feet inside, because they made a statement, made her shop stand out. And now look at her pretty, bowed glass breakfront . . .

A hitching sob caught in her throat, and she felt Cam's arm wrap around her, gently pulling her to his chest. "Shhh, Claire, shhh. 'Twill be all right."

"No, it won't. That breakfront was built in the 1820s. The glass is irreplaceable. Worse, the bastards who did this won't stop . . . not until I pay them."

"Pay them for what?"

From behind him, Brindle said, "Someone's blackmailing you, Ms. MacGregor?"

Loathe to leave the comforting warmth of Cam's arms, Claire did so. This was her problem, not his. "A street gang, Mr. Brindle. Teenage bastards demanding a hundred a week . . . to keep my property safe."

"Have you called the police?"

Claire snorted as she grabbed the tall trash basket, dust pan, and broom from behind her desk. "Ya, three times for all the good it's done me."

Cam suddenly cursed as he knelt before the mirror.

Thinking he'd cut himself on broken glass, she went to him. Instead of an injured hand, he held out a brick, some of its old mortar still attached.

"I believe this is intended for ye."

The blood drained from her head as she read the caulked message.

Until next time bitch.

Oh God, she should have anticipated the threats would escalate. And she definitely had more than broken glass and herself to worry about. She had Mrs. Grouse. What if next time they threw a Molotov cocktail through the door . . . ?

"What's going on?" Brindle asked. "You're as white as a sheet."

MacLeod crossed his arms over his massive chest. "I willna be leaving."

Hearing footsteps on the stairs, slow and soft as spring rain, only the wood straining beneath her weight giving Claire away, Cam peeked at the large French clock quietly ticking in hypnotic fashion to his left and sighed. Here he was, at wits' end with no obvious way out, 'twas three in the morning and the lass had yet to settle for the night, so he might have some peace to think.

If the pattern held, on this her sixth trip down the stairs, Claire would tiptoe across the shop, peer out the windows looking both right and left, test the lock on the barred door—he'd nailed wood from the crates over the openings—then rub her arms, her breath escaping in quick white puffs, as she strained to read the wee thermometer on the wall. She'd then kneel at his side where he lay on a pallet of blankets he'd scavenged from the back room and ever so gently touch his hand, apparently checking his warmth, and then tuck his breachen feile higher about his shoulders. On her last visit, she added a downy counterpane to the mound she'd insisted upon him using, nearly suffocating him.

He watched through lowered lashes as she made her careful progress across the shop, never so much as brushing against an article, so familiar was she with all about her. Apparently satisfied that the street was as she last left it, that the troublesome lads hadna returned, she turned her attention to her odd wee thermometer. Nose crinkled, she shivered and this time gave it a sharp tap, then immediately jerked around to be sure the sound hadn't disturbed him. When he remained still, she quickly padded away. Thinking she was returning to her apartment, he again pictured the library she would take him to on the morrow and all it might contain, but he couldna focus on anything but Claire MacGregor.

She was an odd duck, to be sure. And her expression when she found him on that moving stairs' banister . . . too funny.

Imagining her as she sat across the table from him, her head tipped and eyes narrowed, apparently as confounded as he about his presence in her home, he sighed. What if she couldna reverse the spell? Would he be trapped here for all eternity or just the rest of his life—

Swish, swish.

Ack, not again. 'Twas cotton brushing against long thighs, heading in his direction.

Good God, woman, please go to bed.

He caught the scent of lavender, felt the floorboards beneath him give ever so slightly as she again knelt at his side. He struggled to relax his jaw and breathe in the slow, easy fashion of a man in deep sleep, but then nearly groaned aloud when she lowered a fur pelt over him.

Was she trying to suffocate him?

A gentle finger brushed a lock from his cheek and he caught her hand, cold and white as the snow beyond the panes, causing her to squeak in surprise. "Ssh, lass, I didna mean to frighten ye."

"I'm so sorry. I didn't mean to wake you."

"Ye didna." And neither of them would get any sleep this night if he didna contain her. Before she could rise, he rolled, tugging her toward him. She toppled with a squeal, landing on her right side on the pallet. He wrapped an arm about her waist, pulling her back under his dense woolen breachen feile and against his chest. As he bent his knees, spooning her to him, he muttered, "Sssh, lass, I mean ye nae harm. Just bide a wee, else neither of us gets any sleep this night."

She craned her neck to glare over her shoulder at him, her nails digging into his forearm. "What do you think you're doing? Let me go!"

"Nay. I'm bone weary, lass. In particular, because of yer gadding upstairs and down on the hour, every hour. And ye need some sleep as well."

She wiggled, trying to escape his hold and inadvertently pressed her delicious hurdies into his crotch.

Feeling blood race to his groin—no great surprise given he'd been asleep—hadna apparently tupped—in four centuries, he eased his hips away from her. "Damn, lass, yer arse is positively brumal."

"Brumal?"

"Frigid, lass, like an icy loch."

"It is not and I'll thank you not to swear."

"It is too and *ye* curse all the time."

"I do *not*!"

"Aye, ye do." He hauled the heavy sheep pelt she'd placed on his back over her and muttered into her fine hair, all glossy and lavender, "Now go to sleep or I swear I'll squish ye."

Chapter Eight

Squish her?

What kind of a threat was that? Clout, throttle, beat the crap out of her, whatever, but squish? Not.

Claire craned her neck and found MacLeod's eyes closed, his great, sweeping lashes resting against his chiseled cheekbones. In the glow of the street lamp, she studied the relaxed set of his mouth, his smooth forehead, the arm heavy but loose over her waist. Feeling his chest move, brushing ever so slightly against her back with the long easy breaths of someone in deep slumber, she wondered if he really was asleep.

Whether he was or not, at least she didn't have to listen to his turn-her-knees-to-jelly burr anymore. Not that she'd be getting any sleep anytime soon. Not with all this muscle surrounding her, not to mention the body heat infusing her every pore with the scent of male musk.

God, he smelled good. Even if he had used all her newly purchased Lavender Fields shampoo for limp, fly-away hair. And didn't that teach her to be more succinct?

She'd told him shampoo was for washing his hair, never imagining he'd use it wherever he had hair . . . which, if memory served, was pretty much everywhere except his back, which was really a good thing. She wasn't into furry backs, no matter how soft the hair might be, which was really a *very* good thing because his type—the strong, silent, total hottie type—didn't go for the likes of mousey-brown her. They went for the golden Tracy Simpsons of the world.

She let out a wistful sigh, one her mother, had she heard it, would have criticized with *Dreamers never get anywhere, child.*

She never should have opened that damn box. But she had and there was apparently no undoing it. Or was there?

Thinking to appease Cam, she'd promised to take him to the library after breakfast. Hoped to set him up with every Scottish research book that the library had, then leave him to his own devices for a few hours while she grilled Mr. Brindle again about the money Tavish left her, but perhaps she should do some research as well. On ancient curses. Surely the library would have something useful on the topic. If not, she could always initiate an interlibrary search. Or make a trip to Salem.

Hmm, I wonder . . . "Cam, are you asleep?"

He grunted, sending the scent of chocolate and mint—of Mrs. Grouse's grasshopper pie—across her cheek. "I was."

She grinned. "No you weren't, or you wouldn't have heard my whisper."

"I have verra acute hearing."

She didn't doubt it. "Do you believe in witches? That they're real? I mean do you honestly think they might be more than gifted healers? That they have *powers?*"

He snorted. "I'm here, aren't I?"

There was that. "Would you know a real one from a fraud?"

"I expect so. Why?"

"I know of one . . . in Salem."

He rose up on an elbow to look down at her. "Are ye serious? You ken such?"

She rolled onto her back to see him better and hit the warm spot he'd left. "I don't know her personally, just of her by reputation. The papers always do a story about witches at Halloween—what I think you call All Hallows Eve. I bet we can find her through the Internet."

Elbow still propped, he rested his head on a hand. "I dinna ken this inner net."

"It's part of the computer . . . that box with the map."

"Ah. And she can speak to you through the box?"

"Yes, but given the serious nature of this situation, I think we should meet with her face to face." So the woman didn't blow them off or worse, feed them the canned info she probably sent out to all who made inquiries—maybe a bio and a buy-a-book promo or visit-her-herb-shop kind of crap. And Cam should evaluate the woman. For all Claire knew, the Salem witch was more Shylock than warlock.

"When shall we go?"

"After breakfast. I'll give my friend Tracy a call and ask if she'd mind watching the shop for a while. If she can't, then maybe Victor can."

He leaned forward, close enough to make Claire's breath catch. "Who," he asked, "is Victor?"

"He's my merchandiser, very creative . . . and cheap. The perfect match for a struggling shopkeeper with a limited budget and no natural design talent."

"Match." His brow furrowed and he picked up a lock of her hair. Swirling the tip between forefinger and thumb, he said, "As I recall, ye said there wasna a man in yer life."

"There isn't. Victor is just a friend."

"Hmm, and how long has this friendship been going on?"

"Since the shop opened three years ago. He came in, introduced himself—he lives four doors down—and asked how things were going." She made an unladylike snort. "I told him the truth. He strolled around and said, 'No wonder. This place looks like a convenience store with everything lined up in tight little rows.' Next thing I knew, he was moving stuff around and rearranging everything and voilà, perfection."

He arched an eyebrow. "And in exchange?"

"I hand his business cards to all my customers."

"Has he been having the same troubles that ye're having with windows?"

"No, his studio is in another part of the city, but others on the street have had their windows broken."

"And do they pay the blackmail to these deevil's-buckies?"

"Interesting phrasing. As for the other merchants, I don't know if they're paying or not, but suspect they wouldn't tell me if they were. All I know for sure is that right now, I'm the only one replacing glass every time I turn around."

He nodded, silently studying her, his gaze traveling over her face before settling on her lips, making her heart trip, her stomach quiver. Her gaze shifted to his mouth, his lips, not too full and not too thin, curving up ever so slightly at the corners only a few inches from her own. So close.

Would he kiss her? She wanted him to. The first had been such a shock she hadn't had time to savor it. Just once more, please, so she could have something to remember, perhaps cherish, after he left and she was old and gray.

As if reading her mind, he jerked upright and rocked back on his haunches. Looking out the windows, he said, "Dawn will be breaking shortly and there's a curse to be undone. We'd best get to it."

He rose, taking his warmth and their momentary intimacy with him. Something deep within her shrank.

Towering above her, he held out a hand. "My lady."

Right. If only.

She placed her hand in his. As she came to her feet she glanced at the regulator ticking away above Tavish's ship. Five o'clock. Where had the night gone?

"First, we need to find a coat that fits you. The stores open at nine o'clock. Then we can go to the library. If we don't find what we're—"

"Nay, I havena need of a coat. I have me breachen feile." In a tone that brooked no argument, he added, "First we go to the library, then we find the witch."

"Why you—"

At a loss for words, she snarled and headed for the

stairs. A sudden bark of laughter followed her, but thankfully grew softer, like wisps of smoke drifting up a chimney . . . much like her hopes of someone like him ever finding someone like her attractive.

Peering down the metal rails, Claire muttered, "Please stop fidgeting. People are staring."

"I'm not fidgeting. Auld women and bairns fidget. And I still dinna ken why we have to take yer empty-ay. The library is only a few hectares from here." As for the women staring at him, women always did.

"Cam, the library is a mile away through shoulder-high snow banks. Besides, last I heard you were in a hurry."

Aye, he was. He had to get back to when—and where—he belonged before his clan joined the Stuart, else they take the path of destruction, and he had to do so before he seduced the innocent and naïve Ms. Claire MacGregor.

Christ's blood, had he kissed her in those wee hours as he'd dearly wanted, when she'd looked up at him with those sea green eyes so soft, her chestnut hair spread out like an angel's wings across his pallet, her lips parted, waiting, he would have been more than hard pressed to stop at just a wee kiss. She was too bonnie and he'd been too long without a woman. Worse, she hadna appeared the least inclined to stop him. In fact, he'd have wagered his sword that she'd have gone to her ruin willingly. And that simply wouldna do.

'Twas one matter to lay with a doxy or needy widow,

to take a wee bit of pleasure with a willing companion, but 'twas quite another to take a virginal lass who'd been naught but kind, only to desert her in the end. And leave her he would. And what if he'd gotten her with bairn? Oh, he kenned ways to prevent her getting with child, but could he have pulled away? He seriously doubted it.

The rumble and scrape of metal on metal jerked his attention right, where he found a huge, snaking conveyance lumbering toward them.

When it came to a halt, Claire led the way to an open door. With no small measure of trepidation, he followed her inside where she stopped before a glass and metal box that chinked and clattered merrily as it devoured her coins.

They found a seat toward the rear of the coach, the doors closed without a hand touching them and they were off, the carriage rocking in ever quickening side-to-side motion so unlike that of a horse-drawn coach. Peering out both the front and rear windows, he asked, "What pulls this beast along?"

"Electricity. When we're above ground, the power comes in through a roof-mounted cable. When below ground, there's a live third rail. You never, ever go near the rails while underground. They'll kill you."

Ah, she'd explained electricity—the captured lightning—as she'd tended his wounds. "Like the stun gun?"

"A hundred times stronger than the stun gun."

Humph! Not something he cared to experience again. Perhaps while at the library he should also ask for texts on electricity. If his people could master this energy as Claire's had, 'twould make for a powerful weapon to use against the English. Picturing thousands of clansmen aiming stun guns at unsuspecting Sassenach, he grinned.

The coach picked up speed and the wheels squealed in protest. As the rocking increased to a jarring shudder, he studied his fellow passengers noting their varied countenances, which ranged from apple-cheeked and red noses to those that were nearly pitch black. Few resembled him or his countrymen, a disconcerting sensation.

Apparently noticing he was exchanging baleful stares with a bronze-skinned youth who stood swaying, one hand gripping a strap, his breeches hanging half off his ass, Claire elbowed him and whispered, "It's impolite to make eye contact."

What foolishness was this? "Why?"

"It just is."

"Humph." These people were most bizarre. Meeting a man eye to eye was often the only way for one to measure another's intent, to ken if a stranger was friend or foe. And someone needed to take note of the poor lad, loan him the coins for a belt before his scrawny ass froze off. Had Cam any coins, he certainly would have given the lad a few.

Wheels screeched and their coach slowed as unseen hands applied breaks. Instinctively, Cam wrapped an arm around Claire to keep her from falling sideways. When they came to a stop, passengers began milling. A woman ponderous with child, her arms laden with packages, entered, and Cam rose, indicating she should sit next to Claire. She smiled up at him but before she could angle her way to his seat, a group of youths rushed in, jostling those around them. One, spying the space next to Claire, headed for it and Cam stepped in his path. "'Tis for the lady."

The lad, apparently oblivious to the danger he courted, scowled up at him, one hand slipping into a pocket, mayhap for a knife. Stretched and sneering, he asked, "Says who?"

Beside him, Claire hissed, "*Cameron.*"

Cam held up a hand to silence her, his gaze locked on the cocky, ill-mannered youth. "Says I."

The lad's eyes narrowed, his hand moving within his pocket as he took Cam's measure. It took a moment but the youth finally broke eye contact, shrugged, and then walked away in an odd hitch-and-rock fashion to his companions, who laughed and jabbed his middle.

Bloody hell. First a gang attacked Claire's establishment and now this. Where the hell were the fathers? Someone really needed to take these young knaves in hand and slam some sense into them.

He felt a tug on his arm and turned to find Claire standing at his side. "We get off at the next stop. Come on."

She wedged her way through the packed humanity to the door. When it opened, she rushed down the stairs and nearly fell headlong into a snow bank.

As he steadied her, he asked, "Are you all right?"

"No, I'm *not* all right. You could have been killed! Didn't you notice that kid had a knife? He's a gang-banger, had a tear tattoo. That means he's killed someone."

"Claire, lass, dinna fash yerself." He pushed up his

left sleeve, revealing the foot-long carving knife strapped to his forearm, the one he'd pilfered from her kitchen cabinet. "And all's well that ends well, aye?"

Claire gaped at the blade for a moment, then up at him. "I don't friggin' believe this."

Muttering to herself some words about bales, bonds, and men, she turned and stomped away. Totally nonplussed, he shouted, "What? What did I do now?"

Claire spun, hunched her shoulders and threw her hands in the air as if he were the most hapless creature to ever draw breath. Uncertain as to why—naught untoward, after all, could have befallen him—the gangbanger on the other hand . . .

Deciding there was no kenning the female mind, he heaved a sigh and followed Claire as she continued to stomp, slide, and mutter her way toward the flashing *walk—do not walk* sign, which in his opinion was pure foolishness. If a man wasna bright enough to stay out of the way of an oncoming coach, then he deserved to be run over.

He reached her just as the red hand disappeared and the wee white man appeared and suddenly there before him was the Boston Public Library, or so said the engraving above the wide doors and broad granite steps gleaming wet in the morning sun. Such grandness! The building reminded him of the renderings he'd seen of Rome. Within those dense granite blocks Claire promised he'd find the knowledge he sought. If the information he sought couldn't be found within, Claire had assured him, then it wasn't to be had.

Anxious to start, he took the stairs two and three at

a time only to come to a sudden halt once inside. Ack! Never in his life had he seen such.

Neck craned, he spun slowly, studying the fine frescos on the lofty ceiling supported by columns, admiring the wonderful echoing great hall. He inhaled and caught the scent of old leather and paper, of wisdom. Aye, 'twas definitely the place.

Claire, apparently no longer miffed with him for whatever reason, smiled as she came abreast and motioned to her left. "We have to go upstairs. This," she told him as they climbed, "is the MacKin Building, the original library, but now it houses only the noncirculating collection—the research books. The white building you saw next door houses what we call the circulating collection, the books you can borrow and take home."

A quarter hour later and much to his amazement, Claire had a mountain of books on the broad oak table before him. In awe, he murmured, "So many."

Claire nodded. "We Americans do love the Scots. It's all those hairy knees poking out from beneath yer flashy kilts."

"Aha, ye *can* jest. I was beginning to wonder."

Fighting a grin, she opened the thick volume before her. "Now pay attention. All you have to do is look for *Culloden* in the index. Here's one. Page 221." She flipped the pages, scanned the text, then pushed the book and several scraps of paper toward him. "If you have any questions, write them down. If you want to research specific names or places, write those down as well, and we can ask that nice librarian over there behind the desk to find the information for you."

As she rose, he asked, "And where shall ye be?"

"In the next room. Researching time travel and curses."

Ah, verra good. He shifted his attention back to the text. "Have a bonnie time."

"Ya."

The moment Claire disappeared from view, Cam rose and went to the bone-thin woman with gray hair who sat behind the desk. "My pardon, mistress."

She looked up, blinked, then suddenly smiled, a hand slipping to the bun at the back of her neck. "How may I help you?"

He leaned an elbow on the counter and flashed the smile he used whenever he needed to wheedle a boon out of Minnie. "Would ye happen to have any books on electricity or on combustible engines?" That's what Claire had said powered the taxis and buses.

Color rushed into her cheeks. "Why yes, sir, we do. How much detail do you require?"

Claire scanned the titles on the computer screen looking for anything dealing with Celtic curses and puzzle boxes. "No. No. Ah, maybe this one." She scribbled the title and call number and continued scanning. Thirty minutes later, her arms loaded with books, she found an unoccupied table and spread the texts before her.

Somewhere within the pages had to be the answer.

Three hours later, she knew more than she ever wanted to know about Celtic legends, puzzle box construction, and curses—most of which read like bad poetry—but not a damn thing about undoing the curse that had brought Sir Cameron MacLeod into her life.

She heaved a sigh. Good God almighty, what was she going to do with him if she couldn't undo this?

Exhausted, she placed her arms on the table and plunked her head down. And her carving knife . . . jeesh, hadn't he learned anything from his arrest yesterday? What if they'd had to go through a metal detector to get into the library? At the rate he was going, she'd have to put Brindle on retainer—she had the money, thanks to Tavish—but at $400 an hour, how long would that last? And she'd rather not have to do it. She'd much prefer Cam stayed out of trouble.

What would Cam do if she *couldn't* send him back in time? He was so out of his element here. He couldn't live with her forever. And how would he make a living? There wasn't much call these days for men with swords, although he was good with his hands, had sealed her broken door frame in admirable fashion in nothing flat, but he was also used to being his own man. So . . . alpha.

Oh, he had a good heart, had been courtesy itself when dealing with Mrs. Grouse.

As for his awareness of her, he'd been ever cognizant of her safety whenever it appeared threatened. She'd noticed how he'd eased her out of the path of those kids dressed in Goth getups last night, although there really wasn't a need. But then he didn't know that. And his arm, strong and thick, had wrapped around her as they were skidding out of control in the cab. Hell, he'd even decked Brindle, thinking the man had accosted her.

Poor Brindle. She grinned, picturing the attorney as he sat on her sofa, mouth agape, face flushed, listening to her tale of finding Cam naked in her room—but then it hadn't been funny as he bled all over her carpet.

Truth to tell, MacLeod was solid testosterone. Should he really come unglued, she wouldn't be able to handle him and that frightened her. Men in her world just didn't go around chest out and armed to the teeth, looking gangbangers in the eye, ready to maim at the slightest provocation. Well, unless they were cops or drug dealers . . .

Oh hell, who was she kidding? Any woman would be lucky to have Cameron MacLeod, gorgeous and as intelligent as he is, but in his own time and place. Not hers.

"Bloody fuckin' hell!"

Claire jerked upright. Oh God, now what?

The deep-throated roar of outrage was followed by the crash of wood on wood.

She ran, praying Cam had inadvertently knocked something over.

Arriving in the next room, she found the hundred-pound oak table she'd left Cam sitting at upended, books strewn all over the floor, the once hushed room now buzzing. Several patrons, looking pale, were pointing to the mess. The frail but competent librarian who'd helped her when she and Cam had first arrived stood ashen-faced behind her desk, a phone pressed to her ear. No doubt calling security.

Claire raced to the woman. "Where is he? The Highlander. Where did he go?"

The woman pointed a shaky finger toward the stairs and the crowd forming around it.

"Out of my way!" Claire elbowed her way through the milling gawkers and took the stairs at a breakneck pace. In the lower foyer, she found everyone looking over their shoulders at the doors. She hit the doors running and bolted outside, only to have to slow at the top of the wide granite steps to let her eyes adjust to the blinding sunshine. Squinting, she scoured the sidewalks, right and left, then the students before her shifted and the panic that had been building suddenly eased. He stood only a dozen steps below her. "Cam!"

He turned at the sound of her voice and her heart nearly broke, so desolate was his expression.

"Shit." She never should have left him alone with those books.

She raced down the remaining stairs, stopping one step above him, so they were nearly eye to eye. "What's wrong? Talk to me."

"They were all killed, Claire. *The Butcher* . . . his name was Cumberland. The battle was over in less than an hour. Seeing as he was winning, he ordered his army to spare no one. *No quarter* were his words. Not a clansman was allowed to surrender. More than a thousand, able-bodied and wounded alike, given the ax after . . . after . . ."

He took a shuddering breath and his eyes—already glassy—flooded. "Da, my brothers—slaughtered." He struggled to clear his throat. "Rubha. They razed it. Minnie, even the bairns . . ." He took another shaky breath, blinking back tears. "I have to get back, Claire. I have to get—"

His voice cracked and the tears he'd valiantly managed to hold at bay suddenly spilled, wet traces flowing sideways into laugh lines, then slipping like thieves, flat and low over the high planes of his cheeks, and she did the only thing she could do. She wrapped her arms about him. There before God, the pigeons, and a group of owl-eyed Brownies, she held him and wept right along with him.

His arms about her waist, her arms about his neck, with only the irregular bone-cracking heave of his chest against her breasts telling her he sobbed, she held tight to him and wept for him and for herself. Having been the one to find her mother's body, she'd been too stunned and horrified to grieve and later too filled with fury to give in to the heartache.

When their shaking subsided, became only random jerks, she pressed her cheek to his and whispered, "You will go home, Cam. I promise. I will get you home."

Chapter Nine

A step ahead of her, Cameron opened the door to Applebee's anteroom and she was immediately assaulted by the delicious aromas seeping from the kitchen.

She inhaled and grinning, murmured, "I'm starved and this place has the best burgers and fries in the city."

"What are burgers and fries?" He looked over her head at the darkened interior, the colorful signs, and lights.

"Beef and potatoes, but cooked in a way you've never had before. To die for, truly."

"I hope not."

Augh! God, she could be *sooo* insensitive at times. "I'm sorry. That was thoughtless of me."

"Claire, please . . . dinna fash. What came to pass was none of yer doing."

"I know, but—"

"Welcome to Applebee's. How many in your party?"

Claire swallowed the rest of her apology and told the smiling hostess, "Two."

They were led to a front booth where they settled, sitting across from each other with menus in hand. Claire scanned hers despite having already decided on a deluxe bacon cheeseburger and fries. As she perused the selections, Cam pulled napkins from the holder and thoroughly examined the condiments nestled beside the mini placard touting Applebee's decadent desserts. "Please order whatever you like."

Cam opened the menu and scowled, his finger running down the far right-hand column. Ah, he was worrying about the prices, considering he was used to pennies a loaf.

Flipping to the last page he asked, "Is milk shake butter?"

Claire grinned. "No. It's just shaken milk with flavoring—like chocolate or strawberry—but frappés are better."

"How so?"

"Frappés are made with ice cream."

"I've had iced cream . . . at Stirling. They'd brought snow down from the mountains and mixed it with preserves and cream."

"It's very much like that only richer and thicker."

"Ah."

Claire closed her menu to study Cam and found his brow still furrowed but his eyes clear as he pondered the menu. No one would ever guess that he'd just experienced the worst morning of his life. That he'd been wracked with grief just hours ago. The bus ride from Boston to Salem had helped. It was all she could do to keep him from hanging out the window like a dog, so stunned—or should she say *enthralled*?—was he by their speed coming up Route 1A. She couldn't begin to imagine his reaction to a high-speed inter-state. She'd likely have to shackle him to his seat. No, she wasn't looking forward to it.

Cam muttered something in Gaelic under his breath just as their waitress arrived.

"Welcome to Applebee's," she said, her smile directed at Cam. "I'm Tammy and I'll be your server today. What can I get you guys?"

Claire rolled her eyes. What was she? Wallpaper? "We'll have two deluxe cheeseburgers, well done, fries, and I'll have a glass of the house merlot." She arched an eyebrow at Cam.

His gaze was locked on the girl's scarlet and black outlined lips. "A tankard of ale, if ye please."

Tammy nodded. "Guinness, Brock, or Stout?"

Cam looked to Claire, so she responded, "Guinness will be fine."

Tammy, still grinning at Cam, picked up their menus. "Your meals will be out in a few minutes."

When she sauntered away, Cam crossed his arms on the table and leaned forward. "My thanks. Yer English . . . 'tis verra confounding at times. And why was the lass painted so?"

"She thinks the makeup makes her pretty."

"Humph. Someone should do her the kindness of telling her otherwise."

Well, that certainly answered one question. Claire propped her chin in her hand. "I hope this witch can help us and we're not on a wild goose chase."

"Aye." Cam took the article Claire had printed from her computer—another thing he found amazing and couldn't wait to tell his father about—from his pocket to again study the photo of Sandra Mariah Power, high priestess and elder of her craft in Salem, her pretty face partially covered by a black cat mask. Would this woman have the power to break the bonds that held him here . . . with her?

After rereading the first page, he whispered, "I still canna believe she's told the world she's a witch. Had she done so anywhere in Scotland I dare say she would have been tried for heresy."

"That's the reason this country was founded on religious tolerance. We have no official religion. Our Constitution explicitly forbids it. Citizens can practice any religion they choose."

"Hmm, mayhap Scotland should do the same. God knows the churches' struggle for supremacy is at the very heart of Scotland's sorrows." After a moment he asked, "And what if this witch isna what she claims?"

"Then we'll just keep looking until we find someone who is."

"Aye, 'tisna wise to fash about what we canna change."

"Good thinking. Now to find her." They'd left the house before Ms. Power had apparently had a chance to respond to their e-mail query. Claire spread the map she'd taken from the bus stop across the table. "We're here," she tapped the map, "and that red box is the House of Seven Gables. It's the closest historic site. We can ask there. Surely they'd know where we can find her. If not, we can walk to the Salem Historical Society and ask them."

"And if they dinna ken her whereabouts either?"

"There are more places where we can ask. See, they even have a witch shop that sells potions, witch's balls, and the like."

"Ye canna be serious?"

She laughed. "Oh but I am. You can even buy a broom there according to their Web site."

"This place never ceases to amaze me."

"Oh, good, I'd hate for you to get bored."

"That, my dear lady, couldna happen should I be trapped here for life . . . which I have nae intention of being."

No, he was hellbent on getting home and she couldn't blame him. But she'd miss him, despite all the aggravation he'd caused her. The simple truth was having him here had brought her back to life, one she hadn't even realized she was missing. Tracy had been right. All work and no play had made Claire MacGregor a very dull girl indeed. And speaking of Tracy . . .

"What did you think of Tracy?" She introduced them, then realized she'd left the computer printout with Sandra Power's information on it upstairs, so she hadn't seen them interact.

One corner of Cam's lips tipped up. "She's fair and fulsome, to be sure."

"And . . . ?"

"The lass struck me as being a bit of a kelpie, neither fish nor fowl."

Huh? "I don't understand."

"I dinna mean to be unkind, for she is yer friend, but she appears to be of two minds. On one hand, she's verra much taken with herself—one need only take one look at her to ken that. On the other, she dislikes herself, mayhap for what she's become inside. I wouldna be surprised to learn she wishes to be someone else entirely."

Oh my God. "And you sensed this how?"

He shrugged. "Mayhap it was the way she sought mirrors as she talked, then fidgeted before them. Mayhap it was the way she stood, flirted."

"*Flirted.*" Well, what else did she expect? Maybe a little loyalty from a friend? A little hands-off-the-best-friend's-merchandise? Grrrrrr. Not that she and Cam were an item, but really.

She looked up to find Cam grinning at her, deep dimples making caverns in his cheeks and accentuating the cute dimple in his chin. "Does something ail ye?"

"I'm fine. Just fine." Not.

"Tell me of yer parents."

"My parents. Mom committed suicide eight years ago. I was the one who found her."

"Ack, lass."

"She overdosed on her antidepressants . . . her medicine. She'd been fighting so much sadness for years, but I hadn't realized just how far out of control her world had spun. I found a letter of termination and an eviction notice when I was cleaning out her apartment, that dingy hell hole I grew up in. Apparently, the dry cleaners that she'd worked at for the last fifteen years had closed and with her being sixty and riddled with arthritis and on medication, she couldn't get any work."

Claire scraped the confetti that had once been a paper napkin into a neat pile. "More than once I'd begged her to come live with me, but no, she was too damn proud to live off her daughter." Claire brushed a truant tear from her cheek. "She should have told me."

Cam reached across the table and covered her hand with his. "Yer Mam was a widow then?"

She guffawed, an ugly sound coming from somewhere deep and dark. "No, my father's in prison. Burglary, drugs . . . you name it, he did it."

"Ack, lass, I'm so sorry."

"Don't be. I hope he rots in there." What he and his addictions had done to her mother had killed her as surely as if he'd held a gun to her head and pulled the trigger. It was just too bad she hadn't been able to convince the courts that he'd committed murder. Although God knows she'd tried.

Augh! She'd just spewed out stuff she'd never even told Tracy. What the hell was the matter with her?

Claire gave herself a good shake and embarrassed, reluctantly pulled her hand from beneath Cam's, regretting the loss of contact the minute she did it. Thank God he'd had the wisdom to mask any pity he might have felt.

"Now that I've totally ruined your day, enough about me." She looked about for something, anything, to divert his attention and spotted their waitress balancing a large tray on her shoulder. "Oh good, here comes the food."

He looked away as she'd hoped and straightened. "Ye promise I'll like this?"

She grinned. "If you don't, then there's something seriously wrong with you."

Ten minutes later Cam had cleaned his plate—ketchup apparently his newfound love—and was surreptitiously eyeing her French fries. Already satiated, she slid what fries remained on her plate onto his. "I take it I didn't lie?"

He flashed great dimples at her as three of her fries disappeared into his mouth. "Nay, lass, ye spoke God's honest truth."

"Good. Next time you'll have to try pizza. There's a nice little Italian place right around the corner from us that makes the best pepperoni and sausage in all of Boston."

Had she just said *us*? Yes, and she'd better knock it off. Thinking in those terms would put her in a world of hurt should this witch really be able to undo what she had done.

With the realization that Cam could be gone—could just disappear as miraculously as he'd come within the hour—black spots suddenly appeared before her eyes and with them came the erratic thuds beneath her ribs.

Don't panic, Claire. You know what to do. Take a deep breath. That's it. Now let it out slowly.

The last thing Cam needed right now was for her to black out.

Deep breath, relax. That's good. It's only a stress-induced arrhythmia, like before, just like the doctor said. It will go away just as it always does if you just stay calm.

As she focused on her breathing and seconds ticked by, the thuds became less frequent and her heart slowed; the scary irregular beats that had started the runaway rhythm giving way to normalcy, to her heart resuming its silent rhythm she never gave thought to. *Okay. See you're okay.*

She took a deep breath.

Wow, her heart hadn't gone that crazy since she'd stood at her mother's open gravesite. Victor and Tracy, thinking she was having a heart attack, had raced her to Massachusetts General, where she learned what was really wrong. "More commonly seen in women, nothing to worry about, unless it continues," the doctor had told her.

"Are ye nae feeling well, lass?"

"I'm fine." She smiled, having done another mental systems check. "I'm fine." And she was. She would handle his going away just as she had every other disaster in her life. By taking it one day at a time.

As their waitress passed, Claire held up her arm. "Tammy, would you please bring us one of those brownie desserts?" Cam couldn't leave without having at least tasted that.

"Sure. Be right with you."

Claire turned her attention back to Cam and found his elbow on the table, his chin resting in his hand, grinning at her. "What?"

"Ye're truly remarkable."

That compliment came out of nowhere. "Thank you."

"Aye. Ye find a naked stranger looming over ye in yer bedchamber one day, ransom and clothe him the next, and now ye're gallivanting all over kingdom to see his needs met. Quite remarkable."

She laughed. "It's not like I have a lot of choice in the matter."

"Ah, but ye do. You could have kicked me to the street that first day or told the sheriff who summoned ye that ye didna ken me from a hole in the ground. Ye did neither."

"To tell you the truth I was too frightened to think and just reacted. You are a bit intimidating."

The right corner of his mouth twitched as he arched an eyebrow. "Me? Never."

She laughed again. "Ya right. I'd hate to meet you in your element—in your world—with a sword in hand."

"Ack, ye'd have naught to fear. I do so admire fine hurdies."

"And what pray tell are hurdies?"

"Ye're sitting on them."

"Oh." Her ass. "Thank you . . . I think."

"Ye're most welcome." He looked about, studied the other diners for a moment, then told her, "I need tell ye I'm a bit torn, uncomfortable with leaving ye."

"Why?" Just an hour ago he'd been hellbent on returning to Rubha.

"I'll be leaving ye defenseless against the deevil's buckies, and I dinna like that. Not a bit."

"Oh." Not because he'd miss her, was feeling the same emotional tug she was feeling, but then she should have expected as much. "I'll be fine. Mr. Brindle will speak with the police. See if he can get more police presence in the neighborhood."

"But what if they come in, Claire? Ye're not strong enough to fend off one, much less several. Ye could do with one of those stun guns. A pistol at the least."

The very thought of a gun under her roof caused her skin to pebble like that of a plucked goose, and she rubbed her arms. "There's no need to worry. The alarm will go off if anyone so much as touches the doors or windows."

"Humph."

Hoping to change the subject, she asked, "What will you do when you get home?"

"Find Da and convince him to hie home. That our joining the Jacobite cause will only prove disastrous. Then get the women and bairns up into the mountains with enough stores to get through the coming months. Only then can I—we—turn our attention to fortifying Rubha." He blew through his teeth. "'Twillna be an easy task, believe me."

"How many women and children are you talking about?"

"Hundreds."

"Oh." Picturing herself holed up in a damp cave with several hundred women and children, all worrying themselves sick over what was going on below for months on end, living on the bare necessities of life, fearing being discovered, she shuddered.

"Here you go," Tammy said as she set their dessert and two forks in the middle of the table. Again looking at Cam, Tammy asked, "Can I get you anything else?"

"Nay, thank ye."

"You're from Scotland, aren't you?"

Apparently shaking off his dismal thoughts, he hit Tammy with a thousand-watt smile. "That I am, lass."

Tammy, not the least immune, beamed back. "I knew it!"

Duh.

Her attention still on Cam, Tammy asked, "Are you

here for the psychic fair? It's a lot of fun. All the witches will be there."

Both she and Cam straightened. Claire asked, "Where?"

"At the Museum Mall in the center of town."

As she gave them directions, Claire scribbled on her place mat. "Thank you, Tammy. We'll just take the check whenever you're ready."

"Oh, okay."

When she walked away, Claire grabbed a fork. "Eat up, MacLeod. We have a fair to go to."

A minute later, Cam was grinning from ear to ear. "This is pure decadence."

Pleased that he liked it, Claire mumbled around a mouthful, "Absolutely."

Their dessert devoured and the check paid, Cam tossed his tartan over his shoulders, she donned her coat and they headed for the door.

Just as they entered the anteroom, a stream of laughing teenagers rushed through the exterior door leading to the parking lot. Beyond the glass stood a tour bus and dozens more teenagers heading for the door.

Cam's arm wrapped around her as he backed up, pulling her out of the way and into a corner as kids, mindful of no one but themselves, continued to push in. In the process, she stomped on his foot.

"Sorry."

"Dinna fash. There's no help for it." He relaxed, settling his hips on the windowsill, his legs spreading, his face now only a few inches above hers. "We're going to be here a while."

She looked left into the restaurant where the

frazzled hostess was trying to gain control, then over her shoulder to the long line still trying to press through the doors and out of the wind, pushing her closer to Cam. Unable to back away, she looked up and found him studying her through lowered lids, his expression thoughtful.

"Sorry about this."

"I'm not." He tucked a lock of her hair behind her ear before his hands slipped beneath her gaping jacket, his long fingers splaying across the small of her back, sending a shiver up her spine.

Uhmm, she wasn't sorry either, but . . .

Then, despite there being no space, more kids piled in, and Claire was forced between Cam's spread legs. As the volume of chatter grew, he said something. Unable to hear, she shook her head in response. He bent and pressed his lips to her ear. "Are ye warm enough, lass?"

Oh, ya. Too warm, in fact. Her hands on his chest, pressed belly to groin now, she could feel his growing arousal. Yup. Right there before what appeared to be the entire sophomore class of Waterboro High, Sir Cameron MacLeod was turned on. Just thinking about it sent heat racing to her cheeks and into her lower belly. God, he felt so extraordinarily good. And nice to know he felt something for her beyond the gratitude he'd expressed earlier while they were eating. Not that this would be going anywhere, but still, it was nice to know before he disappeared . . . to face God only knew what hardships and dangers over the coming months.

Her Highlander. *Please, God, keep him safe.*

She was staring at the beautiful curve of his lips, marveling at the shape when he said, "I'll miss ye, Claire."

Oh, how sweet of him to tell her. "I'll miss you too." More than she would have thought possible when he first appeared, his hand clamped across her mouth to keep her from screaming. "Doesn't seem possible we've known each other only a few days, does it?"

"Nay," he murmured into her ear, "but then we've shared a year of experience in these few days."

She nodded. More like a lifetime. "Every time I think about you sliding down that escalator I can't help but laugh."

His eyes crinkled at the corners as his dimples took shape. "Yer world is a wondrous and confounding place, Claire." His right hand slipped from beneath her jacket, leaving the place where it had rested cold and desolate and came to rest on her jaw. As his thumb brushed her lower lip, he asked, "Will ye promise me ye'll be careful?"

Her heart racing, feeling fuzzy-headed with the intimacy of his touch, she murmured, "I will."

Without warning he leaned forward and his mouth gently came in contact with hers, hot and soft.

Oh, yes, Cam. Do.

She'd been hoping—no, praying—he'd kiss her again, wanting to relish the taste and feel of him a final time.

Chapter Ten

God's teeth, she felt so good in his arms. He wanted to delve deeper, relish the heat and sweetness. She might curse him later, might rail at him a moment from now, but he had to ken what might have been.

She melted against him, causing his heart to soar. *Aye, we might have made a wondrous pairing . . .*

Feminine giggles slowly penetrated the mental haze that holding Claire so close had caused. The lass near his elbow whispered, "Hey, check out the old guys."

Ack!

Reluctantly, he raised his head and glanced left to find a gaggle of lassies grinning at them.

The blonde standing at his elbow smiled up at him. "Hey, don't stop on our account. You were doing just fine."

"Thank ye." Cheeky wee twit.

He turned his attention back to Claire and found her scarlet. "Sorry, lass." He straightened to look over the heads of the whelps filling the wee hall. "Let's get out of here, shall we?"

Without waiting for an answer, he took Claire's hand and wedged his way through the crowd, muttering "Excuse me" as he went, elbowing bairns aside as need be.

When they broke out into fresh air, he took a deep breath, then raked a hand through his hair, mentally cursing the jeans she insisted he wear and the stranglehold they had on his poke of sweeties. "Sorry about that. I shouldna have—"

Claire, still apple-cheeked, pressed a finger to his lips. "Don't worry about it."

He wrapped his hand about hers. "Ah, but I do. Ye've a reputation to maintain."

She surprised him by laughing. "Me? Pah-leeze." She then turned to look about. With her back to him, she murmured, "I enjoyed it." Before he could tell her he had as well, although she would have to be dense as oak not to realize it with his shaft pressing into her as it had, she pointed to her left, saying, "The mall is that way. We'd best get going. I don't know how long the fair will last."

Aye, the witch awaited.

Cam glowered as he looked down the line of colorful booths. Twenty-odd witches and not one of them the high priestess Sandra Mariah Power. Where the hell could she be? "Claire, I dinna think she's here."

"Me either."

Mayhap, if they ceased being so circumspect and just asked someone where she was . . .

"Look." Claire pointed to a purple tent before a

two-story brick shop touting fine clothing. "The sign says she's a psychic. If she is, then she should know where we can find Ms. Power."

Cam warily eyed the tent and the woman sitting at a small table deep within the shadows. "What's a psychic?"

"A soothsayer, someone who can see what others can't, often sees things in advance. Some supposedly read auras."

What the hell was an aura? Cam heaved a sigh. "Fine, let's ask her." Fey, after all, was fey no matter its manifestation and they had naught to lose but more precious time.

Claire stopped before the ten-foot-square tent with its flaps tied back allowing only an upside-down V for an entrance. "Twenty dollars for a reading. Nice money if you can do two or three an hour."

Losing patience—gloaming was fast approaching—Cam grumbled, "After ye."

The psychic, a striking woman with waist-length jet black hair and matching eyes, smiled from behind her white, cloth-covered table as they entered. Cam nodded. "Mistress."

On the table before her sat a deck of large cards and to her right on a wee corner table sat three candles encased in glass chimneys, which explained why the close air hung heavy with the heady scent of sandalwood and something else he couldna identify.

Waving to the two chairs before her, the psychic said, "Come in, come in. Don't be shy. Please take a seat."

Claire smiled as she shook her head. "I'm sorry but we're not here for a reading. We're looking for someone. Sandra Mariah Power. Can you tell us where we might find her?"

"May I ask why?"

Cam snorted and whispered into Claire's ear, "Shouldna she ken that already?"

Hissing, "Behave," she swatted his middle with the back of her hand, then smiled at the woman. "We really need her help."

"For what purpose?"

Ack! "I'm not of this time and need get back to where I belong. To do so, I—we—need Mistress Power's help."

The woman, her high forehead now furrowed, came out from behind her table and held out a hand to Claire. "I'm Julia Browne."

Claire shook the woman's hand. "Hi, I'm Claire MacGregor and this," she waved her free hand toward Cam, "is Sir Cam MacLeod of Rubha, Scotland."

The woman held a hand out to him. He heaved a sigh, took a gentle hold of her delicate bones and bent over them, bringing her knuckles against his lips. *What a bloody waste of time.* "Mistress, 'tis my pleasure."

She studied him for a moment, her pupils taking up the entire of her irises so he couldna tell their color, and laughed, the sound rich and throaty. "You lie admirably, Sir MacLeod. Truth is you're aggravated beyond endurance but that's to be expected, I suppose, given your circumstances."

Cam arched an eyebrow. "And what might that be?"

"You're very uncomfortable here."

Tell him something he didna ken. "So Mistress Power isna here?"

"No, she's not. As a high priestess, she's currently preparing for the Full Moon ceremony."

Of course. "So where might we find her?"

"Patience, Sir MacLeod." She resumed her seat behind the table and waggled a finger at Claire, bringing her closer. She again took Claire's hand in hers, asking, "Is he always so gruff?"

Claire peeked over her shoulder at him and blushed. "No, not always."

The psychic nodded, then shooed Claire away.

"You'll find Sandra on Gallows Hill." She gave them directions.

As they walked away, Cam grumbled, "What was all that about?"

"I haven't the foggiest."

"Well, at least we didna—"

"MacLeod!"

Cam spun at the sound of the psychic's voice to see Julia standing just within the tent, her hand on the flap. "Aye?"

"Forgive her," Julia said. "She was terrified and rightly so."

"I bear no ill will toward Cl—"

"I speak of Minnie, Mhairie."

The Scots tripped on air and the hairs on Cam's nape rose, then quivered like dried reeds before a wind. His skin crawled as the tent flap fell and the psychic disappeared. His mother, Mhairie Stewart, had been in his thoughts only a moment ago; her and what he intended to do to her when next he laid eyes on her.

"Cam, it's getting late, we need to go."

"Aye." He shook like a wet dog, took Claire's hand in his and strode as fast as her shorter legs would allow toward Gallows Hill.

Two minutes later, he happened to look left over a single-story shop and spied what appeared to be mast tips. "Claire, do my eyes deceive me or is that a ship yon?"

Claire craned her neck to look around him. "Ah, ya, that's the *Friendship*. She's a three-masted merchantman, a replica of her namesake which was built in 1797. A few Christmases ago, I donated some money in Tavish's name to help build her. Thought it would please him. He was so into shipbuilding."

Ack! The woman would be the death of him. Here she had knowledge and access to a ship—of a variety he kenned well—and had said naught. "Come on."

He strode seaward down the next side street. At Water Street, before the harbor, he turned left and all but ran past dozens of stately brick homes that faced seaward with their picket fences and what Claire called widow's walks. They passed half a dozen stately government buildings with plaques in front of them, but he only had eyes for the pier and the sleek black-and-white *Friendship*.

"Cam! Please, slow down. It's not going anywhere."

Aye, the pier did lack the usual clamor and cargo. He slowed. "Why is it not?"

She took a huffing breath. "Because the *Friendship* is a U.S. Coast Guard training vessel and living museum."

"I dinna ken yer meaning."

"I mean it spends more time at anchor in harbor—either here or in Boston—than it does anything else."

"Is she nae seaworthy?" She certainly looked seaworthy. Newly launched, in fact.

"Oh, she's definitely seaworthy, although she was struck by lightning a while back. Blew the hell out of one of her masts and some decking, but the damage has been repaired."

Aye, ships did get hit on occasion. He'd spent the better part of his youth on one or another of the two frigates his clan, a seafaring sept, owned. He kenned the dangers well.

He slowed as they approached the end of the pier. "Do ye ken the master?"

"No, Cam, I don't. I just wanted to contribute to help build her." Trying to catch her breath, she asked, "Do you want to go on board? It only costs a few dollars."

"They charge ye to simply look?" What nonsense was this?

"Yes. To walk through history."

Humph. History, his arse. She was a living, breathing vessel straining at her ropes. He looked at the queue of waiting citizens, then at the ship. All on the deck appeared to be in order. The reefed canvas was new, the paint fresh, the blocks sound, and the rigging well-oiled. Examining her interior could wait. With any luck, the witch would ken how to break the curse and he'd have no need for the *Friendship*. But should he, he at least now kenned where to find her. Garnering a crew to man her would be another matter altogether . . .

"Claire, we need find the witch."

* * *

Gallows Hill, a rocky prominence covered in wild grass and sparse trees, site of the 1692 witch hangings, stood cold and bleak. Its naked trees rattled branches in counter time with their steps as they climbed.

"Are ye sure this is it, Claire? I dinna see a gallows."

Claire laughed as she puffed at his side. "They're long gone, MacLeod."

"Ah, and the land is going to waste." The rest of Salem, now alight and sparkling like a fairy land below, was packed wall to wall with houses, some so close they barely had space to breathe.

"This is a historic site. I imagine they've placed restrictions on land use."

Something moved at the crest. "Look, to the right. That must be her."

As they approached, the shape became a woman in a long black cape. Lord, please let this be the woman they sought.

Claire waved. "Hello! Miss Power?"

The woman, her hands buried within her cloak, waited for them to come to within six feet of her before saying, "Yes?"

Cam wasn't sure what he'd expected but finding a fair and fulsome woman of middle years, of about five and a half feet with flashing eyes that were first ringed in amber, then green and finally blue, wasna it. He bowed deeply. "Mistress, 'tis my honor. This is Claire MacGregor of Boston and I, Sir Cam MacLeod of Rubha, Scotland. We're here to seek yer assistance in a most pressing matter."

"How did you know where to find me?"

Claire waved in the direction of town. "Julia Browne told us."

The woman smiled for the first time. "Julia sent you?"

Cam grinned. "Well, *sent* wouldna be entirely accurate. We told her why we were looking for ye and she told us where we might hope to find ye."

"I see." She studied them for a minute more in the rays of the setting sun, the light playing tricks with her eyes, changing them from mainly blue to green. "Julia is new to our community, but she's very astute and I trust her judgment. Come along then."

They silently followed the witch to the base of the tree where she stopped before what looked like an altar. "Tonight," she told them, "we celebrate a full moon. I have only one more thing to do, then we can talk."

They stood in respectful silence as the woman went about her work, setting several candles and a large bowl on the altar. Finished with her preparations, she said, "Since Julia has already vetted you, shall we retire to my home? We'll be able to speak in greater comfort there."

Humph. The psychic had asked only two questions of them, but no matter. "Thank ye."

He took Claire's gloved hand and they followed the witch down the hill. As gloaming passed into night, Claire whispered, "Wonder what her home looks like?"

"Nay doubt much like yers. No one would ken from Minnie's croft that she's a witch."

Claire faltered. "You never told me your mother was a practicing witch . . . a Pagan."

He shrugged and tugged her along. "Was there a need? I said she'd placed a curse on me."

"Yes, but I'd assumed . . . oh, never mind."

At a brown two-story home—what Claire called a salt box—the witch opened her windowless front door and bid them enter.

After taking his breachen feile and Claire's coat and hanging them on hooks in the front hall, she shed her cape exposing her waist-length gold and amber curls, then led them into her colorful parlor. It no more resembled Minnie's sparse quarters than day did night, save for the fact that Mistress Power's ceiling beams were also low and he had to duck.

She waved to the sofa and chairs before her hearth. "Please make yourselves comfortable while I make some tea."

"'Tis no need." He really wanted to get this done.

"Of course there is."

Claire immediately settled onto the red settee before a lower table and patted the cushion beside her. "Don't be rude, Cam. Sit."

He huffed. Deciding the two chairs before the window were too fragile to bear his weight, he settled on the settee next to Claire. "I pray she can undo this."

Looking none too happy for some reason, Claire muttered, "We'll know soon enough."

"Aye." A soft almost inaudible padding caused him to look to the door through which the witch had disappeared. A cat, fluffy and white and as fat as a pigeon, entered the parlor. When it stopped before him and began to purr, he leaned forward. "Good eve, puss. I take it ye're her familiar."

In response, the cat rubbed in serpentine fashion against his outstretched legs. Assuming that meant aye, he reached down and scratched it beneath her chin. "Ye need one of these, lass. To keep ye company."

Claire frowned as she warily eyed the cat. "No, I don't. It would only scratch up my furniture and leave hair all over the place."

"What's a few hairs between friends? Besides, she'd warm yer lap on these cold nights."

Claire shuddered. "I'm not looking to become the neighborhood cat lady."

"How would having one cat—"

"Ah, I see you found Ghost."

At the sound of her mistress's voice, the cat scampered across the room to greet her.

Once they were settled—they with their tea, the cat with a saucer of milk—Mistress Power asked, "How may I be of help?"

Cam took a deep breath. So much rested on his being articulate, on her believing his and Claire's tales. "I respectfully request that ye break the curse binding me here, mistress."

To his relief she didna so much as arch an eyebrow but said, "Go on."

Relieved she hadn't scoffed, he told her all he kenned from the moment he awoke in Claire's bedchamber to the present. Claire then told her how she came to be in possession of the chest and how she'd opened the puzzle box. When at last they grew silent, the witch asked, "Did you bring this puzzle box with you?"

"Yes." Claire's hands were shaking as she reached into her purse. "And the scroll his mother had written. I've repeatedly opened the box, said the same words, but nothing changes."

Mistress Power grinned. "Why would you expect it to? That which was once inside is now out." She smiled at Cam.

The witch did have a point. He was as out as out can be. "But can ye undo this curse, mistress? Send me back from whence I've come?"

"May I examine the scroll and box?"

Claire handed them to her. After reading the scroll, Mistress Power studied the intricate carvings as she quietly hummed to herself, whether in ritual or from habit, he couldna tell.

To Claire, she said, "Could you please show me the pattern you used?"

Claire did as the witch bid, explaining her logic, which caused the witch to grin, though he couldna find the least humor in it.

The witch finally placed the box and scroll on the table before them and folded her hands in her lap. "I wish I could be of help but I can't undo this."

"But—" How could she not? Cam bolted to his feet, startling the cat, who'd been complacently licking its paws.

Nay. They'd come all this way. She simply had to help.

Claire placed a hand on his arm. "But surely, Miss Power, there must be some way—"

Mistress Power held up a hand to silence her. "This curse, as you call it, has already been undone." She looked at Cam. "I assume that your mother fully intended to release you when she thought it was safe. Unfortunately, she died prior to doing so. Claire came along and undid it. There is nothing for me to undo."

Ack! He should have kenned better. No wonder these witches could tout their so-called skills so publicly. They had none, so the church and elders hadna reason to fear. Worse, he'd wasted precious time.

"Do not despair, Mr. MacLeod. Fate may have cast a cruel blow but has seen you to a good place and surrounded you with caring friends."

"Ye dinna ken the heartache this duplicity has caused, Mistress."

"I think I do. Not so long ago in the greater scheme of life, three frightened girls set in motion a lie that took twenty innocent souls to the gallows . . . right here on this very hill. Not one of those souls was a witch, yet the girls claimed they'd been bewitched."

He raked the hair off his face as the squat clock sitting on the mantel ticked away minutes, stealing time like water from a poor spigot. "Mistress, not twenty but *thousands upon thousands* are going to die if I dinna get back to where I belong."

Mistress Power sighed, her lovely multicolored eyes growing glassy, shifting to green as tears welled behind her thick lashes. "I'm so sorry, Mr. MacLeod. Even if I were able to reduce you again to essence . . . soul . . . and place you in that box, what then? The box is simply a box that has passed from hand to hand for generations. There's no more magic in it than there is in my having my great-grandmother's spell book over there." She waved in the general direction of bookcase to his right. "If I did send you back to Scotland, there's no one awaiting you there. Those who knew you and the magic are long gone.

"I do empathize with your plight, Mr. MacLeod, I truly

do, but there is no way to undo this. More importantly, we can't change history. We can only learn from it."

"*Nay*! I willna accept this."

The witch cast a worried look toward Claire and rose, her hands clasped before her. "Mr. MacLeod, you have no choice but to accept it. I wish you well."

"To hell with ye!"

Blood roared in his ears as he stormed from the room. Had he remained, he'd have started smashing things . . . starting with that bookcase and her bloody book of spells. Great lot of good they could do him.

Biting cold slapped his face as he crossed the witch's threshold. Piercing, frigid, and laden with the tang of salt, the wind tasted and felt like home. Of Rubha.

He had to go home.

Behind him, Claire's mumbled apology was caught by the wind and then tossed away to be replaced by the sound of the thick door closing.

A moment later, her hand settled on his forearm. "Cam, I'm so sorry, I thought . . . I'd hoped . . ."

He shook off her hand. "I have nae need for sympathy, Claire. I willna be taking this lying down."

Chapter Eleven

"Cam, where the—"

Oh God, she was going to be sick again.

With her head killing her, Claire had no time to do anything more than lean over her kitchen sink. In what felt like a lifetime later, she was finally able to raise her head and turn on the faucet. Holding her breath, she flushed away the mess she'd made, rinsed out her mouth, and settled on a kitchen chair, her head in her hands.

"I'll have to get better to die."

When the world stopped spinning, she snuffled and made her way to the bathroom. "Aspirin. I need more aspirin."

She flipped on the light. Through gritty eyes, she stared in disbelief at the white towels strewn on the bathroom floor, then at the whiskers and soap scum coating the hand-painted peonies lining her sink. "I take back every wistful thought I ever had about you, Cameron MacLeod."

Not only did he take up more space in a room than

any decent man ought, but was sloppy and he'd become reticent since meeting with the witch. Worse, he went through cola and shampoo like they were water—which he spent far too much time singing in. And she didn't want to even get started on the thermostats. If he turned them down one more time, she'd run him through with that bloody sword of his should they ever get it back.

Augh!

She kicked the towels out of her way—her head pounding almost too hard for her to breathe, much less allow her to bend over and pick them up—and opened the medicine chest. She cracked open a new bottle of aspirin and took three, reasoning they were small. The last two hadn't done a thing to relieve the throbbing in her head or her stiff muscles, which ached unmercifully from all her shivering.

A pill caught at the back of her throat. Gagging, she flipped on the faucet and gulped water from her hand. God, she felt like shit. Flu. Had to be. And no small wonder after all the running around in the cold she'd been doing.

I never should have brought him to Salem.

She should have gone by herself, but no, she had to do show and tell. Moreover, had she gone alone, he never would have had an opportunity to kiss her, and she wouldn't have melted into it, gotten lost in the dark and sweet, wet and wild of it. Dumb, dumb, dumb.

And what on earth had ever possessed her to think their living together—albeit, celibately—would work? He might have the most beautiful male body she'd ever laid eyes on, but that didn't make for compatibility. He awoke before the birds to tear through the books she'd pulled from the library each day long before any decent person even thought to open their eyes, and then he'd disappear after supper saying he had to get some air and wouldn't return until two in the morning. What the hell was he doing night after night until that hour? She needed eight hours of sleep. She needed order. She needed her down time after dealing with customers and bills all day. But not Cam. He read, he ate, he puttered, and then paced the city. So needless to say, she didn't unwind and didn't get any sleep. She worried, and quite naturally, about what trouble he'd get into next.

God, why had she told him as he sat on that bus regarding the world in miserable, stony silence that he'd have a place with her for as long as he needed it? Until she could get him home?

She huffed. Because she was half in love with loud, sloppy yet incredibly sexy—and in his own way charming—Cam MacLeod, that's why.

Another chill raced down her spine causing her already-sore muscles to contract and her teeth to chatter. Great, her fever was back. She looked about. Why was she in the bathroom? Oh ya, she needed aspirin.

She opened the medicine cabinet and dumped two pills, then another into her palm. Take three, they're small.

She shivered again, flipped off the light and stood in her bedroom doorway looking at her big comfy bed. Maybe she should lie down for a minute, just one minute to let the pills take affect. Then she could go back to work. Another shudder wracked her. Ya, just rest for a minute.

Teeth chattering, she jerked back the quilt and climbed into bed. As she curled into a ball facing the window and the frigid night beyond, the glow from the street lights below seared the back of her eyes. She closed them.

Cam, where the hell are you?

Cam cursed under his breath when a drunkard shouted, "Closer, baby" to Claire's near-naked friend, Tracy Simpson.

Christ's blood. Would he ever get over his shock of this place Tracy . . . and now he . . . worked in? More alarming was discovering half these lasses were married. What kind of man would allow such?

Tracy, dressed in little more than high-heeled silver shoes, knelt and thrust her hips forward in hopes of receiving another tip, as she called the notes strangers pressed between her breasts and into her scant whatever.

Realizing the drunkard stood empty-handed and was about to grab Tracy's bare arse, Cam stepped forward and grabbed the man by the scruff, hauling him backward. "Ye were warned, sir. No one touches the lasses."

The drunkard, tottering sideways, swung an impotent fist. "Get your goddamn hands off me!"

Cam tightened his hold and shoved the well-dressed man who'd been tossing whiskey back for the last three hours toward the door. "Out with ye."

Halfway across the showroom, the drunkard slung another fist, trying to shake Cam off. "Let go of me!"

In response, Cam twisted his wrist, tightening the man's collar and effectively shutting off his air and any fight the sorry sot might have in him. By the time Cam pushed him through the Purple Pussycat's front door, the drunkard's face was purple.

On the stoop, Cam released his grip and gave the man a shove, sending him flailing into the parking lot. As the man gasped and regained his footing in the slush, Cam checked the parking lot for trouble, but found only steam, lavender in the glare of the Purple Pussycat's sign, rising with the ease of ghosts from the sewer opening ten feet away and a nearby streetlight blinking as it crackled. Somewhere to his right, wheels whined as they spun on wet pavement. At a distance, a siren whooped. He shook his head. God, what a place. The sounds of man and his machines, not nature, were the constant.

The drunkard, wavering, then falling to the slick pavement, cursed as he tore his pants.

"Be gone with ye, and next time keep yer hands to yerself."

The man flung out an arm as he staggered to his feet, his middle finger extended in the air. "Screw you!"

And the same to ye, ye friggin' idiot.

Cam stood at the door until the man stumbled away, in no hurry to go back inside—the noise the owner had the bollocks to call music giving him a monumental headache. The place was almost empty and the lasses would soon be done with gyrating on their golden poles and on men's laps. He shook his

head. That one of the lasses was Claire's friend was
beyond his ken. But then, Tracy had been the one to
call and tell him about this bouncer position. Although not work he would ever have sought, it was
the only labor he apparently qualified for in this
world, since he had no driver's license or guild mem-
bership. At least it paid well and for little more than
towering over patrons and glowering, so they'd stop
annoying the lasses and arguing amongst themselves.
On one occasion, he had had to slam a fist into a
man's middle to get his attention, but generally—

The door behind him burst open and raucous
music filtered out and with it the Purple Pussycat's last
three patrons, laughing and hooting.

Cam closed the door behind them. "Good eve, gentlemen."

One yawned. "Same to you, big guy."

When they drove away, Cam went inside and bolted
the door behind him. In the main room, he found all
the lasses in one state of undress or another, lined up
at the bar with drinks before them, counting their
tips. He leaned over the bar and waved to get the barkeep's attention. "Mike, please, I beg ye, turn off that
racket!"

The barkeep laughed, threw a switch and the
Purple Pussycat grew blessedly silent.

"Thank ye. My head was about to explode."

Now if he could just get Tracy to drink up so he
could see her home and then get home to Claire. The
poor wee lass had been feeling odd for the past two
days and was now decidedly peaked. She'd barely
touched her supper. More worrisome, she'd been

growing more and more terse and that wasna the least like her.

As he lifted the first of the chairs onto a table for the cleaning woman, Tracy spun on her stool to face him. "MacLeod, thanks for taking that guy off me tonight."

"Ye welcome, lass."

"It's payday. Better come get your check before Mike decides to keep it."

Verra good. He strode to the bar where Mike, the owner and barkeep, held out a piece of paper to him.

Cam looked at it and, scowling, handed the check back. "Ye said fifty a day. Four days at fifty should be two hundred. Nay this. Do it again."

The man thrust the check back at him. "I had to take out Social Security and taxes, man. Sorry. It's the law."

Cam looked at Tracy for confirmation. She shrugged. "It's true, MacLeod. The man's not trying to cheat you."

Hell's hatches! 'Twas highway robbery.

He snatched the check from Mike's hand, shoved it into his pocket and reached for another chair. At this rate, he'd never repay his debt to Claire. These people should have themselves another revolution. Ack! So he'd need the bucks after all. As soon as he got home, he'd query Mrs. Grouse and learn all he could about the Franklin Park. For now, he would contemplate transporting and storage.

By the time he lifted the last chair onto the last table, he had the venison storage worked out, and Tracy was dressed and standing by the door.

"Ready?"

"Aye." Well past ready.

Outside, Tracy slipped her arm through his. "Thanks for walking me home. I really appreciate it. It can be scary out here sometimes."

"Ye're welcome."

"Have you told Claire yet that you've found a job? That you're working here?"

"Nay, and she'd best not learn of it."

Tracy squeezed his arm as she laughed up at him. "She won't hear it from me, but why haven't you told her?"

Because all but pimping women wasna what any God-fearing man worthy of the name would do. "How I earn my bed and board is my concern, not Claire's."

"She's charging you rent?"

"Of course not. But I wish to repay her kindness as quickly as possible."

And before she learns how he'd managed it. Before he left as suddenly as he'd come, for go home he would.

As a car swished past, spraying gritty slush all over their boots, he said, "Speaking of bed and board, ye need to be giving some serious thought to doing something else. This dancing isna good for you." For any woman for that matter.

"Why, Cam MacLeod. How nice to know you care."

"Ye ken my meaning, lass. 'Tis neither safe nor . . . healthy."

When they rounded the corner onto Tracy's street, she slipped, regained her footing and shifted her hold, pressing a breast against his arm. Grinning, she said, "I won't be dancing at the Pussycat much longer. I haven't had a chance to tell Claire yet, but I got the role in the summer theater production of *Grease* that I'd been after. I'll be in Salisbury by March first, that's when rehearsals begin."

"Ye'll be an actress? On stage?" 'Twas going from the skillet into the fire.

"Isn't it great? I'm so excited I could just scream."

He could, too, but for another reason entirely. Dare he ask if she'd be clothed at least?

Grinning up at him, her eyes glowing in the lamplight, she asked, "Would you like to come up for a nightcap, to help me celebrate? I have some Guinness, that dark ale you like."

"Nay, thank ye. Claire is waiting for me."

Tracy laughed, her voice ringing sweet and clear in the cold air, a sharp contrast to Claire's more husky tones. "No, she's not. She's sound asleep. Has been for the last four hours at least, if I know my friend."

Humph. If Tracy were truly a friend she wouldna be batting her lovely blond lashes at him and trying to coax him into her apartment. Not that he and Claire had done anything more than kiss, although he certainly wouldna mind if they did, the more he thought on it. And the longer he stayed, the more he thought.

Aye. Claire was definitely driving him wode as she stumbled about each morning in her furry robe and stocking feet, her hair every which way, smelling of warm sheets and woman, grumbling that he was making too much noise while surreptitiously watching his every move. Aye, he'd seen how she watched him, how her eyes locked onto his arms or chest as he moved about. Devil that he was, he'd occasionally flex or stretch when he had no need just to watch the fine blush rise in her cheeks. Aye, the lass was every bit as aware of him as he was of her, although she'd likely deny it with her dying breath. And given his situation, well she should.

"Can I take your silence for a yes?"

"Nay, I'm afraid not. I'm tired and need get home."

"Aw, just a wee drop. I promise to be good."

He could well imagine. He'd caught a glimpse of Tracy's lap dance earlier in the evening and kenned expertise when he saw it. There wasna a way he'd be dipping his wick into that oil lamp. "I canna."

"Okay, but I won't take no for an answer next time."

Ack.

When they reached her door, she stretched and kissed his cheek. "Good night, MacLeod."

"Good night, Tracy. Be sure to lock the door behind ye."

She made her way up the salted steps and once inside, waved. When he heard the lock click, he turned toward home and Claire.

Thirty minutes later, Cam scowled looking into a well-lit Velvet Pumpkin. Now why had she left the lights on? He shrugged and, key in hand, reached for the brass handle only to have the door swing wide with the mere touch of his hand.

Hearing silence, his heart jolted. She'd never leave the door unlocked, nor would she go to sleep without turning on her alarm.

Giving only a cursory look at the door frame, noting that it hadn't been forced, he strode in, looking for any hint that she'd been harmed, but all appeared to be as it should. "Claire!"

Had she fallen and broken her neck? He ran to the back room. Finding all as he'd left it—the chair he was mending still on the work bench, the tools precisely where he'd left them, Tavish's possessions still in the process of being inventoried, but no Claire—he took the stairs two and three at a time.

At the top, his heart beat a frantic tattoo against his ribs as he threw open Claire's apartment door. "Claire!"

Seeing nothing amiss in the parlor or in the kitchen, he strode into her dark bedroom. By the light of the streetlights, he finally saw her in a tumble of bed linen.

"Claire?" Wondering how the hell could she sleep through all his bellowing, noting the room was unusually hot and the air acrid with the smell of sweat and vomit, he reached for her bedside lamp.

"God's teeth!" Claire, her eyes sunken, lay deathly pale in a wad of damp sheeting, blood oozing from her nose, her hair matted with sweat. He grabbed her arms, alarmed to feel heat pouring off her as he hauled her onto his lap. How long had she been like this?

"Claire." He patted her cheek in hopes of rousing her but her head only lolled onto his chest. "Claire, wake up! Can ye hear me, lass?"

Not daring to leave her alone, Cam scooped her into his arms and rushed out of the apartment where he spied Mrs. Grouse, her robe in hand, struggling up the first of the steps leading to the third floor. "Mrs. Grouse, 'tis Claire. She's burning and willna wake."

"Calm down and come."

Mrs. Grouse headed back to her apartment and Cam followed. Inside, she pointed to her sofa. "Put her down there."

He shook his head. He wasna putting Claire down anywhere. He sat, Claire cradled in his arms. "What's wrong with her?"

Mrs. Grouse clucked repeatedly as she gently touched and prodded Claire. Finally, she straightened, her lower lip caught in her teeth, which did naught for his peace of mind. "I don't know," she murmured, "but she needs a doctor." She picked up her phone. A heartbeat later she said, "210 Dartmouth. My neighbor Claire MacGregor, she's unconscious. No wounds. No, no diseases that I know of. No, she's burning with fever and there's blood coming from her nose. No, this isn't an overdose, you idiot! She doesn't take drugs. Yes. Yes. Okay."

She dropped the telephone and reached for her coat. "The ambulance is on its way, Cameron. We need to take her downstairs."

He rose. "Where will it take us?"

"Probably to Brigham, that's the closest hospital."

Oh God. Hospitals were for the dying. As his throat constricted, his hold on Claire tightened. "Nay. Ye need tell me where I can find a doctor so I can bring him here."

Mrs. Grouse grabbed her purse. "Cameron, they have doctors at Brigham who'll take very good care of her. It's one of the best hospitals in the city. Come."

"But—"

"Trust me. I've been a patient there myself. Now

come on. We don't have time to argue. The ambulance will be here any minute."

Torn, wanting to trust the woman but not sure that he should, Cam reluctantly followed, Claire in his arms.

At the front of the shop, Mrs. Grouse mumbled what sounded like a curse. "Cam, we need her insurance card." She pointed to a velvet sofa to her right. "Please lay her down there, then run upstairs and grab her purse. I'd do it but it might take all night. It should be next to the coffee table. All her identification is in it."

"Why would they need identification? We both ken her."

"Cam, this is very important. They won't treat her without her card. I promise I won't let anyone touch her until you return. Now hurry."

Muttering every expletive he could lay tongue to, Cam lowered Claire as gently as possible to the sofa only to have her groan when her neck came to rest on the sofa arm. Ack, whatever was wrong with her, please God let her survive.

The unmistakable throbbing whoop of an emergency vehicle brought him to his feet. As it grew louder, he ran for the stairs.

Chapter Twelve

A woman in blue materialized in the waiting room doorway and shouted, "Mr. MacLeod?"

Cam jerked to his feet—the sheriff they'd placed at the door after he'd gone into a rage when they'd taken Claire away also stood, but Cam ignored him. "Aye."

The woman waved him toward her. "You can come in now."

'Bout bloody time! He and Mrs. Grouse had been fretting for hours. "Is she all right?"

"The doctor will speak with you now."

Not liking the evasive response, Cam motioned toward Mrs. Grouse. "Can she come as well?"

Claire's intrepid tenant had skillfully lied for him, claiming Cam and Claire were betrothed and then had guided him through the maze of documents they'd asked him to sign. Now, fearing he wouldna understand all that the doctor would tell him, that he'd not ken enough to ask the right questions, he needed Mrs. Grouse at his side.

"Yes," the nurse said, "she can come as well."

He helped Mrs. Grouse rise—the hard chairs had done naught for her aging hips—and followed the nurse into the mysteries of Brigham Hospital's emergency room.

The woman led them into a small, well-lit room where, to his great relief, he found Claire breathing—albeit amidst a myriad of beeping machines. After glancing at the instruments hanging from the wall and at the large needles sitting on a metal tray, he took Claire's hand in his and brushed a lock from her pale cheek, alarmed to find that she was still unconscious.

"Ack, love, ye look terrible."

"Mr. MacLeod, I'm Dr. Willis." A gray-haired man in a white coat held out a hand and Cam shook it. "Your fiancée appears to have a serious case of influenza."

Influenza. The word rang like a death knell in Cam's head. The disease had killed Margie and many others in his clan.

"And how do ye ken this? Could it not be something else?"

"We've done blood work and a throat culture and won't have the results for another day or so, but I feel fairly certain—given her symptoms—that we're dealing with the flu."

"So this liquid," Cam nodded toward the water bag suspended above Claire, "will heal her?" Why else would they have it connected to her?

"No. We can't use antibiotics. They have no effect on viruses. Viruses have to run their course and die a natural death. The fluids just hastens the process and makes her feel better."

Anti-bite-tocks and viruses? Why in hell could this man not speak English? "But after this . . ." Cam waved a hand, at a loss to describe all that he was seeing, "then she'll be well."

"We have every reason to believe so. She's still very dehydrated, still febrile—feverish—so we need to watch her for a few days in the hospital."

Cam took Claire's hand in his. "When will she wake?"

"She already has, once while we started the IV and again while we drew blood." He examined the machines, then touched Claire's brow. "Her room in the Progressive Care Unit should be ready shortly. The nurse will let you know when they're ready to move her upstairs."

The man turned to leave and Cam grabbed his arm, needing to make one more thing clear. "I'm staying with her."

The doctor looked at Cam's hand then into his eyes and smiled. "That's fine. She'll be in a private room."

Cam let go, and the doctor left, leaving Claire, much to his consternation, to the machines and their worried selves.

"Mrs. Grouse, do ye believe him?" Claire's lips and skin were so dry and pale, her eyes so sunken, she looked like she'd been bled thoroughly, although he could find no evidence of it.

Mrs. Grouse moved to the opposite side of the strange bed and took hold of Claire's other hand. "Yes, I do. She's young. It will just take a little time."

Aye, but how much?

* * *

Never patient with incompetence at the best of times, Cam huffed watching the two wee nurses struggle to get Claire shifted from the emergency room bed to the one in the room. Annoyed they should even try, he growled, "I'll do it."

Looking relieved, they stepped back and Cam scooped Claire into his arms and swiveled toward the bed only to have the dark-skinned nurse say, "Whoa, not so fast. I don't want you pulling out her Foley."

She bent and a moment later tossed a bag with a wee bit of deep amber liquid in it onto the new bed.

Ack, more tubes. "What's that?"

"A urine bag. We'll take out the catheter when she's able to get up and go to the bathroom."

Incredulous that he'd heard correctly, Cam gently lowered Claire onto the crisp white sheets, then examined what came from under the hem of her hospital gown. "Are ye telling me that this hose is inside her, uhmm . . . private place, and that this dark liquid is *piss*?"

"That's precisely what I'm telling you. Now, if you'll please step out, we'll get Miss MacGregor situated."

Good God almighty. Imagining what the insertion must have felt like, Cam shuddered and joined Mrs. Grouse in the hall just outside the door. Pointing back into the room, he asked, "Is this right? That they should do this . . . this fooly to her?"

Mrs. Grouse nodded as she yawned hugely. "Cam, it's a Foley catheter and it's fine. I had one when they took out my gallbladder." She then looked at her watch. "Would you believe it's taken them seven hours to get her up here?"

Nay. And the poor auld woman looked nearly as rough as Claire. She should make her way home now that Claire was supposedly in capable hands, but how? He wasna about to leave Claire, nor could he let Mrs. Grouse go abroad on her own. She could slip on the ice, fall prey to a street gang—

"Cameron, I hope you don't mind but I called Victor, Claire's designer friend, to come pick me up and take me home. I'm sorry, but I'm so tired I can barely stand."

Ah, a problem solved. "I canna thank ye enough for coming with us. Had ye not—"

"I'm glad I could be of some help. She's like a daughter to me."

"I'll not let any harm come to her."

She patted his cheek. "I know, dear. You're a good man."

Kenning better, he remained silent.

The nurses came through the door, their arms loaded with damp linen. The youngest, a blonde no higher than his elbow said, "You can go in now."

"Thank ye."

He settled Mrs. Grouse in the bedside chair and took Claire's hand only to find a wee red light attached to one of her fingers. Now what? From the neck of her gown sprang a new series of colorful wires connecting her to a machine similar to the one that had beeped at her side downstairs. All puzzlements with no apparent end, but all he'd soon learn.

He rubbed his thumb across her palm. Did her skin

really feel a wee bit plumper or was that just wishful thinking on his part? Damn.

Someone rapped on the door frame, Cam turned—dreading whatever the nurse had coming next—and found a worried-looking man of middle years, an enormous bouquet of flowers in hand, standing in the doorway.

The man smiled as he came forward. "Cameron MacLeod, I presume. I've heard a lot about you from Tracy. I'm Victor Delucci, Claire's friend."

Shorter than Cam by a hand, lighter in weight by four stones, dark-haired and handsome, Delucci stuck out a hand and Cam clasped it, discovering the man had a good grip, but had palms as smooth as Claire's. Obviously not a swordsman.

Delucci greeted Mrs. Grouse. "Hey, Mrs. G." He bent and kissed her cheek. "How's our girl doing?"

Our girl? If the man and Claire were close, why then was he meeting Victor for the first time?

Mrs. Grouse rocked to her feet. "She's doing as well as can be expected, I think." After relating all the doctor had said, she reached for her purse. "I'm ready to go whenever you are."

Delucci placed the flowers on the side table, leaned over the bed rails, and to Cam's consternation kissed Claire's forehead. "Sweet dreams, sweetie. I'll drop by tomorrow."

After Mrs. Grouse did the same, they'd left, but his and Claire's quiet was short lived. The dark-skinned nurse returned, shot something into the water bag above Claire's head, then rapidly went through the workings of Claire's bed, the TV, telephone, the emergency light in the garderobe, and what he should do with the items she placed on the bedside table.

By the time the woman left, Cam felt much like he did after an all-day battle. Exhausted. He pulled the chair closer to the bed and took Claire's hand in his. "Well, lass, 'tis just ye and me against the wee viruses now."

Aye, and he'd never felt more useless in his life, a warrior armed to the teeth without a visible foe.

He lowered the bed rail and ran a finger along her jaw. So soft. "Woman, ye have to cease frightening me so. I dinna ken how much more I can take."

He fingered a lock of her hair, recalling the first time he'd laid eyes on her, big-eyed and teary. If he lived to be one hundred, he'd never forget how she'd bounced onto her bed and challenged him, demanded that he give her back his sword. "Ye were a sight to behold, lass, you truly were, hissing and spitting, thinking I was robbing ye blind."

And then on a whim he'd kissed her. And she'd responded with a kiss that had haunted him until he'd done it again. And still he wanted more.

He brought her fingers to his lips. "Love, ye have to get well, do ye hear?" She simply had to. She had so much yet to accomplish. Hell, she'd yet to marry and have bairns . . .

Ack! Ye're a bloody arse, MacLeod.

They'd been living under the same roof and breaking bread together for days and he still had no idea if she even wanted such for herself. He'd been so bloody focused on finding his way home, learning about this new world, that he'd never even bothered

to ask how she felt about him living with her, much
less asked what she might want out of life, what she
dreamed of. Hell, he'd had to check her license to
learn her age and date of birth for the clerk below.

Sighing, he rested his forehead on his folded arms;
the realization that he'd simply taken from her day in
and day out, as if it were his due, but not given back,
caused a burning at the back of his throat and eyes.

But no more. Should she survive—please, God, let
her—he would do his utmost to pay back her every
kindness, and to that end, he'd learn all that he could
about her, even if it meant dogging her every step day
and night.

Chapter Thirteen

"Cam . . ."

"I'm here, love." The warmth encircling her hand became a gentle squeeze.

Ah, finally, he's home. And had he just said *love?* Deciding she'd been dreaming, she grinned or rather tried to. Augh, her tongue and teeth felt like they were coated in moss. "Thirsty." She should get up and drink something.

Before she could open her eyes something wet and slimy smelling of lemons stroked her lips. *Auuugh!* She knocked it away and opened her eyes, blinking at the brilliant sunshine pouring through the curtained window. What the—?

There were no curtains in her bedroom.

Claire's eyes flew open. As her gaze flew around the room, she struggled to sit. *Oh my God, I'm in a hospital*!

Cam's strong arm came around her and the head of the bed started to rise. "Easy, lass. Ye've had a nasty bout of influenza, but ye're doing just fine."

Yes, she'd been sick as a dog. "But—" She waggled

the clip attached to her right index finger, then, feeling something tug on her chest, peered down the front of her hospital gown. She was wired. She squinted at Cam. His eyes were bloodshot and his hair, normally neat and in a queue, hung loose and looked like it hadn't been brushed in a month. "You need a shave."

He ran a hand along his scruffy jaw. "I thought I might grow a beard."

Ewww. "Please tell me you're kidding."

The corners of his eyes crinkled as he grinned. "I havena had a chance to shave."

"How long have I been here?"

He adjusted her pillow, then pressed the nurse call button on the side rail. "Just a day and a wee bit, though I must tell ye, finding ye unconscious like I did scared the sh—stuffing out of me."

Unconscious? Wow. "I'm sorry. I've had flu before and thought if I could just get some sleep . . ."

He leaned forward and kissed her forehead. "Dinna fash yerself, love, it's over, although I'd greatly appreciate it if ye didna get it again."

"Me, too." And he'd called her *love* again. Knowing she shouldn't dwell on the endearment, that he probably called every woman in his life "love," she looked around the room again, this time seeing numerous bouquets lined up across a dresser. "Wow, the flowers are lovely. Who are they from?" There were so many it looked like someone had been planning her wake.

"The red roses are from Mrs. Grouse and the pink ones from Victor. Tracy sent the daisies." He plucked the card from the huge display of yellow carnations on the end. "This one came in this morning, says 'Get well soon. I need the money, the Cocky Rooster.'"

Her laugh sounded more like a croak. "That's the pub down the street. Tracy must have told them I was in here. I eat there . . . well, I used to eat there two to three times a week. Their clams aren't as good as those at the Union Oyster House, but they're cheaper and I adore clams."

"Humph. So why dinna ye eat there now?"

Because you're here, and I enjoy watching you devour everything I put before you. Nope, not going there. "Because it's Christmas and with my later hours it's just easier to fix something at home rather than go out."

His eyes narrowed. "Humph."

"You say that a lot."

"What?"

She imitated his *humphing.* "So who is the cute teddy bear from?" Huge and white with a big red bow around its neck, the bear grinned at her from behind the blooms.

"Me." With the admission, a lovely blush colored his cheeks.

Surprised, she smiled. "You?"

"Good morning."

Claire looked to her right and found a curvaceous brunette in navy scrubs, a stethoscope slung around her neck, her arms full of linens, smiling at them from the doorway.

"Good morning." And it most certainly was. Cam had given her a teddy bear, of all things.

"I'm Suzy. I'll be taking care of you today. How are you feeling?"

"Better, thanks." Although she doubtless looked like hell.

"You look a lot better." The nurse grinned at Cam, then dropped the linens on the chair he'd been sitting in. Checking Claire's IV, she asked, "Do you think you can handle some fluids this morning?"

Claire nodded. "I think so."

"Great. I'll order a tray. If the clear fluids stay down, we'll pull the IV and give you some real food." She then stuck a scope in Claire's ear, a minute later announced that a normal temperature, took her blood pressure, and then bent down. "Your output is great. I think we can pull the Foley as well."

Augh! She had a catheter? She twitched her bottom. Yup. And Cam had been sitting next to . . . *Ewwwww*. God, how embarrassing.

"Cam, could you please excuse us for a few minutes? Go down to the cafeteria and grab a cup of coffee or something."

"Are ye sure ye'll be all right?"

"Yes, I'll be fine. Do you know where the cafeteria is?" Did he even know what a cafeteria was?

"Aye. As ye lust then." Looking none too pleased, he headed for the door.

The minute he disappeared, Claire asked, "Can we get rid of this catheter?"

"Sure, if you think you're strong enough to make it to the bathroom."

"I am." She'd crawl on her hands and knees if she had to. Anything to get the tubes out and her nasty self into the shower.

As Suzy closed the door, she said, "I *love* his accent. I could listen to him all day."

"Me, too."

Suzy flatted the bed. "How long have you two been together?"

"A few weeks." Which sounded better than eight days.

"And you're already engaged?"

"Uhmm . . ." So that's how Cam had managed to stay at her bedside. He'd lied. "We're not officially engaged. We just live together."

"That's quick, but it's obvious he cares for you. He growls like a bear every time anyone comes near you with something new in their hands that he hasn't seen before. But once satisfied, all is well and he does turn on the charm. He's had the entire staff in a lather since you came in." She sighed a bit wistfully. "It's not often you see someone that cute, buff, and straight walking around single. Where did you find him?"

"He found me. Just sort of popped into my life one day."

"Lucky girl."

The jury was still out on that.

Three hours later—her catheter out, well showered, and her clear liquids consumed and still hanging in—Claire drummed her fingers on her overbed table. Where the heck was he?

Having nothing better to do and needing a distraction—she'd begun imagining every kind of horror Cam could have gotten himself into—she turned on the TV and caught the tail end of the weather forecast. The guy in the bowtie pointed to an ominous white circle over Canada and then at another coming up the east coast. "These lows," he told her, "have the potential for becoming the storm of the century."

Oh great. So much for her hopes for any customers this weekend.

The man had the audacity to grin. "Better get the wood and candles laid in, folks. We could be facing up to two and a half feet of snow by Friday."

"Augh!" She wanted to cuff him . . . and Cam. Where the hell could he be for this—

"Second Hand Rose" suddenly rang out from somewhere deep inside her bedside table.

Praying the caller was Cam, fearing that it might be and he was in some kind of trouble, she pawed through the dresser, found her purse and flipped open her cell phone. "Hello?"

"Claire?"

"Cam! Where the hell are you? You left here three hours ago."

"Aye."

He heaved a sigh as someone near him shouted and a door slammed, echoing in the background as if he were in an underground tunnel.

"Cam, where are you?"

"The man said Ipswich Central."

Picturing MTA stops and drawing a blank on any Ipswich Central, she asked, "Ipswich central what?"

"Ipswich Central Police Station?"

"*What?*"

He heaved a monumental sigh. "Love, would ye happen to ken the number of that barrister, Mr. Brindle?"

Chapter Fourteen

What kind of a friggin' idiotic country was this that a man had to have a *license* to dig a few clams? And how the hell was he supposed to ken there was a *season*? He'd never heard such blather in his life. Next they'd be telling him he needed a license to breathe. And he hadna resisted arrest. Ack!

Cam crossed his arms, leaned against the bars and stared down the corridor, his hopes for help arriving anytime soon slowly dwindling.

"Hey, man, what you in for?"

Cam glanced sideways at the thin, runny-nosed man leaning on the bars next to him, then back to the door at the far end of the hall. "Reiving."

The man sniffled. "Reefers. Cool. I'm in for possession, too. They caught me with two bags of coke." He cursed and sniffled again. "Just watch, I'll get twenty years hard time. Shit, I'll be fifty before I get out from behind bars this time."

Cam stared at the man. He loved cola. Praise be to Saint Bride that he'd not been caught coming home from a shop with an arm load. There'd be no explaining a twenty-year imprisonment to Claire, though why she hadna warned him—

"MacLeod! You have a visitor."

Hope soaring, Cam stepped back away from the bars. The young officer who'd questioned him on arrival fit the key in the lock and opened the door. "Hands out."

Cam did as he was told and cold steel clamped around his wrists.

The officer waved him out and pointed left. "Through the door."

He was led down a gray corridor and into a small gray cage where he found a frowning Mr. Brindle sitting at a gray metal table. As the barrister rose, the officer said, "You have fifteen minutes."

When the officer left, Mr. Brindle waved toward the chair across the table from him. "Take a seat and tell me what happened."

Cam sat, the cuffs on his wrists clanging as they came to rest on the table. "How's Claire? Is she verra upset?"

Brindle scowled at him. "What do you think?"

"Ack, she should be resting, garnering her strength, not fashing over me."

"I know." Brindle shuffled the papers before him. "Says here you've been charged with trespassing on private property, unauthorized use of a boat, clam digging without a license on a state wild life preserve, and resisting arrest. What do have you have to say for yourself?"

"I say naught that I'm charged with is my fault,

leastwise, it shouldna be. I didna ken the law about digging, didna ken that the wee boat wasna there for the using, and I certainly didna resist arrest." He rubbed his breast bone, the place where the Boston officer had hit him with the stun gun and grumbled, "I learned that lesson the hard way."

By sheer providence he'd been burrowing in a deep hole, trying to pry out a tenacious clam with his knife when the sheriff happened upon him and he'd been able to kick sand over the blade or he'd be facing more charges. But then Brindle didna need to ken that.

Cam placed his elbows on the table and leaned forward, his hands open in supplication. "Sir, I just wanted to get some clams for Claire. They're her favorite food and the sea salt would have aided her healing. I'd gone to the public house she liked but they wanted a king's ransom for just a wee handful. So I thought to dig some myself. I went to the shore and dug but to nae avail. Seeing the boat up the beach, lying face down as it would be at home for any to use when its rightful owner wasna using it, I borrowed it and rowed out to the far point thinking I'd have better luck where fewer people tread." He shook his head still not believing he was in trouble with the law yet again. "I would have brought the bloody boat back. I'm nae thief."

"I didn't say that you were. So then what?"

"So there I was digging away and before I had a dozen clams in my bucket, the gaming sheriff—and who kenned ye could have so damn many bloody kinds of sheriffs—grabs me and slaps me in irons."

Looking dubious, Brindle pushed his glasses halfway down his nose to look over the rims at him. "Says here you struck the game warden."

Cam reeled back in his chair. "I did nae such thing! The man was naught but a wee shit. Had I struck him, I'd have leveled him and been on my way and not sitting here in irons. Nay, I just grabbed the bucket back from him after he'd taken it from me. I'd dug the damn clams. They were mine."

Brindle rolled his eyes and took off his glasses. "Well, we've got some time before your arraignment. I'll see what I can do to placate the boat owner . . . see if I can get him to drop the charge. Then I'll speak with the game warden. I'll explain that you're new here, didn't know that there were restrictions on clamming, and with any luck, I can get him to back off."

"And if he willna?"

Brindle put his glasses in his coat pocket and reached for what Cam now knew to be a briefcase. "Then you and I, MacLeod, have another date at court."

Claire glared at Victor as he sat across from her perusing an old *Architectural Digest*. "They should have been back by now."

"Relax, Claire. These things take time."

"Yes, and I'd know precisely how much time if you'd brought me to the court house like you promised you would. I don't like being duped."

"The doctor said he'd release you only on the

condition that you went straight home to bed." He looked up at her. "You'll note you're not in bed."

"Screw you." What if they wouldn't release Cam on his own recognizance? What if he needed a character witness?

"You're turning into a potty mouth, Claire."

"Screw you *and* the horse you rode in on."

As she reached for her cell phone, Victor put down the magazine. "Go ahead. Call Brindle. Annoy the man some more, so maybe he'll walk out and leave MacLeod to his own devices. That what you want?"

Claire slapped the phone closed, tossed it onto the coffee table, and picked up the teddy bear Cam had given her. "Sometimes I hate you, you know that?"

"Hate's an awfully strong word, sweetie. And beside, I know it's not true. You love me." He picked up the magazine again. "I'm still waiting to learn how you met this Highlander. He doesn't strike me as your sort."

"What do you mean by that?" Why wasn't he her sort? Because he was handsome?

"I mean I've never seen you eye construction workers. I do, but you don't. All that raw, pent-up macho, that buffed and tanned muscle, has never been something you've been drawn to. You ogle the civilized guys in suits."

"You're so full—What makes you think Cam's not civilized?"

"An idiot could take one look into those steely blue eyes of his, grab hold of his callused paw, and know he's pure blue-collar-and-beer and damn proud of it.

He's probably been in more bar brawls than you've got teeth."

Claire pulled up her knees, pressing the bear to her chest, Victor's assessment hitting a little too close to home. Cam did like his ale, and God only knows how many battles he's fought. And she did too ogle construction workers. Sometimes. But not overtly, unlike some people she could mention. "I'll have you know he speaks four languages and has very good table manners." So there.

Victor arched an elegant black eyebrow. "Great, he can order wings in every dive from here to Bangkok, but he'll still have beer with them and you're still in over your head."

"You're such a snob."

"No, I just grew up near the docks and know my men." He rose and then settled at her feet, taking her right hand in his. In as gentle a voice as she could ever remember him using, he asked, "Sweetie, has he shared his past with you? Have you met his family? Or even his friends?"

"No." And she never would. And that made her sadder than anything else. Made her heart ache, bleed for him. He was so *alone.* So very, very alone.

"Oh my God, you're in love with him."

Claire tried in vain to blink back the tears that suddenly sprang from out of nowhere, then giving up, buried her face in the bear's soft belly. "Seriously dumb, huh?"

"Oh, sweetie, I'm so sorry." Victor's arms wrapped around her and her week's worth of worry and fear took shape in chest-wracking sobs.

God, the whole situation with Cam was so appalling, and as impossible as it was improbable. She was in love with a man who needed her, might even care for her, but wasn't in love with her and certainly had no intention of staying with her.

"Please tell me you're not sleeping with him. You've only known him a week, don't know where he's been . . ."

She pressed a finger to his lips. Poor Victor. He lived in mortal fear of getting AIDS, got tested every six months even though he'd been in a committed relationship for years. *Just in case.* To ease his worry, she would have loved to tell him that Cam was probably the safest partner on the planet, but her dear friend couldn't keep a secret to save his soul. "No, we've kissed but that's all."

And that's likely all they'd ever do, so hellbent was he on finding his way back to his own world. He hadn't done more than kiss her forehead since they'd spoken with the witch and then only because she'd been at death's door.

And wishful thinking has never gotten you anywhere, girlfriend.

She scrubbed her eyes with the heels of her hands, sniffled, and attempted to straighten the bear's now soggy red bow. "I'll be fine." And she would be.

"I'm ready to hear from the defense."

Wesley Brindle nodded to Judge Harry Brown, then leaned toward his client. "Remember, MacLeod, this is just an arraignment. Not a trial. Say nothing unless the judge or I ask you a direct question. When you respond keep your answers to yes or no. Is that clear?"

MacLeod nodded, and Wesley wiped the sweat from his palms and stood. "Your honor, I'm Wesley Brindle—"

"I know who you are, Mr. Brindle. I'm surprised to see you in my courtroom."

"So am I." He hadn't set foot in a courtroom since he'd broken the back of the prosecution's case against Donald Ripper, thereby setting him free. To his everlasting regret, not four hours after walking out of the court house a free man, the bastard Ripper held up a convenience store and killed the owner and an employee, a mother of three.

"I thought you didn't take on criminal cases any more."

"I don't." Translation: My client is not a criminal . . . although he's walking a fine line.

"We'll see about that. Proceed."

Since he'd gotten the boat owner to drop his complaints, Wesley only had to deal with the resisting arrest charge and opened with, "Your honor, there is no crime here. My client, Cameron MacLeod, is the victim of an overzealous game warden." He related MacLeod's version of events as his client had related them to him. "A newcomer to our shores, he didn't know there were regulations regarding public land use or use of a neighbor's boat. He'd never imagined there might be, having been raised on an isle off the coast of Scotland where men fished and gathered as they could, where they had no electricity or indoor plumping. In truth, he's a man out of his element."

As he waxed on about his client's good points—which were far too few in Wesley's estimation—he detailed his client's experientially limited adulthood, never lying but stretching veracity to the point of incredibility, while the judge kept his gaze on the defendant.

Finally, the judge held up a hand. "Enough, Mr. Brindle. I get the picture." He then addressed Mac-Leod. "Mr. MacLeod, if you had no electricity, how did you see at night?"

"Oil lamps."

"And what kind of oil did you use?"

Shit. The judge was trying to trip up his client. Before he could register an objection, MacLeod responded, "Whale oil."

"And how did you acquire this whale oil?" The judge looked directly at Wesley and arched an eyebrow, all but saying *I have the son of a bitch now.*

Wesley started voicing his objection to relevance, and MacLeod caught his arm. "Nay, I'll answer the man." To the judge he said, "We caught them."

The judge grinned, obviously enjoying himself. "And how did you catch these whales, pray tell?"

As titters erupted in the back of the room, MacLeod said, "With our ships, of course. We have two."

"Ah. Could you describe these ships, please?"

MacLeod shrugged. "Aye. Seventy-eight feet by thirty-six, single hulled, triple masts, their average tonnage is three thousand pounds—one slightly more, the other a wee less due to the cabins. They averaged eight to ten knots, but we could get twelve out of *The Bride* if the wind was blowing up her arse."

The room erupted into laughter and the judge

banged his gavel to regain control. "Any more outbursts and I'll clear the court."

Looking none too please with anyone, Judge Brown turned his attention back to MacLeod. "So how did you get the oil out of the whales?"

"Beggin' ye pardon, sir, but 'tisna *in* the whale, sir, but *'tis* the whale."

MacLeod launched into his clan's method for stripping the fat—including all the tools needed.

Wesley was about to interrupt, then realized his client was just warming up to his tale, had started throwing in humorous anecdotes to balance all the gore and stench he was describing in graphic detail. As MacLeod went on, giving them tips on the proper disposal of entrails, Wesley leaned back in his chair and relaxed. MacLeod, a one-man show, had his audience in the palm of his hand.

Within ten minutes the judge, looking a little bilious, held up a hand. "Enough. Thank you, Mr. MacLeod." To Wesley he said, "Mr. Brindle, your client has proved your case. Case dismissed without prejudice."

He slammed down the gavel and immediately bolted from the courtroom.

The audience erupted with hoots and applause, and MacLeod leaned toward him. "What now?"

Wesley opened his briefcase and shoved in the documents he'd prepared but would have no need for now. "It's over. You're free to go."

MacLeod looked astounded for a moment, then broke into a broad grin and held out his hand. Wesley shook it, pleased that a client had handled himself well for a change. The judge had been right. MacLeod had won the case. Wesley had simply been window dressing, which suited him just fine.

"Thank ye. Truly."

"You're most welcome." Not a bad day's work, all in all.

But they still had another trial ahead of them. Perhaps if he donated a healthy sum to the police department's Widows' and Orphans' Fund, he could get them to drop the concealed weapons charges. Handling the officer with the fractured nose would be a bit trickier, but . . .

Still grinning, MacLeod asked, "How much do I owe ye?"

Wesley smiled as he snapped his briefcase closed. "Not a thing. It's been taken care of."

Rather than looking pleased by the news, MacLeod's brow furrowed and his jaw tensed. After a moment, he relaxed and asked, "Would ye happen to ken the easiest way to the Franklin Park Zoo?"

"You just take Route 1 South to 203 East and follow the signs. Why?"

Chapter Fifteen

"Claire! We're home!"

Claire flew off the couch as bounding footsteps echoed up the stairwell. Before she could get to the door, Cam burst into the living room, smiling from ear to ear.

"I'm free, lass. Free!"

"That's wonder—"

The breath swooshed out of her as he scooped her into his arms and laughing, spun her. Without thinking, she wrapped her arms around his neck and his head bent toward hers. Expecting a quick smacking kiss, she puckered up, only to have his lips land firm and smooth, unhurried on hers. As she marveled at the deliberateness of his kiss, luxuriated in the surprise of it, his hand slid to the back of her neck, and his tongue swept across her lips. Mindless and melting, she opened to him on a sigh.

God, he felt *sooo* good. And he was safe and free.

"Uhmm, I guess we can discuss this another time."

Mr. Brindle?

Claire reared back from Cam as if his kisses had seared her—which in a way they had—and found Mr. Brindle standing in her doorway grinning. As heat raced up her neck, she swatted Cam's arms. "Put me down!"

When he did, she waved Brindle in with a shaking hand. "I'm so sorry. I didn't realize you were standing there, Mr. Brindle. Please come in."

Cam laughed. "Aye, Brindle, come in. We've much to celebrate." Taking Claire by the hand, Cam acknowledged Victor's presence with a nod and led her to the couch where he sat on the arm.

"Brindle was positively brilliant, Claire. Ye should have seen him. But how are ye feeling? Is the fever gone?" He placed a hand on her forehead. "Ye look a bit flushed, lass. Are ye all right?"

Oh, better than all right and her flush had nothing to do with the flu. "I'm fine, Cam." To their attorney she said, "Please take a seat and tell us what happened. Victor and I have been biting our nails."

Victor, eyeing Cameron with overt suspicion, muttered, "Speak for yourself, sweetie."

Not about to have her dear friend put a damper on her or Cam's high spirits, she said, "Be nice, or I'll recommend you highly to Sara Townsend. She's remodeling. Again."

Mrs. Townsend, a too-rare customer, was an infamous micromanager when it came to any purchases for her home, truly believing she was blessed with exquisite taste. If she did, it was all in her mouth. She'd tried to buy Claire's baroque mirror, but on learning the woman planned to knock it apart and use the framing for a doorway, Claire refused to sell. And when everything went wrong with her decorating, which it invariably did, she blamed the decorator in stage whispers all across town. She could ruin a good reputation in days, the public taking socialites at their word.

Victor shuddered. Claire smiled. *Gotcha.*

Cam reached into his pocket and pulled out what looked like a driver's license. "Look, I've an identification card as well now."

She gave Brindle a questioning look and he shrugged. "I figured while I had him I'd kill two birds with one stone. At least now if he's arrested again, he'll have something to hand over."

Claire scowled at Cam. "But there won't be anymore arrests, right?"

One corner of his mouth lifted and a single dimple took shape. "I pray not. In any event, we should celebrate. May I pour some of that wine ye're hording in yer cabinet over the food box?"

Her jaw went slack for a moment. "You've been looking in my cabinets?"

Totally nonplussed, he nodded. "Aye. Had to do something while ye slept and what better way to ken the way of things here?" With that he strode to the kitchen.

While he banged cabinet doors, she mumbled, "The man is impossible."

Brindle nodded. "Yes, but very true to his time."

Frowning, Victor asked, "Which time? The Jurassic?"

Shooting a warning glance at Brindle, Claire said, "He means Cam's more like his predecessors than he is his contemporaries."

"Didn't I just say that? The man's beer and wings, Claire. Even his attorney agrees with me." Victor held out a hand to Brindle. "By the way, I'm Victor Delucci, Claire's friend and until recently," he slid a scathing look in her direction, "her closest confidant."

As Brindle and Victor shook hands, Cam returned with four wineglasses and an open bottle of merlot. He poured a splash in one glass and handed it to her. "Just a wee bit for you, lass, until ye're on yer feet again." He poured healthy amounts into the rest, handed them out, then slapped his forehead. "Ack, I forgot Mrs. Grouse!"

When he ran out the door, Claire put down her wineglass and clutched her hands in her lap. Dreading the answer but needing to know, she asked Brindle, "How did it really go today?"

"Much to my surprise, he did very well, answered honestly, and had the court eating out of his hands by the time the gavel came down and the case was dismissed."

"Did he tell you why he stole the boat and went to the bird sanctuary?" Brindle had told her that much during her third call to him. That's when she'd also learned Cam had been charged with resisting arrest. Again.

"Yes, but it comes under the heading of attorney–client privilege."

"You've got to be kidding." She was the one writing the checks . . . via Tavish. Sort of. "He's a breathing anachronism with a short fuse and I assume the arresting officer was armed, yes? Someone could have been killed."

Brindle shook his head. "The incident wasn't that dramatic. MacLeod merely snatched back what he thought was rightly his from the warden. That ticked the man off and suddenly our boy was in cuffs."

"Oh." Cam hadn't come out swinging like he had the last time, which boded well for his future here, should the witch be right and there was no *returning* for Cam. And well for her, if for no other reason than she wouldn't be bailing him out of jail every time she turned around. "Do you expect the March trial to go as smoothly?"

"We can only hope."

Before she could ask him about strategy, Cam returned, saying, "Mrs. Grouse will be along shortly."

He disappeared into the kitchen and returned with a bottle of Guinness. As Cam popped the top off the ale, she risked a glance at Victor and found him giving her his *I told you so* look. Annoyed he'd actually gloat, she turned her back to him and found Cam smiling at her, his gaze slipping from her eyes to her lips, which caused her stomach to inexplicably flip. She found herself suddenly wishing their company away.

As if reading her mind, Cam winked and heat rose up her neck. Hoping a distraction would work before anyone noticed she was turning red, she raised her glass. "A toast to the best lawyer in Boston!"

After everyone cheered and sipped, Victor rose and raised his glass. "I have an announcement as well. You're looking at the new designer for the Berkley Hotel."

Claire squealed, "Oh, Victor! That's wonderful news."

He bowed, grinning from ear to ear. "Thank you. It's a dream come true."

"When do you start?"

"I've already started. Haven't slept a wink since I received the call."

"So you're not going to Los Angeles tomorrow?" To Cam and Brindle she said, "Victor is one of twelve designers who've been invited to do competitive showroom displays for the Design Convention. The winner receives a spread in *Bella Homes and* an all-expense-paid trip to some exotic place like Maui or the Virgin Islands."

Victor grinned. "I'm going out to L.A. The hotel owners actually insist upon it. They know my winning would add cachet to their project."

"That's fabulous." She raised her glass again. "To Victor's new hotel and to hopes of his being named Designer of the Year!"

After a second round of cheers, Victor pawed through his coat pocket. "Before I forget, I wanted to give you the keys to the truck, just in case you sell that lovely armoire downstairs and need to deliver it before I get back." Keys jingled as he told her, "Remember to pump the gas pedal three times if you want it to start and for God's sake park on the right side of the street. They're predicting more snow this weekend and I don't want it towed."

"You're so sweet! Thank you. But how will you get to the airport?"

"I'll take a cab."

As he set the keys on her end table, Mrs. Grouse

came toddling through the door, her divine German chocolate Bundt cake in hand. "What did I miss?"

An hour later, Mrs. Grouse had returned to her apartment and Cam was waving good-bye to Brindle and Delucci, a man he was developing a decided liking for despite Delucci's obvious distrust of him. The man did care deeply about Claire's welfare, and he'd inadvertently solved Cam's transportation problem. Aye, a lovely man, that Delucci.

After locking the door and setting the alarm, Cam took the stairs two and three at a time, looking forward to some time alone with Claire.

He found her in the kitchen, cake plates at her elbow, her hands in her sink full of bubbles and goblets.

Ack! "Drop the goblet, lass." He scooped her into his arms, making her squeal.

"Put me down!"

"Nay. Leastwise not until I have ye where I want ye."

He carried her into the living room and settled at one end of her deep-seated sofa, his back resting on the padded arm, his legs stretched out on the cushions, then made room for her betwixt them. As he wrapped his arms about her, he said, "Comfy?"

She huffed but settled, her back to him, her head resting on his shoulder. "You like having your own way, don't you?"

He grinned. "I'm a man."

"That you are." She looked up at him then, a mysterious smile taking shape.

"A bodle for yer thoughts, lass."

"I was thinking about how much my life has changed since you arrived."

"Greatly, I should imagine."

She twisted sideways, her hand settling at his waist, her fingers playing with the buttons on his shirt. "It's been a long time since I've had to think about anyone besides myself, you know. I'm not saying I prefer being alone. I don't. That's just the way things turned out. I'm used to eating out more often than in because I can't justify messing up the kitchen just for myself. I did laundry on Mondays, paid bills and did banking on Tuesdays, Wednesday I check the paper for coupons . . . well, you get the idea. You could set your watch by my schedule."

"And now ye barely ken the day of the week."

She laughed, looking at him through stormy green eyes. "That about sums it up. And you?"

He wrapped a lock of her glossy hair around his finger. "'Tis rare for me to find myself alone. I'm accustomed to the sounds of men and animals, but when need be, I could always find quiet, to think in peace. Here, there isna quiet. Here, there's a constant hum."

She frowned. "It's silent now."

"Not so. Ye canna hear sirens and such at the moment, but if ye listen, ye'll hear water running in the pipes that heat this place or Mrs. Grouse running water. Ye'll hear the hum of the food box and the light buzzing in the kitchen." He grinned as he ran a finger along the fine bones of her wrist. "Even in the dead of night 'tis never truly quiet here."

She cocked her head, listening. "I never heard the refrigerator before, but now that you mentioned it—"

"The constant drone makes it difficult to ponder a heart's desires. And speaking of desires . . . What do ye lust for, lass?"

She sighed, making him that much more aware of the soft press of her breasts against his chest. "First, I'd like my shop to succeed beyond my wildest dreams."

Which wouldna happen unless she had people coming into the shop. Humph. He must think on this. "And?" Surely there had to be more.

"I'd like to marry a good man and settle down in a cute house. One with working plumbing, a fireplace, a rose garden, and maybe a dog in the backyard."

All good wishes for a woman as fine as she. Mayhap if he could make the first come true, the rest would follow naturally.

"And I want to have a child."

"Only one?"

"*No*," she laughed. "I'd prefer a dozen, but don't want to appear too greedy just in case someone really is listening."

Ah, a cautious lass to be sure. "I havena doubt that all yer wishes will come to pass. Ye're a verra bonnie lass, Claire MacGregor, with much to offer."

She smiled but without the usual light in her eyes. "Maybe in your world."

"Nay, in any world." And why—kenning he must leave—did the thought of her lying with another cause something in his middle to churn and curl upon itself like a nest of snakes? Ack.

She threaded her long, slender fingers through his and asked, "So what were your wishes before you ended up here?"

"Dare I admit they amounted to little more than to gorge to my heart's content on battle, food, and lasses?" Pure folly on his part given what he'd learned from the library's books. "My time would have been better spent kenning the hearts and minds of those in power and mayhap none of this would have come to pass."

"So what did you do all day?"

"I trained men for war and led them into battle."

"How old were you when you started this?"

"I was fostered out to the MacDonald clan at the age of seven."

"But you were just a baby!"

"Nay, 'tis simply the way at home. A lad needs to ken all he can and often the father hasna the heart to be as stern as he needs to be or he may not have the skills to train his sons. And, more goes on within the great halls than sons should see betwixt his parents. 'Tis better that they are away."

"Like what?"

He fingered a lock of her hair. "Like parents in their cups. Many a keep has only one main chamber. And many a tupping goes on in dark corners."

"By tupping do you mean . . ."

"Aye."

"*Ewww.*"

"Precisely why 'tis better the whelps are off."

She looked up at him, a frown marring her brow. "Did you have to go to war often?"

"Often enough to ken what I'm about, but our conflicts rarely last more than a week. Most often they're resolved within a day, bloody as they are." When she shuddered, he said, "Dinna fash. More often than not, all is quiet about Rubha and I'd help as needed in the fields and less often on board our ships." He really enjoyed being on board *The Bride*, but rarely had an opportunity to do so. Should trouble strike, he had to be with his men, not out to sea. Or here. He heaved a sigh.

She wiggled until they were nearly eye to eye and touched his cheek. "Cam, what are you going to do if Sandra Power is right? If there is no going back?"

He picked up the hand that touched his cheek and kissed her palm. "She isna. Canna be." His people needed him. Needed the information he'd garnered. He *would* find his way home. There were psychics all over the city. He'd already spoken to several—unfortunately three were outright charlatans and one had told him the same thing the Salem witch had—but there were others. He had another appointment in just a few days. Surely she—a witch too busy to see him sooner—would ken the secret. Which meant he had a great deal to accomplish and precious little time in which to do it.

"But what if—?"

"No *ifs*, love. Only when." He ran his thumb over the soft fullness of her lower lip, his blood heating as he did so. God, she was lovely. And because of it, he could do naught but tell her, "I will be loathe to leave ye."

Her eyes became a bit glassy as she looked deep into his and admitted, "I don't want to see you go. I'm growing accustomed to having you around."

I shouldna, I really shouldna.

Aye, but she was his for the taking. He could see it in her bonnie green eyes. And he wanted her, desperately wanted to run his hands over the length of her sleek thighs and up onto her fine hurdies to ken if they were as wonderful to touch as they were to look upon. Wanted to feel the weight of her wee breasts in his palms, to ken whether or not her nipples were cinnamon or as pink as her lips. Aye, he wanted her with a yearning he'd not experienced in years, which rattled him.

"Cam." Her gaze shifted from his eyes to his lips as she cupped his cheek in her hand. Watching her tongue peek out, then disappear before she caught her bottom lip betwixt her teeth, his groin swelled uncomfortably. "If you're thinking what I think you're thinking, I should tell you that I'd love you to kiss me again, but we'd better not. I don't want you to catch the flu, too."

"Lass, ye forget I'm invincible."

Kenning any reservation on her part stemmed from her concern for his welfare, the door to his conscience slammed shut. Hungry for a taste of her, he lowered his mouth to hers. Tasting wine and woman as her lips parted on a sigh, he delved deeper, relishing the slick softness of her mouth, unable to keep from wondering if he'd find the same sweetness between her thighs.

As his kiss deepened, Claire twisted and stretched out along the length of him and her hands found their way to his neck where they tugged on the ribbon holding his hair. When it fell away, she buried her fingers in his hair and he pulled her closer as he'd been dreaming of doing since he'd kissed her oh-too-briefly in Salem.

She tasted sweet, of wine and Mrs. Grouse's cake.

Delightful. His hand slipped up her ribs, seeking her breast. A heartbeat from his goal, she suddenly jerked upright.

"*Aa-ah CHOO! CHOO!*" She gasped, then coughed, a wracking sound that made him cringe.

God's teeth, what an arse he was!

He gently thumped her back. "There, there, lass." Here she was barely out of hospital and he had naught on his mind but tupping her blind.

Scarlet, her eyes watering, she flapped a hand at him. "I'm . . . fine. I just need to catch . . . my breath." She swung her legs off the couch and sat, elbows on her knees, with her head in her hands. "Damn. I'm so sorry. I thought . . ."

Claire shook her head. Hell, she hadn't thought at all. She just wanted Cam, wanted him on her, in her, with a yearning that had made her mindless and selfish. And because of it, he'd likely get the flu now, too. *Dumb, dumb, dumb.*

She sniffled and straightened. "Sorry. I thought the worst was behind me."

He rubbed her back. "Ack, ye poor wee thing. 'Tis all my fault. I never should have kissed ye in the first place, ye still being as sick as a dog and nae in ye right mind."

Her laugh came out in a bark and started the coughing all over again.

Why me, Lord?

When she was finally able to breathe again, she looked around the living room wondering where Victor had put her prescription.

Cam jumped up and headed for the kitchen. "I'll get ye medicine."

"Thanks." The man was not only incredibly sexy and a great kisser but a mind reader as well. What more could a woman ask?

He returned with the amber bottle and spoon in hand. Scowling at the label, he read, "Phenergan expectorant with codeine. Take one teaspoon every six hours as needed. No refill." He held them out to her. "Take four. 'Tis a wee spoon."

Imagining what four would do to her failing common sense, she laughed again, which set off another coughing fit.

"Easy, lass." He grabbed the bottle from her, and muttering under his breath in Gael, poured a dose into the spoon and held it to her mouth. "Open wide."

She opened like a hatchling and the liquid hit the back of her tongue, making her gag. God, it was putrid. Seeing him tip the bottle over the spoon again, she held up a hand. "Enough, Cam. Please, no more."

"But—"

"Trust me. One is plenty." Any more and she'd be tossing cake all over her worn but lovely Persian carpet. Heaving a sigh, she came to her feet. "I need to lie down for a while."

"Of course." He followed her into her bedroom and pulled back the covers. As she kicked off her shoes he fluffed her pillows. "Lass, I'm glad yer home."

"Me, too."

When she settled into the deep feather mattress, he

covered her and tapped the tip of her nose. "Sweet dreams, love."

Because he'd called her *love* again, because he'd stood guard over her at the hospital, because her toes curled and shivers ran down her spine whenever he kissed her, she took back every evil thought she'd ever had about him. Even about him being arrested. Again.

As soon as he closed the bedchamber door, Cam strode to the kitchen to take a second look at Claire's calendar.

Humph! He *had* seen a pattern when he'd first glimpsed it. Every Sunday and every other Thursday for the last month Claire had called a glazer to come and repair her windows, which meant the deevil's buckies would likely hit again tonight.

Ack! So much for his plans for making a raid on the game park. 'Twas just as well, he supposed. He needed to practice driving a bit to be sure he kenned the way of it. The last thing he needed was to be caught by the police with reived venison and then have to face Claire's wrath atop it. But on the morrow he had to make the raid, come hell or high water. A storm had been forecast for Sunday.

He opened Claire's knife drawer, pulled out a short and long blade and tucked them beneath his belt since the wide silver tape—what Claire called duck tape, though why he couldna imagine, since it no more resembled a duck than he did a feather—was sitting on her workbench downstairs.

Armed as best he could manage, given his blades were still held by the sheriff, he tiptoed to Claire's room and peeked inside. Seeing her breathing had settled into the deep, easy rhythm of sleep, Cam closed the door, scooped up the keys Delucci had left on the side table and headed for the stairs.

At the second-floor landing, he pressed an ear to Mrs. Grouse's door. Hearing the tee-vee, he knocked. A moment later, she opened the door.

"Cameron, is something wrong with Claire?"

"Nay, she's fine and asleep. I dinna mean to alarm ye, but I think the lads who've been breaking her windows will strike again tonight. I intend to nab them before they can throw another brick but will need to lurk outside to do it."

Her hand flew to her throat. "Oh my! Do be careful, dear. They might be armed and I don't want to see you hurt."

He cocked an eyebrow. "Mrs. Grouse, do I look like a man who'll be either careless or harmed?"

She smiled up at him. "No, dear, you don't."

"Would ye be kind enough to keep an eye on Claire, keep an ear to the door should she call out?"

"Of course. Oh! I almost forgot. A package and letter arrived for you this morning. Wait right here and I'll get it."

A moment later, she handed him a box and missive, both addressed to Cameron Grouse. Ah, 'twas the supplies he'd ordered from You Shop tee-vee. When the helpful sales representative had asked for a security number, Cam, not kenning her meaning, had asked Mrs. Grouse for help. She'd supplied the number, one her husband had once apparently owned. Verra considerate of her, truly, else he wouldna have been able to acquire the special card.

As he headed downstairs, his package in arm, she called after him, "Do be careful, dear."

He waved over his shoulder and lied, "Always."

In Claire's work room, he pocketed the glossy credit card, then cut open the box and found the blades he'd ordered. Pulling them from the wrapping, he discovered they all could do with a wee bit of honing but were adequate and sturdy nonetheless. He pulled Claire's carving knife from his belt and replaced it with the foot-long blade the salesman had called a *buoy* knife, of all things. The shorter blades he secured to his upper arms beneath rings of duck tape, then grabbed the cast iron bar Claire used to pry open crates.

Outside, he spied a large white truck bearing the sign VIVID DESIGNS BY VICTOR parked at the far right corner. "Thank ye, Victor."

Inside the vehicle, it took him a moment to get comfortable and to pump the pedals three times as Delucci recommended. When the engine roared to life, he blew through his teeth. So far so good.

He pulled down on the stick as he'd seen the taxi driver do, only to have the truck growl in response. Humph! Mayhap he needed to press a pedal as well. He pressed down on the go pedal, the truck unexpectedly charged backward, and a godawful crack ensued. Startled, he jerked his feet off the pedals. The engine coughed, sputtered and finally fell silent.

Shit! Who would have kenned driving could be so difficult?

He got out.

The steel pole supporting the light looked none the worse for his ineptness, but the same couldna be said for the tail end of Delucci's truck. Ack. He should have noticed the front wheels were cocked.

He climbed back into the truck, straightened the wheels and turned the key again, thankful when the engine roared back to life.

This time, he jerked the stick as fast as possible past the R—which apparently meant *retreat*—and down to the D, which he prayed meant drive.

To his monumental relief, the truck lurched forward.

Hallelujah!

He made his way out onto Huntington Avenue where he managed to turn right clipping a snowbank but missing the parked cars. Two streets later he turned left. A short while later, his confidence growing, he turned left once again.

As he rolled along at an amazing speed, he blew through his teeth. 'Twasna so hard after all.

When he rolled past the Velvet Pumpkin, he laughed. Claire would nay doubt pitch a fit if she could see him sitting in the driver's seat.

He drove by three more times, then pulled into the place he'd vacated, shut off the engine and got out, only to see he'd placed the truck too far from the sidewalk. Ack!

He got back in and moved the stick to the R. After a good bit of lurching forward and back, he got out and was pleased to see the truck was reasonably close to where Delucci had placed it.

Ha! No moss on this stone.

Now to find a good spot to wait out the deevil's buckies.

Crouched next to the stairs fronting the house facing Claire's home, Cam tensed each time a vehicle turned onto the street. Seven rolled past without incident before a long, blue car came into view. When it slowed and red light fanned out turning the snow-packed street crimson, Cam shrugged off his breachen feile and pulled the long blade from his belt.

When the car door closest to Claire's shop flew open and the driver turned his attention to the passenger, Cam bolted from his hiding place. Three long strides and he wrenched open the driver's door.

"What the—"

Cam grabbed the driver by the throat before he could finish his exclamation and hauled him out, his blade to the lad's neck.

Hearing his friend cry out, the lad standing on the curb with a bottle in his hand spun around to face him.

Cam glared at him. "Put it down or I slit yer friend's throat."

Bug-eyed, the bottle-wielding youth froze, his gaze darting from Cam to his friend, then back again.

The driver, his back straining to ease the pressure Cam was exerting on his neck, shouted, "Do as he says, man!"

"Slowly," Cam informed the youth on the sidewalk, "or blood spews."

The youth, his gaze locked on Cam's blade, held

out both arms and slowly lowered the bottle to the sidewalk.

"Back away."

The youth did as he was told, and Cam marched the driver, now reeking of fear-laden sweat, around the car to where the tall uncapped bottle stood. Seeing a thick green liquid inside, his heart tripped. "Ye marly pokes of shit!"

The bloody bastards were going to throw a fire bomb. Picturing the chaos and flames, imagining Claire and Mrs. Grouse trapped above, Cam growled deep in his throat and wrenched the lad's jaw to the side, ready to cut.

The youth standing on the sidewalk, apparently kenning his intent, shouted, "No, man! You can't kill him for throwing paint! It's paint, man! Just paint."

Cam's head jerked around. So they weren't trying to burn Claire out? Just wanted to make more of a mess? Not trusting them, Cam picked up the bottle and threw it into the car's open door.

As green liquid splashed in all directions coating the interior but naught else happened, the youth in his grip keened, "Shit, man! My mother's gonna kill me."

Ha! Were he at Rubha he'd do more than kill the pair. He'd take a whip to them, then throw them in brine. But he wasna home and should call the police, but then he'd have to explain his blades and would likely end up being arrested again himself. Humph! What to do, what to do?

Aha. "Yer wallet. Now!"

The driver yelped, reaching for his back pocket. "Shit, man, you're cutting me!"

"I'll sever yer friggin' head if ye dinna make haste."

The lad finally held out his purse. "Take it all, man. Just let me go!"

"Take out yer license." When he did, Cam barked, "Hold it up where I can see it."

Cam memorized the name and address, noting as he did that Manuel Gaza was sixteen years old, auld enough to ken better. He grabbed the wallet and pulled out the thin bills, not bothering to count them. "The bank notes," he hissed, "are restitution for the windows ye broke in the past." He spun the lad, lifting him off his feet, one hand clutching his collar so he could look the bastard in the eye. Glaring, his teeth bared, Cam growled, "I ken where ye live, ye wee bastard. If I so much as catch scent of ye again, I'll go to yer home and destroy it and *all* yer mother holds dear, ye included. Do I make myself perfectly clear?"

The lad, decidedly pale in the lamplight, swallowed convulsively. "Ya, man, real clear."

Cam shoved the driver backward, sending him sprawling at his friend's feet and threw the license and wallet after him. "Now get yer sorry arses out of here before I change my mind and kill the pair of ye where ye stand."

They scrambled into the car and were gone, their wheels squealing. Watching tail lights flare as they slid around the corner, Cam tucked his knife into his belt.

"The wee bastards should be conscripted onto a bloody man-of-war." There was naught like trying to stay alive to focus a man on what was really important.

Inside, he placed the bank notes in Claire's money drawer and headed upstairs where Mrs. Grouse greeted him at the first landing, her eyes wide. "Oh my word, Cam! I saw the whole thing through the window. Very impressive dear, but why did you let them go?"

"I've had my fill of police, Mrs. Grouse."

"I quite understand, dear, but you let them off too easy." She crossed her arms over her ample chest. "I'd dearly love to call their parents."

"Ye can do that?"

"Yes, if I knew where they lived."

Cam laughed. He really should get some sleep for he'd get none on the morrow, but then there was still much to accomplish this night. "Mrs. Grouse, may I come in? We've a call to make. I also wanted to talk to ye about a plan I have for bringing more people into Claire's shop."

Chapter Sixteen

Claire stretched, her breast aching, her middle cramping with need, her mind filled with images of Cam as she'd seen him that first night, naked and glorious . . . only this time they were making love. God, he was beautiful. She rolled, seeking his warmth, and instead felt cold sheets and sunshine.

Damn, she'd been dreaming again.

She opened one eye and looked at her clock.

Eleven! She bolted upright, listening for sounds of her housemate as she looked around the room. She *never* slept in and here she was lying abed, while the shop remained closed with only two weekends left before Christmas. She'd be bankrupt by month's end.

In and out of the shower and dressed for the day in record time, Claire made her way to the kitchen where she found hot coffee in the pot, the paper looking read, but no Cam. Praying he wasn't getting into more trouble, she headed downstairs with coffee in hand, only to hear female laughter as she opened the door to the store room. Thinking it might be Tracy and Mrs. Grouse, she walked through the doorway to her shop and came to a startled halt.

The place was buzzing with customers, most of which were female, many with Velvet Pumpkin gift bags looped over their arms. As she made her way to Tracy, who wasn't supposed to be there, she caught sight of Mrs. Grouse sitting in the far right-hand corner at a small table for four, her head wrapped in a turban and a fringed shawl wrapped around her shoulders. Before her sat a giggling young woman of about twenty, a porcelain tea set between them.

More women stood in line at the counter where Tracy—obviously in the weeds—was taking their cash and bagging purchases as fast as her inexperienced hands could manage.

Claire slid behind the counter and took the gift wrap from Tracy's shaking hands. "Good morning."

"Oh, thank God. I was afraid you'd sleep the day away."

"What's going on?"

Her friend smiled at the customer before her as she handed the woman change, then nodded toward the door. "After you finish wrapping that silver crumb buster, look outside."

Claire laughed. "It's a silent *butler*."

"Whatever." Tracy took the flow blue platter from the woman now standing before her, removed the price tag from the back and handed the platter to Claire for wrapping. Taking it, Claire nearly sighed aloud. She loved the platter, had dusted it with loving hands for months.

The platter wrapped in a pound of pumpkin

embossed tissue and caught with the Velvet Pumpkin's gold and purple seal—extravagances she shouldn't have made but did when she'd first opened the shop—she handed it to the woman. "It's a lovely piece. I hope you enjoy it."

The woman grinned from ear to ear. "It's for my daughter-in-law. That handsome gentleman outside said she'd much prefer it over the crystal bowl I'd initially chosen, the platter being something she could use every holiday. Creates memories for the grandchildren, you know?"

Claire nodded. If anyone understood the importance of memories, it was Cam. And speaking of him . . .

"Tracy, can you handle this for a moment?" Only two more people waited in line, one holding four cinnamon bun candles, the other holding a small perfume bottle, neither of which required elaborate gift wrapping. "I'll be right back."

She went to the door and peered out. At the foot of the steps she saw Cam, his hair loose, dressed in his tartan, brass cuff and all, beaming at a gaggle of women who were looking up at him, their adoration obvious even at a distance. Behind him stood a huge wooden sign reading *Free Fortune Reading by the Incomparable Madame Grouse.*

Augh! Were they out of their minds? Mrs. Grouse was no more a fortuneteller than she was. She flung open the door and stomped down the steps. By the time she reached the bottom, she wished she'd grabbed her coat.

Wrapping her arms around her middle, she smiled

at the women clustered around Cam, then hissed, "May I have a word, please."

He looked down at her and beamed. "Ah, lass, ye're awake finally." He wrapped an arm around her shoulder, pulling her to his side. "Ladies, this is the Velvet Pumpkin's proprietor, Miss MacGregor. Please go on in and make yeself at home. Madame Grouse will be with ye as soon as she can."

Casting appreciative glances in Cam's direction, the women ran up the steps.

When they were out of earshot, she asked, "What in hell is going on?"

"Ack, lass, ye'll catch ye death. Best we talk inside."

Claire shrugged off his arm. "You better start talking."

Chuckling, he pressed a hand to her back and steered her toward the stairs. "'Tis simple really. Ye're offering free readings in the spirit of the season. 'Tis the season for giving, after all."

She gaped at him. "You don't see any incongruity in that? For God sake, Cam, this whole thing is so . . . *bogus.* Mrs. Grouse can no more tell fortunes than you can."

"Shh, love, I'll explain more fully in a moment." He pushed open the door and ushered her inside, only to have two women rush toward him.

The woman holding two walking sticks—one with a sterling silver handle and the other with a carved mahogany dog's head—elbowed the woman holding two silver-plated ladles in an effort to get in front. "Mr. MacLeod, which do you think my husband will like best?" She held the canes out to him.

Cam examined both, then flashed his dimples. "The silver. For a man of simple but refined taste."

"Oh, you're so right. That's Edgar to the ground. Thank you so much."

As she rushed off, the woman with the ladles came forward. "Cameron, I can't decide between the two for my sister. Which do you think will appeal to her more?"

Claire gaped. How the hell would he know?

Cam arched a brow, dimples flashing again. "'Twill depend."

"On what?"

"Is she as lovely as ye with the same exquisite taste?" To Claire's disgust, his gaze traveled over the woman from furry hat to black patent leather boots, before it rose again and he winked. "If so, then ye have nae choice but to go with the more elaborate of the two, mistress."

The woman, pushing seventy if she was a day and fighting it every inch of the way, almost swooned as color flooded her already too rouged cheeks. "Thank you. You've been such a help."

Cam took the woman's right hand in his and brought it to his lips. "My goal in life, madam."

Claire had all she could do to keep from guffawing.

When the woman turned away, Cam placed his hand on the small of Claire's back and pushed her toward the back room.

"That was so, so . . ."

Words failed her.

"Aye, but she'll buy both in order to have an excuse

to come back on the pretext of returning one. And with any luck, she'll bring her sister with her."

Claire rolled her eyes. No one was that stupid. But she glanced at the counter and sure enough, there was the woman in line with two ladles in hand. Shaking her head in disbelief, Claire shifted her attention to Mrs. Grouse where she sat staring into a teacup. Oh my God, she was pretending to read tea leaves. Augh!

Cam closed the door between the shop and storeroom. Poor Claire. She looked about to explode.

Hands on hips, she glared at him. "Whose bright idea was this?"

Get huffy with him when he had only her best interests at heart, would she? Ha! He hadna been given his looks and charm for naught.

He closed the distance between them, forcing her to back up. As her hurdies hit the workbench, he murmured, "'Tis a clan effort if ye must ken. I came up with the fortunetelling and made the signs and Tracy jumped in to handle the sales since neither I nor Mrs. Grouse had any idea how ye handled yer taxes."

"Cam, you've got sale signs everywhere but there's nothing on sale! The candles were $12.00 apiece before the sale. They're now four for $48.00. Read my lips. There's *no* difference!"

He grinned as he leaned toward her, his hands settling on the bench to either side of her, effectively trapping her between his arms. "Brilliant, no?" He flexed at the knees, his hips coming into gentle contact with hers. "What say ye, lass?"

Claire's breath caught as he'd hoped, she swallowed and blinked. "To what?"

He leaned in and brushed his lips ever so lightly over her neck just above her collar bone, something he'd been dreaming of doing for days. As her skin pebbled, he could almost see the chills dancing over her skin before he latched onto her neck, gently sucking, applying pressure with his teeth—the threat of a bite there but not. A groan escaped and her knees buckled.

To keep her upright, he slipped his hands beneath her jeans-clad hurdies, his hips pressing into hers. Lord, he loved when a woman suddenly went limp. Made blood rush to his groin, pushing the predator in him to the fore. But then he was leaving.

He released her neck and brushed his lips along her jaw. "Claire?"

"Hmm?"

"Are ye still angry with me?"

Eyes closed, Claire's hands eased around his waist. "Okay."

MacLeod, ye still have the touch. He kissed the tip of her nose, straightened and reluctantly stepped back. "We'd best return then or Tracy will have our hides."

Claire blinked. "Huh?"

Regret making hollow his victory over her anger, he whispered more to himself than to her, "Ye're a bonnie one to be sure, lass." He took her hand in his. "Come."

"I'd love to."

* * *

One deep, heart-reaching kiss and she'd been ready to drop to the storeroom floor, her common sense, her pride, and her customers be damned.

Claire tossed the frying pan into the drawer, still not believing she could have behaved so, so . . . sluttily. Was that a word? If it wasn't, it should be.

And hallelujah, she'd finally realized Cam had been deliberately using his body to befuddle her. Oh ya. Any time she became miffed with him about something, he'd close the distance between them and get that look in his eye, the one that made her toes curl and her knees weak, and made her all too aware of him as a man. Worse, he didn't even have to kiss her. Just catching the scent of him turned her brain to mush. Oh, he knew what he was doing, all right. Augh!

And where was Mr. *I-can-get-into-your-panties-whenever-I-want* anyway? It was almost midnight.

She tossed the dish cloth onto the counter and strode into the living room where she plopped down on the couch and stared at the cash, checks, and receipts lying on the coffee table. A phenomenal three thousand and ninety-five dollars—what amounted to her mortgage payment and then some—all in one day and all thanks to one gorgeous Highlander and his way with the ladies. Lord, he could work a crowd. Watching him hit his stride had finally clued her into just how well he'd been manipulating her.

She huffed and picked up the receipts. She had three hundred dollars she couldn't account for and she should be looking for the receipts, not worrying about Cam.

Instead, she looked at the clock again. *Please God,*

don't *let him get into any more trouble*. Her heart couldn't take it.

Brrrrring

Claire flew into the kitchen and snatched the phone from the cradle. "Cam?"

"No, it's the other man in your life."

"Oh. Hi, Victor. How's California?"

"Warm and expensive. How's everything in Bean Town?"

"Cold and expensive." And a lot better if she knew where Cam was. "Why are you calling so late? Is something wrong?"

"Everything's great except that I just realized I left my Palm Pilot on the front seat of the truck. Would you be kind enough to get it before somebody steals it? My life is in it."

"Sure. No problem."

"Thanks. You're the best. So, how's everything going with your houseguest?"

"Fine. We had a great day."

After a brief silence, Victor said, "Just be careful, sweetie."

He knew her too well. "I will."

After listening to his itinerary, Claire wished him luck, hung up, and returned to the living room, only to discover the truck keys weren't where Victor had left them. "Crap."

Had Mrs. Grouse moved them as she cleaned up after their impromptu party? Claire looked under the furniture and cushions hoping they'd simply fallen, then scoured her kitchen, and still not finding them, decided she might as well look in the truck. If the

Palm Pilot wasn't visible, then finding the keys could wait until morning when she could ask Mrs. Grouse where she'd hidden them.

Three minutes later, standing at the end of the street, her shoulders hunched against the wind, her hands deep in her pockets, the fine hairs on the back of her neck standing on end, Claire ground her teeth. No keys, no truck, and no Cam could mean only one thing.

I'm going to kill him. I swear to God I am.

His morning coffee in hand, Wesley Brindle glanced at his watch and deciding he had time, turned on the TV hoping to catch the traffic report before he charged out the door. He had a big day ahead of him. Today his client TeknoSystems would learn if they'd won their lawsuit against their competitor New Age. If they had, Wesley was looking at a half-million-dollar windfall.

"Officials at the Franklin Park Zoo," the news anchor informed him as he took a mouthful of coffee, "have just released this security tape in hopes that someone in our viewing audience will recognize the perpetrator and call the Dorchester police."

Coffee spewed as Wesley watched the grainy footage. Even head down, face hidden from the camera, there was no mistaking his client Cameron MacLeod running hell for leather down the Franklin Park driveway, a twelve-point, wild-eyed buck draped over his shoulders.

Chapter Seventeen

"Claire!"

Claire bolted upright, her eyes flying open as her apartment door flew open and Mrs. Grouse came running in. "What . . . What's wrong?"

She looked around befuddled until she realized she'd fallen asleep on the couch waiting for Cam.

Mrs. Grouse reached for the TV remote. "You have to see this."

"What time is it?"

"Six. Now watch."

"The spokesman for the Zoo," the TV reporter said, "said Zoo security personnel were at the back of the facility assisting the veterinarian with capturing several loose lemurs when the break-in occurred." Before she could ask Mrs. Grouse why she found this so important, the scene changed to the security camera footage. Recognizing Cam despite the poor black-and-white image, she gasped, "Oh my God."

"I told you—"

Claire flapped her hands. "Shhh!"

"Zoo officials are asking anyone who recognizes the perpetrator to notify the Dorchester police."

"Oh my God." She gaped at Mrs. Grouse. "But why? How?" Without waiting for an answer she turned her attention back to the TV and found the reporter interviewing a small, sniffling child. With tears streaming down her little cheeks, the toddler cried, "He took Santa's reindeer. Now Santa won't be able to find us."

"Oh, Cam." Where they'd found a child at this hour was anyone's guess, but the move had been brilliant. The child's pain was palpable, really tore at the heart strings. Practically guaranteed Cam would get twenty to life when they caught him.

Getting to her feet, she asked, "Have you seen him? Is he home?"

Mrs. Grouse nodded. "He came in about an hour ago."

Claire stormed toward the door, and Mrs. Grouse blocked her path. "Step aside."

"Now, dear, I know you're upset but give the poor man the benefit of the doubt. After all, he did risk his life the night before last confronting those hoodlums."

Claire stepped back. "What are you talking about?"

"The gang that's been breaking your windows. Cam caught them outside the night before last. I saw the whole thing from my window. Terrifying to say the least," she shuddered, "but I can assure you they won't be bothering you again."

"He confronted them? He could have been killed! Tell me precisely what happened."

Mrs. Grouse's recitation had barely begun when the phone rang and Claire held up a hand. "Don't go anywhere. I want to hear the rest of this." In the kitchen she picked up the phone. "Hello?"

"Get me MacLeod. Now!"

"Mr. Brindle?"

"Yes. Is he there?"

"I don't know. I haven't gone downstairs yet." Trying to buy time, knowing the answer, she asked, "What's wrong?"

"Turn on the TV. Channel 5."

Claire took a deep breath. Should she admit she'd seen the coverage or pretend not to have seen it and let Mr. Brindle do all the talking? She opted for the latter and walked into the living room, where she saw the station was running the security tape again. Still shocked, the mantra that had been running around in her brain for the last three minutes came out. "Oh my God."

Into her ear, Brindle shouted, "I doubt even He could help MacLeod now! I have an appointment at ten that I can't get out of, but I'll get there as soon as I can. If you find MacLeod before I get there, do not—I repeat, DO NOT—let him out of your sight. Chain him to a radiator if you have to."

With that, he hung up.

Oh shit! "Mrs. Grouse, I have to find Cam. Please stay by the phone. If anyone calls, you know nothing. Just take a message."

A sharp blow to his left hip had Cam rolling to his feet, the blade he kept beneath his pallet in hand.

"Cameron MacLeod, you better start talking!"

Surprised to find his assailant was Claire, he blew through his teeth and palmed the blade before she could see it. As he raked the hair out of his eyes, he glanced out the windows. "God's teeth, woman, the sun's barely up. What in hell is wrong with ye?"

"*You*, that's what's wrong with me." She started pacing in front of him, the cane she'd apparently hit him with slapping her right leg with each step. "Where were you last night?"

"Out."

"Out where?"

Uh-oh, had she discovered the truck missing? 'Twas altogether possible, but he'd better be vague until he kenned what really had her in a snit. For all he kenned, it could be she'd discovered he'd eaten the last of the ice cream. Good stuff, that. "I had an errand." When she just stared at him, waiting, he added truthfully, "Across town."

"And you needed the truck to do it."

Oops. "Aye."

"Ah, and did this errand happen to have cloven hooves and antlers," she flung out her arms, "this wide?"

Ack! How could she possibly ken this? He started to rise, being one who always thought faster on his feet. "Now Claire, dinna get yerself—"

The blade within the cane was suddenly pointed at his heart. "Do *not* 'now Claire' me. I want an explanation and I want it now. Your face is all over the damn television. I'm surprised the police haven't already raided this place."

"But how?" He'd been most careful, had watched

the guards, had executed the distraction perfectly—a brilliant move letting those leaping, ring-tailed beasties loose if he did say so himself—and had come and gone without a soul inside or out catching sight or scent of him. So how could this be?

Apparently reading his thoughts, she shouted, "Security cameras, Cam! They're mounted all over the zoo property. They have pictures of you with the damn deer slung around your neck like a muffler." She threw up her hands. "Where's the deer? And please *do not* tell me you killed it."

"Ack! How could ye even think such a thing? Tisna a game park, this zoo of yours. 'Tis a bloody menagerie. And not until I found their pen and the beasties came up and tried to eat from my hand did I realize it."

And what kind of place was this anyway that they spied on each other? He heaved a sigh and waved toward the alley. "The truck is in yon alley."

"You parked the—come on."

Out the loading dock door they went, Claire muttering every step of the way. At the back of the truck, she said, "Open it."

He did as she bid, opening one side carefully.

She stuck her head in and pulled it out so fast, she nearly toppled. Looking horrified, she yelped, "You stole *two!*"

He shrugged. "The buck wouldna stop bleating, so I grabbed another. For company. But they only had the one buck—"

"So you took the doe."

"Aye. Are they worth as much?"

"What the hell are you talking about?"

"Ack, woman, are ye dense?" He pushed the hay he'd also reived over the threshold and closed the door before a beastie could make an escape. "Ye use cards, bank notes, and bucks as barter. Is the doe of any value? Or would it be better if they go as a breeding pair?"

Claire stared at him blankly for a moment, then went down on her haunches, her head in her hands. "I think I'm going to be sick."

Suddenly worried, he squatted next to her. "'Tis the influenza again? Should ye go to the hospital?"

She looked up at him, tears streaming in twin burns down her cheeks. Something hot tightened about his chest, nearly squeezing the air out of him. "Please, lass, talk to me."

She looked up at him, her misery as plain as her red nose. "A *buck* is our slang for a *dollar*. You're going to prison if they catch you with these deer, and there won't be a damn thing I or Mr. Brindle can do to help you. You have a record, Cam, and you have yet to go to trial on the assault charges."

"Oh."

She sniffled as she came to her feet and headed for the shop, her arms wrapped about her ribs, as if to shield herself. Over her shoulder she asked, "May I ask where the hell you were planning on keeping the deer until you could sell them?"

He followed, wondering why life was never simple. "In the storage room at the Purple Pussycat." Thinking the deer were wild as they are in Scotland, he'd planned to butcher them and put the meat in the cold storage at the club, but that was before he discovered they were friggin' tame.

She stopped and stared at him. "Why on earth would you put them there?"

Ack! His life was apparently determined to go to hell in a sporran. He might as well tell her the whole truth, bad as it was. And better that she hears it from him than Tracy. "I work there."

She scowled, as well she should. "Doing what?"

Crusty buggers, this is a bitter mouthful to swallow. "I'm a bouncer." Now she kenned the worst of it.

Owl-eyed, she looked at him. "You are not."

Reluctant to admit it again, he simply nodded as he opened the door for her. "Ye can speak with Tracy. She got me the darg."

"But if you already have a job, why did you steal the deer?"

"Humph!" *Stealing* was putting too fine a point on his acquisition, but arguing the subtler points of reiving would likely only get her in a worse snit.

Following her up the stairs to her apartment, he grumbled, "I only earn fifty dollars per day and they take a goodly amount of it back in bloody taxes. I owe ye thousands, Claire, and at the rate I'm earning I'll be long dead and still owing."

"But you don't owe me—"

He took hold of her arm, making her stop and face him. "Nay! I *do* owe ye. I've never been a beggar and willna start now. I pay my way whatever the circumstances."

"Okay, okay, I didn't mean to call your manhood

into question. I just thought you should know that
Tavish left money—"

"This isna a discussion. I'm simply telling ye."

"Oh, you are, are you?" Growling something under
her breath about male craziness she continued her
rapid climb up the stairs. "We need to get rid of the
deer before Brindle or the police come."

"But where? We canna just turn them loose."

"Oh, yes we can."

Mrs. Grouse greeted them as they rushed through
the door. "No phone calls and nothing new on TV."
Giving Cam a worried look, she handed them each a
cup of coffee. "Now what?"

Claire took a sip, then reached for her coat. "We're
off to hide a couple of reindeer in plain sight."

"A couple?" Mrs. Grouse tsked but with a twinkle—
what one might even call admiration—in her eye as
she waggled a finger at Cam. He shrugged, one
corner of his mouth lifting in a rueful grin.

He's going to be the death of me. Or I of him.

Claire reached for the truck keys which had magi-
cally reappeared on the end table. "If Brindle shows
up, feed him some coffee cake and tell him—oh hell,
I don't know what to tell him. Make something up.
We'll be back in an hour."

Mrs. Grouse nodded. "And if the police come?"

"You know *nothing*. Less than nothing. You just
woke up." To Cam she said, "Come on."

With Cam in the passenger seat and her behind the
wheel, both of them bundled and gloved, they

headed downtown. They hadn't gone two blocks when the wind kicked up, sending fat flakes swirling around them.

"Ugh, just what we don't need right now." A blind man would be able to follow their tracks across the Common. The police would be lifting the tire prints. Turning on the windshield wipers, she mumbled, "Why me, Lord?"

As if reading her mind, Cam said, "'Tis good. The snow will hide our tracks."

"From your lips to God's ears." The way the wind was blowing, she seriously doubted it.

Fifteen silent minutes later as they traveled up Boylston, approaching the smaller of the two sections that made up the fifty-five-acre Boston Common, her stomach flipped and hands began to sweat. Only one more block and they'd be there. She could do this. She could. She just had to back the truck into the roadway the maintenance people used and then open the doors. The deer would bolt for the trees where they could root around until someone spotted them and called the zoo. It was a good plan. Reindeer were Laplanders. They liked snow. The blizzard wouldn't do them any harm. And she'd still be functioning in the gray—no, call it charcoal—zone.

She crossed Charles, which bisected the Common and slowed as she came abreast of the larger of the two parks. Where was that drive? The heavy snow earlier in the week had already turned the Common into a beautiful but unfamiliar fairyland. The blizzard now raging beyond her windshield made it more so.

Focused on finding tracks or a break in the curb,

some hint of the turnout that marked the maintenance drive through worsening visibility, she startled when Cam hissed, "Up ahead to ye left."

A police cruiser, its motor running, was parked in the turnout she'd been looking for. Crap!

Claire eased off the gas. Now what?

Having no choice, she rolled past the cruiser, rounded the corner onto Park and came to a stop. She exhaled audibly, surprised to hear Cam do the same. "What a pair we make."

"Aye. I had visions of us wearing naught but yellow and steel."

"Me, too." And yellow was not her best color. "What now?"

"The Purple Pussycat. We have nae choice."

Picturing the deer running amok inside the club, alarms blaring, Claire shook her head. "No way."

"Aye, way. There's a storage building at the rear. We can put the deer in it for now and come back later tonight."

Splendid, just what she wanted to do. Make a night raid on a strip club to retrieve two reindeer. Resigned, she muttered, "I guess we have no choice."

When the Purple Pussycat came into view, Cam said, "Go past and then turn left. 'Twill lead to the back."

Behind the club, Cam pointed to a decrepit building that hadn't seen paint in a decade. "There."

She backed up to it, and Cam jumped out. Before she could get to the rear of the truck, he had the shed door unlocked and open. How he'd come by the skill she didn't want to know.

He took hold of the truck's door handle. "Stand there betwixt the truck and the shed door. I'll stand guard on this side where there's greater space. We dinna want the beasties to hie off."

"Right." *I so don't believe I'm doing this.*

He turned the handle. "Ready?"

"Yes." Sort of.

She held her breath, her heart beating so hard she knew she'd break a rib, and Cam jerked the door open.

And nothing happened.

She looked at Cam and he looked at her. Apparently also fearing the worst—that the deer had asphyxiated—they both leaned over to look inside. At which point the deer bolted.

Claire, seeing nothing but huge furry antlers, screeched and ducked as the buck, sleigh bell collar jangling, sprang over her. The doe, apparently not to be outdone, followed suit, catching Claire on the rump with a hoof as she went.

"Son of a bitch!"

Claire, her arms crossed over her head, twisted to look under one arm to see what was happening and if it was safe to rise. Cam stood with his hands on his head staring after the reindeer hauling ass around the corner, their tails high, flashing them as they went. He cursed again before reaching out to help her to her feet. "Are ye all right?"

Hands shaking with an hour's worth of fear-induced adrenalin, Claire shoved the hair out of her eyes and shouted, "Are you out of your ever-loving mind? I'll never be right again!"

Chapter Seventeen

Cam looked around the alley. "Where are we?"

Claire shut off the truck. "At Victor's studio. Come on."

Worried that she'd said naught since leaving the Purple Pussycat, he silently followed. Inside she rooted around a storage room much like her own, only this one was loaded from floor to ceiling with huge bolts of cloth, before handing him a broom.

"Sweep the hay out the back of the truck while I find something for us to eat. My head's killing me."

Though sweeping was woman's work, he thought it best not to argue. Claire wasna in a good frame of mind. Truth to tell, she looked ready to kill.

The truck swept clean, he went back inside. Not finding Claire in the storage room, he climbed the stairs.

In the large, well-lit loft, he found Claire, her chin resting in her hand, sitting at a table, a plate before her. She looked up as he approached. "All I could find were some crackers, pâté, and cheese. Bon appétit."

Ravenous, he murmured, "Thank ye." When their meager meal was done, he pulled the shears from the container at his elbow. "Is there a mirror anywhere?"

She immediately straightened, looking from the shears to his hair. "Do you really have to?"

"Ye saw the teevee. Ye tell me."

She heaved a sigh and held out her hand. "I'll do it."

Ten minutes later, he ran a hand over his head and grumbled, "I now ken how the poor sheep feel."

Claire caught her lower lip in her teeth, fighting a grin. "It looks good. Very modern."

"Humph! I seriously doubt it." He'd taken pride in his hair, having a full mane of it. Unlike the Sassenachs who had to wear wigs to cover their bald pates.

"Thanks for taking care of that gang that's been harassing me."

"Ye heard about that, did ye? Mrs. Grouse, I presume?"

"Yes. She couldn't wait to give me the details."

"'Twas my pleasure." And it had been. 'Twas a man's duty to protect and serve after all.

He strode to the windows and found the storm intensifying. "We'd best be going before we get trapped here. And we'd best leave the truck and take the emtyay. No point in giving the police more ammunition should they find me." He turned to find her studying him, her expression pensive. "What ails ye?"

"I'm frightened."

Ack, poor Claire. He strode across the room and wrapped his arms around her. Resting his chin on the top of her head, he whispered, "I'm so verra sorry, lass. Ye didna ask for any of this."

He should see her home and then disappear. The

police would doubtless question her, but without her kenning his whereabouts, surely they'd leave her be. He would leave his check and credit card as partial payment toward what he owed her. All he really needed was his identification card. He could live off the land as need be. 'Twouldna be the first time and likely wouldna be the last. He could manage until he met with the new psychic. Then he'd be home . . . where he belonged.

His decision made, he lifted her chin with the crook of his finger so he could look into her eyes and found them as wet and glossy as rain-soaked ivy. "Lass, ye'll be fine. Ye have naught to fear."

"It's not me I'm worried about. It's you!"

"Why ever would ye be fashing over me?"

She slapped his chest with both hands. "You're a duck out of water, a cat on a—a fucking *bicycle*, Cam. You're totally clueless and you're driving me crazy!"

He couldn't help it. He laughed.

Claire bared her teeth, apparently frustrated beyond endurance with him, and tried to pull away but he wouldn't let her. "Aye, love, I am all those things, to be sure, but not for long. Soon I'll be home and this will be but a dream we've shared. Ye do have to admit it has been one hell of an adventure, aye?"

She huffed but finally relaxed against him. "I suppose so. If I live to be a hundred, I'll never forget the look on your face when the deer bolted." She giggled for a moment then sobering, straightened and patted the front of his shirt. "And not to beat a dead horse, but what if there really is no going back?"

Then he'd still leave. He'd brought her enough heartache.

Fighting a head wind, they made it to the end of the block and headed down the stairs into what Claire called the underground, where they became two people in a mad crush of bodies wanting to ride the coaches which Claire again reminded him traveled on the lethal third rail.

Looking around, he asked, "Why are there so many about at this hour and in such weather?"

"A lot of businesses are still open. Hotels, hospitals, and the like."

A high-pitched screech of metal on metal emanated from the tunnel and those around them shifted forward. The coaches came to a shuddering halt, the doors opened, and the people behind them pushed forward, barely giving those in the coaches time or room to get out.

Finding only standing room inside, crammed hip to hip with their fellow passengers—one particularly odiferous—Cam grabbed the last free strap hanging from the ceiling and wrapped an arm about Claire. The train lurched forward. Bodies made larger by well-padded coats careened sideways, forcing Claire even closer to him. Liking the feel of her thighs pressed to his, he asked, "Comfy?"

Claire's nose twitched, apparently catching the odd stench coming from the man standing next to them. "Only you would ask that."

He grinned, happy his nose was a good two feet

higher, and turned his attention to the map mounted at eye level on the wall directly before him. Mass Transit Authority. M.T.A. Not empty-ay. Humph! And why had he not noticed this map when they'd gone to the library? Would have saved him a lot of aggravation and walking if he had. "Claire, which color track is yer home?" He could tell from the station signs that they were riding the red line.

"On the green. We'll change tracks under the Common."

Picturing the deer, they exchanged worried looks.

Chapter Eighteen

"Mrs. Grouse, we're home!" And none too soon. They'd only walked a block and Claire felt nearly frozen solid thanks to the wind.

She looked around as she hung up her coat, then shrugged. "She must have gone downstairs. I wonder where Brindle is? He should have been here by now."

She'd been greatly relieved not to see a cruiser parked out front and the police camped on her couch.

Cam nodded toward the coffee table. "There's a missive for ye."

Claire collapsed on the nearest chair and started pulling off her snow-caked socks. "What does it say?"

He turned on a lamp and picked up the letter. "Dear Claire, Mr. Brindle called to say he can't make it today but would come as soon as the roads were passable and that you are not, under any circumstances— she underlined that—to let MacLeod out of yer sight." He chuckled. "Trusting soul, that Brindle." He looked down again. "He also wants you to know that he managed to get the other charges against Cameron dropped, so there won't be a March trial although why he bothered he can't imagine and I quote 'given MacLeod's penchant for grand theft.'" Cam laughed. "Ah, my property will be returned to me. Great news that."

"All wonderful news." For a change. It probably also meant she'd get the bond money back, but likely not for months.

He scanned the rest of the letter. "She goes on to say the police havena called nor come by. And her daughter called. She'll be coming home for Christmas." Cam dropped the letter onto the coffee table next to the pile of receipts. "That should please her immensely."

"Yes. She's probably in a cleaning frenzy as we speak." Claire rose and not seeing the checks and cash on the table wondered where Mrs. Grouse had hidden them. She went into the kitchen, turned on the tea kettle, then peered into the cookie jar. Nope, not there. She drummed her fingers on the counter. Where would you hide money if you were a bank-phobic eighty-five-year-old woman? She checked the bread box and heaved a sigh of relief. There it all was. Now to check her stores. The power would be going out sooner rather than later the way the snow was coming down, and thanks to Cam, she hadn't done anything to prepare.

Hearing the TV, she shouted, "Have they found the deer?"

"Aye!" Barefoot and grinning, he came into the kitchen. "The buck and his doe are running hither and yon all over the park with dozens of police chasing after them. Funny to watch, really."

He *would* find it funny. "I'm glad they're okay."

"The man said a veterinarian is coming to fetch them home. Did ye ken a reindeer can run 50 miles per hour? Aye, that's what the man said." Cam shook his head in apparent wonder. "'Tis faster than we traveled on the way to Salem." He pulled a box of crackers from the cabinet. "And I saw myself on teevee and suspect ye've been fashing for naught. I wouldna have kenned it was me had it not been for the buck."

She gaped at him. She could only name *one* six-and-a-half-foot Scot who could run flat out with one hundred and fifty pounds of wild-eyed, thrashing reindeer on his shoulders.

Growling under her breath, Claire opened the freezer. Two weeks ago, she would have known what was inside down to the last cube without looking. With Cam around, it was anyone's guess. She opened the fridge. "I hope you like chicken." If not he was shit out of luck. She had chicken breast, chicken thighs, and a whole chicken in the freezer and leftover fried chicken in the meat keeper.

"I adore it." He came up behind her to have a look for himself and reached over her shoulder as he moved condiments and plastic containers around.

He's doing it again, getting in my space.

"The weather person said ye can expect three feet of snow by evening. Ah, look, ye still have some spaghetti. 'Twas verra good, by the way."

"Thank you." She did make a mean sauce and he smelled wonderfully masculine as he hovered over her, which she shouldn't even be thinking about. "We'll have it for lunch."

She mumbled, "Excuse me," to get him to back up and pawed through her junk drawer for matches. "Will you do me a favor and check on—"

Grrrrrrring, grrrrring

They both jerked and stared at each other. Claire murmured, "Oh God. What if it's the police?"

Cam strode into the living room and looked out the windows. "There isna a police car outside and no one is standing on the stairs."

Grrrrrrrring, grrrrrrrring!

Cam growled deep in his throat. "I'll wager 'tis the bloody deevil's buckies again."

As he jerked open her apartment door, she placed a hand on his arm. "Promise me you'll be careful."

He tapped the tip of her nose. "Aren't I always?"

"No."

Blade in hand, his gaze locked on the hooded figure beyond the glass, Cam crossed the darkened shop on silent feet. As if sensing his presence, the figure straightened. Ack, 'twas the Salem witch. But why on earth was she here, and on a day fit for neither man nor beast? His pulse quickened. Had she found the solution to his dilemma? "Please, God, let it be so."

Hope soaring, he punched in the alarm code and pulled open the door. "Mistress, come in before ye catch ye death."

"Hello, Mr. MacLeod." Her expression serious, Sandra Power glided over the threshold.

"To what do I owe the pleasure?" As her hood fell back sending a wee flurry over the floor, he rushed to close the door, only to hear a woman behind him squeak, "Not so fast, young man!"

A dozen women covered in a healthy dusting of snow were marching up the steps. Not having kenned their presence, the hairs on the back of his neck quivered. As they filed past and into the shop, he recognized the blind psychic he'd met in Salem who had told him to forgive Mhairie. To Sandra he asked, "Mistress, what goes on here?"

"Patience, Mr. MacLeod."

When the last woman crossed the threshold, he peered outside to be sure nothing else was heading his way, then closed the door. As he reached for a nearby table lamp, Mistress Power said, "That won't be necessary."

"As ye lust." He stepped into their midst. While his gaze raked over the women ranging in age from lasses to crones, from beauties to plain, each studied him in turn. Recognizing a woman of middle years whom he'd consulted with just days ago and who'd told him precisely what Mistress Power had, he scowled. "My lady."

"Mr. MacLeod, good to see you again."

He seriously doubted it, given he'd stormed out of her establishment.

"Mr. MacLeod," Mistress Power said, drawing his attention away from the last psychic he'd visited, "Discretion is paramount to us, but not apparently to you. Learning you've been running from pillar to post, from frauds to witches with your tale is alarming enough, but to see you on television . . ."

Humph! "If ye're here to chastise me or to tell me to cease—"

Both her hands flew up, palms to him, as did those of the women on either side of her. Within a heartbeat, the air felt charged as if before a powerful storm. The crystals on the chandelier above his head rattled and the hairs on his arms and neck immediately rose. Sensing imminent danger from all quarters but most strongly at his back, he spun and found the women behind him also had their palms to him. One, the crone, was scowling at him.

A heartbeat later all returned to normal and Mistress Power said, "Mr. MacLeod, you can relax. We mean you no harm."

Keeping the auld woman in his peripheral vision should she take it into her head to lunge, he muttered, "And why should I believe ye?" Every instinct within him warned otherwise.

"Because many of us empathize with your plight and the rest simply believe it's safer for all concerned if you're where you belong. What you see before you are the most gifted in the craft, of our kind. Like a rope made up of multiple strands, we're hoping to be stronger together than we are as individuals. What you just experienced was a collective energy. Are you ready?"

"For what?"

"To experience our full power, to return from whence you've come *if* it's at all possible."

"Now?" But he'd not said goodbye to Claire. He

couldn't simply disappear without a word. She'd fash herself sick wondering what had happened to him, and he had yet to tell her how much she'd come to mean to him, how much he truly appreciated all she'd done for him. That he'd grieve the loss of her, miss her more than he would have ever thought possible just weeks ago. "I need to say my fare—"

"Now or never, Mr. MacLeod." She cast a wary glance at the other women and he followed suit, only to realize that some were here under duress, that they'd just as soon walk out the door.

He took a deep breath. 'Twas, in fact, now or never. "Ye'll tell her what happened? That I care deeply and shall miss her?" He reached into his pocket and pulled out his cards and the check. "Please give these to her. And tell her to keep her trust in Victor for he loves her like a brother. And . . . tell her to get a cat. Lovely and honest, gentle and kind, she's still . . ." His voice cracked. "She's still lonely, mistress."

Sandra Power's features softened. "I will."

"Then so be it."

Who was he talking to?

Praying it wasn't the gang who'd been tormenting her, Claire edged in behind the open storage room door and pressed an eye to the crack between the frame and door. Recognizing Sandra Power, her heart began to hammer. Then she recognized two others. The blind psychic and a young girl they'd met in Salem. My God, there were twelve of them!

"Now or never," Sandra told Cam.

"Ye'll tell her what happened?"

Oh dear God! Had they come to grant his wish, answer his prayers?

"That I care deeply," Cam continued, "and shall miss her?"

Ooh, he cared deeply? Then why the hell hadn't he said so before now? Here she'd been thinking the worst. Augh!

Oh, and he thought her lovely as well?

The blind psychic suddenly looked her way. As the sightless black eyes narrowed, Claire's heart—already going insane with what she was seeing and hearing—slammed against her ribs. Had the woman sensed her presence? Panic closed Claire's throat as an invisible band tightened around her chest and caused her heartbeat to grow ever more erratic. Black spots started dancing before her eyes.

Do not panic. It's just the stress arrhythmia. Take a deep breath.

Praying the woman hadn't sensed her—that whatever the witches were doing in the shop would continue for Cam's sake—Claire backed away from the door, pulling deeper into the shadows toward the stairs.

Oh God. This was really happening. He really was leaving her. Now, before she'd had an opportunity to tell him she loved him. Every fiber in her wanted her to make herself known. To go into the shop and put a stop to whatever Cam and the witches were doing. But would he willingly remain—turn down the witches' help—if he knew she loved him? Or would he still go despite knowing?

She'd never know, because she wasn't running in there. He'd been too distraught learning about his family, had begged for help. And here it was in the form of twelve witches.

At the foot of the stairs, she hesitated, listening to the odd droning. She took a deep shuddering breath, tasted ozone, and looked back over her shoulder. Yes. Better that she not know if he'd remain or go.

The tears that had been building coursed down her cheeks. This was his wish, his life, not hers. And his leaving without him knowing the hopes and fears she harbored meant she could pretend that Cam would have remained had he known she loved him.

The drone followed her up the stairs growing louder instead of softer as she climbed. As she rounded the second-floor landing, the light above her blinked erratically and her footsteps faltered. *Please, God, keep him safe.* He'd be going into battle if he couldn't dissuade his father, would be one of thousands joining the Jacobite cause. The thought made bile rise in her throat. Even she knew all had been killed on the field of blood called Culloden.

She slipped into her apartment and quietly closed the door. Her heart skipped, then thudded as the lamp blinked out and a deadly silence descended. She grabbed the teddy bear sitting on the coffee table, all she had left to remember him by, and curled into a ball on the couch, her sobs coming in wracking keens as she buried her face in the soft plush. *Oh God, Cam. I'm so frightened for you.*

Chapter Nineteen

Three horrific hours later, Cam pulled the counter-pane from Claire's bed, draped it over her as she lay curled in a tight ball, the bear he'd given her clutched to her chest. He settled in the chair across from her, his head in his hands.

'Twas over. The witches had done their utmost, of that he was certain, and here he still was. Sandra Power had looked almost as bereft as he felt and had apologized for holding out hope where there was none to be had. She'd remained after the others had left to offer comfort, but like her hope, he found none. In the end he assured her he was reconciled to his fate and begged her to leave. Fearing Claire would seek him out when he was fit for neither man nor beast, he'd gone down into the basement where he dealt with his demons and fears, grieved yet again for his family and clan, and then put their ghosts to rest. Or so he hoped.

But now what?

Well trained in the art of war, stronger than most,

a fine horseman, his skills were worth a king's ransom to a liege in Scotland but were totally worthless in this place and time. He'd seen the advertisements for soldiers on Claire's TV. Had stared in awe at this century's armored vehicles, planes, and ships, what these soldiers took for granted as their weapons of war. He had experience with none of it.

But what if he asked to be a mercenary foot soldier? All armies had need of them. One thing was certain, he wouldna continue pimping women. 'Twas barely tolerable for a short period. 'Twas beyond imagining doing so for a lifetime.

Humph, a lifetime. While trying to ease his grief, Mistress Power had listed what she called the positives in his situation. She'd told him he would now likely live to be ninety. Who the hell needed to live so long? Or would even want to?

He needed a drink.

He rose and went into the kitchen where he opened the cabinet above Claire's cold storage and pulled out the remaining two bottles of merlot, then rummaged through her drawer for the wine opener. After two twists, he muttered, "Screw it," and pulled the cork from the bottle with his teeth and sucked down half the wine from one bottle, then returned to the parlor with a bottle in each hand.

"Cam? *Cam!*" Claire, her hair wild, her eyes puffy and blood shot, stared at him for a heartbeat, then launched herself into his arms, wrapping her legs about his hips as her chest hit his. Stunned, his arms came about her.

"'Tis pleased I am, lass but—"

Her hands cradled his face. "I thought—oh my God! You're still here! I was so scared." She kissed him, hard and sweet.

Without thinking, needing comfort as much as she apparently did, he opened to the caress of her tongue, her lips a balm for the wound too deep to touch.

Their kiss unbroken, he carried her to her bed-chamber, pausing only to drop the bottles onto her dresser, then collapsed onto the thick ticking and down, taking her with him. As he braced his arms to cushion the impact, her fingers locked behind his neck and her legs rode up and settled at his waist.

He ran a hand up her ribs to the fine fullness of a breast, something he'd been longing to do for days. A perfect palm full. She groaned into his mouth at his touch and he repaid the compliment, groaning as well, desperate for more. He plunged into the warm depths of her mouth and tasted salt and that which was Claire alone. With each breath he wanted more.

He broke the kiss so his lips might travel to her jaw and heard a soft keen. Ah, he well understood, but his mouth couldna be in two places at once. Her breasts with their taut nipples his goal, his lips traveled down the smooth contours of her neck, then hesitated where her pulse bound beneath his lips. He licked and traveled on. Buttons. Tiny pearl buttons blocked his way. His fingers, never designed for such a small task, fumbled with the glossy pink nuisances. He hated buttons, he truly did. He heard her wee keen and her fingers, fine and delicate, slid past his and within seconds the fabric parted exposing slick white fabric and soft curves. Nothing in a shop window could compare to the sight, this lovely warm flesh encased in smooth satin. Not lace, not feathers.

He slid down, forcing her legs to loosen their hold at his waist so he could capture her breast in his mouth. As he did, she arched and fingers threaded through what remained of his hair. Hair that should have been brushing her breasts and making her keen but was sadly no more.

He blew a hot breath across the tip of her right breast as he slipped the straps from her shoulders. He wanted in. Desperately.

He spied the clip between her breasts, squeezed and the fabric separated. Smooth alabaster mounds tipped by large caramel nipples came into view. A groan escaped him. Aye, 'tis better than he imagined. He latched onto one peak and suckled as a babe might, hot blood pumping into his groin. In. He needed in.

As if reading his mind, her hands started tugging at his sweater. He reared up and ripped it over his head and tossed it onto the floor. Claire, panting, her gaze locked on his, shrugged out of her delicate shirt and under thing, then reached for the button on her own jeans.

His hands closed over hers. "Nay." He wanted to unwrap that exquisite package himself and be ready to enter when he did.

He kicked off his sneakers. One button, a zip, a tug, and he was free of the tight garb that bound him, hers for the taking. Fully engorged, he knelt between her legs and placed a hand on her belly, a fingertip resting on the button of her jeans. "Mine?"

Her breath quickened. "Oh, yes, all yours."

He growled deep in his throat. His for the taking and take he would. His fingers made quick work of her button and zipper before hooking the fabric and tugging. The fabric slid easily off her hips and down her thighs. He tossed all onto the floor, then took a moment to admire her in the pale light.

He ran a gentle palm over the downy dark curls at her apex. "Ye're most lovely."

When her skin quivered in response, he placed a finger in his mouth and licked, his gaze locked on hers. His finger moist, he touched the soft puffy fold beneath the curls, and she keened, her hips rising with the touch. "I need ye."

She licked her lips and managed a breathy, "Yes."

His thumb grazed her tender nub as he slid his finger forward and found wet heat. "Ah, lass, ye're ready."

He stroked, watching. Her hands, which had clutched at the sheeting when he'd touched her, now reached up for him, her breath coming in short pants. Aye, lass, now.

He settled over her, his hips coming into perfect alignment with hers, and captured her mouth again with his. As his tongue stroked hers, her hands slid to his shoulders and her legs wrapped around his thighs. He rocked forward, his heart racing as he slid into her warm, wet core and felt her nails digging in. Her breathy keen would have given him pause had she not lifted her hips and slid her hands to his arse, urging him deeper. He thrust again and got lost in the warmth and sweetness, deaf to all but the sound of her panting and the slick slide of their bodies as he rocked above her. To his wonderment, her legs quickly grew taut and her body began to arch, her nails digging into his buttocks. *Oh, lass, bless ye. Ye're coming with me.*

On the brink of exploding, he felt her buck. As the wondrous flesh surrounding his shaft pulsed and she fell over the precipice keening his name, he followed. *Oh, Cam. My word. Who knew?*

Never in her wildest imaginings had she even imagined that sex could be so wonderful.

Her body still pulsing with aftershocks, Claire took a shuddering breath and looked at Cam as he laid eyes closed and panting, half on her, half at her side. Wow. Physically, he was every woman's fantasy come true, but for him to be so, so . . . wow.

She studied the movement behind his closed lids. How could he possibly sleep after so miraculous a happening? And look at his hair, standing up every which way in wavy spikes. She grinned, thinking it kind of cute but suspected he'd be cursing her for cutting it so short before the week was out. And he was still here. But how? Better yet, why?

She ran a finger along his lower lip. "Cam?"

"Ugh."

She laughed and he rolled onto his side, draping an arm about her, pulling her close so they lay face to face. "Shhh."

Claire snuggled into his warmth, her fingers toying with the fine hair on his chest. "Not until you tell me why you're here."

One eye opened and a dimple took sharp in his right

cheek. "I havena the strength to move. Ye drained me of all my vital juices."

"I'm pleased to hear it. But what I meant was what happened downstairs?"

"Naught of any import." His left hand gently stroked her ass as he nuzzled her neck. "My apologies for rushing the loving, lass. Normally I take a good bit more time, but ye ken 'tis been a while. Shall we start anew?"

Shivers ran down her spine as he caught her earlobe between his teeth, his breath hot on her neck.

"Yer skin is lovely, the color of fine ivory."

How nice that he thought so, but he still hadn't answered her question. "Cam, I saw Sandra and the others in the shop. What happened?"

He cupped her right breast and gently rubbed a thumb across her nipple. "Naught to be concerned about."

Deep inside, the hot aching need returned. She was sorely tempted to cave in to the feeling, but no, she couldn't just yet. Something had happened downstairs. She'd heard their conversation and the droning. Had seen the lights flicker out. She leaned back so she could look into his eyes. "They tried to reverse the spell, didn't they?"

"Ack, ye're determined to be the cat at the mousehole." He heaved a sigh and rolled onto his back, an arm flopping over his eyes. "Aye, they did, but it appears I'm trapped here."

While part of her rejoiced at the news, her heart nearly broke at the way he said *trapped*. "Oh Cam, I'm so sorry. I had such hope."

"As did I."

"Now what? What will you do?"

"Let's not fash on that now. I'm starved." He bounded out of bed and headed for the kitchen.

What the hell? "Cam, we need to talk." She grabbed her robe and hurriedly padded after him.

"Nay," he called, "we need to eat."

She found him rooting around in the refrigerator. "We can eat later." She'd just gotten him back. Emotionally, anyway, and she couldn't have him shutting—stonewalling her. "Cam, look at me."

He straightened and smiled at her, spaghetti in hand. "Will yer stove work without electricity?"

Who the hell cared about food right now? "Yes, but we need to talk about this. You have lots of options besides the Purple Pussycat. I can teach you to use the computer and you can do data entry. Maybe construction. We can get you a green card—"

"Humph!"

"Second Hand Rose" chimed loud and shrill through the apartment but she ignored it. "Damn it, Cam, don't roll your eyes at me when I'm—"

"You'd best answer that. It might be Mrs. Grouse in trouble."

Augh. She pointed a finger at his chest. "Don't you dare move."

Claire stomped into the living room and snatched up her cell phone from the coffee table. "Hello?"

"What the hell is going on there?"

"Oh. Hi, Victor."

"Don't 'hi Victor' me. I turn on *Good Morning LA* and what do I see? MacLeod, of all people, running through the Franklin Park Zoo with a fucking two-hundred-pound deer over his shoulders!"

"It was only one-fifty."

"Claire! For Christ sake. Did you call the cops?"

"No! It's a complicated story, but I can assure you—"

"I don't need assurances, Claire. I need you to get him out of your life before you end up in the next cell. Christ, Claire, they could charge you with harboring a criminal."

Ya, and probably with aiding and abetting, too. If Victor ever found out she'd used his truck to transport the reindeer, he'd have a heart attack. "There's really nothing to worry about, Victor. The deer are safe and back where they belong."

"Do you hear yourself? That does it. I'm coming home."

Oh no, he had to stay. "Victor, please, you can't come home. You have too much riding on this competition. You have to stay out there and win. Your career may depend on it."

He heaved an exasperated sigh, and then she heard the sound of shoes pounding on hard wood, could easily picture him pacing, torn between friendship and necessity.

"All right, but listen well, sweetie. I hear word one about MacLeod getting into any more trouble and I call my uncle and put an end to it. I don't give a damn if it bankrupts me."

Claire closed her eyes. Victor's uncle, Tony Delucci, once a union leader and captain, was now a regional crime boss under perpetual surveillance by law enforcement or so Victor had told her in strictest confidence. To her knowledge, the man had only been hauled in once on racketeering charges and been set free, but if rumors were true . . .

"Victor, I promise there won't be any more incidents."

"Claire, there better not be. I love you too much to allow that Neanderthal to ruin your life."

With that, he hung up.

Claire looked at the silent phone. Why me, Lord?

In the kitchen, she found the candles lit, the wine Cam had had in his hands when she'd jumped into his arms sitting on the table, but no Cam. Her heart tripped. "*Cam?*"

"Who called?"

She spun and found him fully dressed standing in the doorway. "It was Victor. He's enjoying California."

"Good. I couldna get the stove to work."

She nodded. "That's because it has an electric ignition. We'll have to use matches."

"Verra good. I shall ask Mrs. Grouse to join us."

And with that, *poof*, he was gone. She held her breath until she heard him pound on Mrs. Grouse's door and her tenant respond.

She collapsed onto a chair. This was not what she expected after their first lovemaking. She'd expected to be held, for them to talk a bit, maybe share a few secrets they'd never shared with anyone else before. Instead, he jumped out of bed and now he was seeking Mrs. Grouse's company instead of hers. It was as plain as the nose on her face. He didn't want to be alone with her. But why? Did he regret making love to her?

She mentally ran through it all. The urgency and passion. The wonder of it. The words of praise he'd whispered. His touch. Then he'd initiated another bout of lovemaking, and then she'd started questioning him and he'd—no, she'd started asking questions and then he'd initiated another bout of lovemaking . . .

"The light finally dawns on Marblehead." He'd started making love to her a second time *after* she started questioning him, to distract her. She stared through the doorway and into her bedroom at the brass bed that had never felt the weight of a man before now, stared at the rumpled bed covers. A burning started at the back of her throat. What wasn't he telling her now?

Chapter Twenty

The storm left the city—normally dirty and littered despite the sanitation department's best efforts—beautiful and clean, buried beneath a pristine blanket of white. And with its passing came the sun, electricity, and blessed warmth. God, she'd never been so cold in her life. She'd invited Cam into her bedroom and he'd come, keeping her warm until sometime during the night when, to her growing consternation, he'd retreated to his pallet downstairs. She'd removed it, told him he had no need for it, and still, he disappeared each night leaving her frightened and worried come morning.

And he'd not eaten more than was necessary to keep him alive in days. At first, she feared he was coming down with the flu, but he had no other symptoms. When she pressed him to talk to her, he'd simply mumble, "I dinna feel like eating."

More worrisome was his reticence to share his fears or plans. Oh, he'd tell her tales about his past life, about the time he broke his arm going over a waterfall in a wine cask or the first time he'd gone into battle, tales about his family, even about the first time he'd kissed a woman—him all of twelve at the time— often in haunted tones after he'd make love to her in slow, wonderful fashion. But he never would speak of the witches and what had happened that night. Nor would she discuss what he planned to do with the rest of his life no matter how she approached the subject. She'd be furious if she wasn't so damn frightened. Something was eating him alive.

The buzzer on her stove went off and she flipped off the oven. Tonight she was pulling out all the stops before he went off to work at the Purple Pussycat, a job she knew he loathed. Roast beef—dark outside, blood red, and all but mooing on the inside—French fries, gravy, and peas. His idea of heaven on earth, food-wise at least.

She pulled the roast out of the oven and checked the meat thermometer—perfect—and turned up the heat on the rest of the meal, then stuck her head out the living room window. "Cam!"

He looked up from where he was shoveling snow and smiled. "Aye?"

"Supper in fifteen minutes."

He waved, then went back to work, the smile gone.

She reached for dishes and the kitchen phone rang. *Please don't let it be Victor. I can't handle any more right now.* "Hello?"

"Hello, this is Sergeant Evans with the Boston Army Recruitment Center. May I speak with Cameron MacLeod, please?"

Deep breath. *No need to panic until you have a*

reason to. "I'm sorry but he's not here right now. May I take a message?"

"Yes, will you let him know that I spoke with my superiors and I'm afraid we can't give him anything in the UK. But I can guarantee him a year in Germany, so he can jump the channel anytime he has leave." He chuckled then said, "We'll start processing him as soon as he comes in. The next basic training course starts in three weeks."

Oh sweet merciful God. Take another deep breath. "Thank you. I'll be sure to let him know."

The phone missed the cradle when she tried to hang up and it landed with a crash on the floor.

Cam! What the hell are you thinking?

She'd never worried about him joining the military—a natural fit, she supposed and an obvious fascination for him as witnessed by his attention to the news and their ads on TV—because she thought there was a law against non-nationals joining the armed forces, but apparently not.

She made a mad dash for the bathroom. By the time she got there, the wave of nausea had blessedly subsided. She leaned, arms braced, over the sink, and looked into the mirror. She wouldn't have recognized the haunted face looking back at her had it been a photograph. "Oh, Cam."

He wanted *home* that badly?

"Claire?"

She jerked at the sound of Cam's voice and shouted, "I'll be right out!" She splashed ice-cold water on her face, then looked in the mirror. "You have to hold it together until you can think of something. He did this because he's proud and homesick and thinks this is the only way he can get home again. Not because he doesn't love you like you love him," which she suspected in her heart of hearts was true but she wasn't going there. Not now. "It'll be okay. You'll think of something."

Please, dear God, let me think of something.

She tapped her cheeks with cold water again and stepped into the kitchen, a smile plastered on her face. "I made your favorites tonight."

Grinning, he grabbed her and slipped his ice-cold hands beneath her sweater, making her squeal. Keeping her trapped, he leaned down and kissed her. "It smells delicious but ye shouldna go to such trouble."

She patted his chest. "Go wash your hands while I set the table."

A moment later, they were situated before a veritable feast. An hour later, neither of them had done much more than pushed their food around their plates.

Cam, looking at her plate, asked, "Are ye feeling unwell again? Should ye lie down? I can make ye a toddy. I have the whiskey."

The Scotch had been the first thing he'd bought after she cashed his check claiming her wine was fine but there were times when a man needed a real drink. "No, I'm just tired."

It had been a long day. Many of last week's customers had returned with girlfriends in tow to ogle Cam under the pretext of shopping or having their fortunes read by the incomparable Madame Grouse. And she couldn't blame them. Cam MacLeod was, beyond doubt, the handsomest man she'd ever laid eyes on, and apparently she wasn't the only one to think so.

"Cam, we need to go Christmas shopping tomorrow."

"For Mrs. Grouse, you mean?"

"For you, for me, and for a Christmas tree."

"But I thought ye didna celebrate Christmas." She'd told him about going home and finding her mother Christmas morning.

"Well, I think it's about time that changed."

With Cam in tow, Claire stopped before the smart Christmas display in the Tall-E-Ho window and pointed to the mannequin dressed in a navy worsted blazer, a turtleneck, and striped shirt. "What do you think? Can you picture yourself in something like that?" It really was handsome. "Cam?"

She looked around and found she'd been talking to air. Cam was nowhere in sight. Where the hell had he gone? He was right behind her a minute ago. "Damn it."

She started backtracking, stopping to look inside Victoria's Secret, a place that held him fascinated for several minutes when they passed it initially. She wound her way through the racks to the back without seeing him.

"May I help you find something?" a young saleswoman in curve-hugging jeans asked.

"I'm looking for a great-looking guy about six and a half feet tall, black hair, and great dimples."

She smiled, "Aren't we all?"

"Ya." Obviously he hadn't been in. She ran out the door and stood on the sidewalk looking right and left. Well, he hadn't walked past her, so she turned left. Seeing the telescope in the Sharper Image window, she grinned and went inside.

"Claire! Ye have to try this."

"There you are." He was sitting in a vibrating chair grinning like an idiot. When his gaze narrowed and traveled over her, she knew precisely what he was thinking. So did the salesman at his side who wiggled a brow at her. Heat rose up her neck. "Come on. We have more shopping to do."

Laughing for the first time in days, he rose and followed. Catching up with her, he wrapped an arm about her waist and nuzzled her neck. "We could have a wee bit of fun in that, no?"

Claire swatted his arm, grinning despite herself. The man was incorrigible.

She dragged him—protesting every inch of the way—into Tall-E-Ho where they found a salesman rolling his eyes while a woman, obviously harassed and jabbering into her cell phone, pointed at several items she wanted.

"Look," the woman growled into the phone as she pointed to a striped tie. "I don't care if he's dying of TB, he has to be at that shoot. No. No. Need I remind you he's under contract?"

When she followed the salesman to the counter, Cam whispered, "A bit of a shrew, aye?"

Claire nodded and steered him toward the sports jackets.

"You tell him," the woman shouted as she faced

them, "I'm suing his sorry—" her gaze raked Cam, "—ass. I'll get back to you." She snapped the phone closed, said something to the salesman, and headed straight for them. Looking at Cam, she smiled and said, "Excuse me, but haven't I seen you before? You're with the Elaine Pummel Agency, right?"

Cam smiled, flashing his dimples. "Nay, I dinna ken such an agency."

To herself the woman muttered, "God, this gets better and better." She held out her hand. "Hi, I'm Maggie Wheaton, Dynamics Inc, and you're just the man I've been looking for."

Cam, his expression now wary, took her hand and bowed over it. "Sir Cameron MacLeod at yer service."

The woman literally beamed up at him. "Would you mind if I took a picture of you?" Before he could respond, she'd reached into her large designer hand-bag—a two-thousand-dollar alligator exclusive if Claire's memory served—and pulled out a digital camera.

"Hi," Claire stuck out her hand. "I'm Claire Mac-Gregor and who are you exactly?"

"Oh, I'm sorry." The woman, forty-ish and dressed head to toe in Ellen Tracy black, reached back into her bag and pulled out two business cards, handing one to each of them. "I'm with Dynamic Inc, the mod-eling agency."

Claire fingered the heavy linen card between her forefinger and thumb as she read the fine embossed print. Maggie was more than *with* the agency; she was vice president. Already knowing the answer, Claire asked, "And why do you wish to take Cam's picture?"

* * *

Thirty minutes later, they were sitting in the Russian Tea Room, the only place Claire could think of in her agitated state that might offer them some privacy to talk. Sitting across from them sat Maggie Wheaton staring at her camera.

"As I'd hoped, the camera loves you. Look." She held the camera out to Cam, who looked at the images, shrugged, and handed it to Claire. She clicked on each of the poses Maggie had taken on the street and with a sinking heart suppressed a sigh. Yup, the camera did love him. No question.

"Given your size, I'll have to work to convince the European designers to let you do runway. They'll have to rethink some styles, rework patterns—" she flapped a hand as if they understood all the nuances of the fashion industry, "but then again, they're not stupid. They'll know that the female buyers will just have to take one look at you and they'll be buying everything you showed." She took the camera back and smiling, scanned the photos again before putting it back in her bag. She looked at her watch. "Damn, I have to run. I have another appointment."

She waved over their waitress and paid their bill over Cam's protests. "My pleasure," she told him.

Maggie rose and Cam did, as well. She held out her hand to him. "As soon as you have a passport, call me and I'll call Brinker and line up a shoot to start your portfolio. We can't do anything without one."

She then shook Claire's hand and thanked them both for their time. Halfway to the door, she called over her shoulder, "We'll go over the contract at the studio."

When the door closed on her, Cam collapsed into his chair. "The woman is a bloody whirlwind. I've never seen the like."

Nor had Claire. "She's from New York."

"And ye ken this how?"

"From her accent and the way she dresses."

He shrugged, crossed his arms on the table, and leaned toward her. "I didna ken half of what she said and dinna believe she heard a word I said."

Oh, she'd heard all right. Maggie Wheaton was just determined that he wouldn't say no. "She believes you have the potential for a very promising career."

He scoffed. "Strutting around like a bloody dandy in someone else's garb? I dinna think so." He shuddered. "Wouldna be the least manly."

Not from his perspective, she supposed. "But it could be quite lucrative."

That caught his attention and he frowned at her. "How so?"

"Some models make hundreds per day."

"Ye mean hundreds per week."

"No. Hundreds per day."

"Humph!" He scowled at her for a moment, then pushed back his chair. He held out his hand to her. "'Tis still foolishness and a moot point in any event. I dinna have a passport."

Her heart skipped a beat. Prayers sometimes were answered.

* * *

The next day, Claire smiled as she held out her hand to Tony Delucci. "Thank you for seeing me on such short notice, Mr. Delucci."

Victor's uncle returned her smile, taking her hand in his, then pulled her into a bear hug. "Please, Claire, call me Uncle Tony, and it's been too long." When he released her, he said, "Let me look at you. Ah, as lovely as ever. It's been what, three years since I've seen you?"

She nodded. "Not since your niece's wedding."

"Far too long. You tell that nephew of mine to bring you around more often." He motioned to the booth. "Sit and join me for lunch. I hate eating alone."

Claire doubted she could eat a thing given why she was here, but nodded and started unbuttoning her coat. A waiter stepped up to assist her. When he walked away, she slid into the white, table-cloth-draped booth opposite *Uncle* Tony and looked around. "It's lovely." And everyone looked normal.

"Is this your first time at Isabella's?"

She wiped her sweating palms on her slacks before resting them on the table, hoping she appeared more relaxed than she felt. Tony Delucci was still smiling but his dark brown eyes were as hard and calculating as she remembered them being the last time they'd met. "Yes, it is."

"Victor should be horsewhipped." He looked at the menu, then grinned. "I can recommend the Clams Casino."

"You remember." The man must have a mind like a steel trap. She'd gorged on them at the wedding reception.

He winked at her. "Of course. A gentleman never forgets a lovely woman's favorite food."

The waiter arrived, he ordered for both of them, and then rested his elbows on the table, leaning toward her. "So, my dear. What brings you here . . . to me?"

Oh God, where to begin. If she lied to this man she'd be buying trouble the likes of which she didn't even want to contemplate. "Did you happen to see the story on TV about the stolen reindeer?"

"Yes, funniest damn thing I've seen in years, watching the cops running and falling in hip-deep snow trying to catch them. Why?"

Here we go. "Well, Cam, my friend, stole the reindeer and I turned them loose in the park . . . sort of."

His laughter rang through the restaurant, heads turned, and he sobered . . . sort of. Still grinning, he said, "I'm sorry. But last I heard, lifting a few reindeer wasn't a hanging offense and neither of you were caught. Why do you need my help?"

"You're going to think I'm insane."

"Let me be the judge of that."

She didn't bother to swear the man to secrecy. Secrets were part and parcel of life for him. When her tale was done, he studied her for several minutes, then said, "It's doable. But it will cost you since it will need to be legitimate and security is tight, as well it should be. He'll have to use it within forty-eight hours or it might be dangerous. Everything is computerized now."

But it *was* doable. Cam could go home. "How much?"

He spread all ten fingers on the table. "Due on delivery Christmas Eve." He took out a pen and scribbled an address on a packet of sugar and slid it across the table to her. "Get him there within the next 48 hours. They'll take the photo."

Before she could get over the shock that it was doable, could even contemplate where she'd get ten thousand dollars, he smiled and said, "Ah, our lunch is here."

The waiter placed her lunch before her. "Lovely. Thank you." Where on earth would she get ten thousand dollars?

As he cut into his veal scallopini, Delucci murmured, "You should know that if it had been anyone else but you asking, for whatever reason, the answer would have been no. You I've known for only a few years but your mother I knew from way back when. You favor her." He looked at her then, his eyes as gentle as those of a cocker spaniel's. "She was a good woman."

Claire looked down, afraid she'd burst into tears. He wasn't doing this for her or Victor or even for Cam. He was doing this for her mother. She was going to cry.

"Here." She looked up to find Tony Delucci holding out a pristine monogrammed handkerchief.

She took it and mopped up her tears before they fell all over her clams. "Thanks."

"You're welcome. Now tell me about your plans for Christmas."

An hour later, Claire stood on the sidewalk, her cell phone pressed to her ear. She'd crossed the line, now stomped flat-footed in the world of black, but she knew precisely where and how she'd get the ten thousand dollars. She could only hope it wasn't too late.

Chapter Twenty-one

Standing in the vacant lot three blocks from Claire's home, Cam shook his head. "Nay, too skinny. Looks as if 'twas chewed upon."

The Christmas tree man, red-faced and rotund even without his winter garb, let go of the tree—the thirtieth Cam had asked him to shake out and hold up for inspection—letting it drop onto the pile. "Then you pick one out."

He'd been wondering how long it would take. Cam pointed to the fat, lovely tree he'd had his eye on all week, since he'd spied the man setting up this Christmas tree shop. "That one. I'll give ye twenty dollars for it." An outrageous price given it was only a tree.

The man snorted. "It's a hundred."

Cam held out his arms. "Look at all these trees. Ye've hundreds of them. Are ye going to turn yer nose up at a sale with only a few wee days left before Christmas?" Cam pointedly looked around. "I dinna see anyone else here buying."

"Seventy-five and you'll be stealing it. It's a blue spruce. From Canada."

Ack! Seventy-five dollars for a bloody tree. But this would be Claire's first personal Christmas tree in more than a decade. A very important thing, according to Mrs. Grouse. And he was feeling flush. He'd received another check from the Purple Pussycat—this one for six days' pay—and was awaiting a call from Sergeant Evans, who'd assured him he'd have no problem entering the army where he kenned he could earn an honest living. Cam had no choice but to claim his birth records had been destroyed in a fire—and for all he kenned, they truly had been, but the photo ID and Mike's letter of reference attesting to his honesty and reliability had eased the way. The sergeant's questions on strategy—what he called *what if* scenarios—had been child's play for a man who'd cut his teeth on *Vegetius* and had battle experience although he couldna admit to it else the sergeant think him daft. His physical soundness may also have helped.

How he'd tell Claire he was going away for a long while was another matter entirely. But for now, he would focus on making this the best Christmas Claire MacGregor had ever had and Mrs. Grouse had promised to help. But back to bartering.

"Thirty and ye can buy yer family the biggest goose in the butcher's shop and still have coins to spare."

The man took a look around his lot, muttered something under his breath then held out his hand. "Done. Thirty bucks cash. No check."

Cam laughed. Bucks. And a dog won't growl at a bone.

He took the man's hand and slapped him on the back. "May ye have a bonnie *Hogmanay*—New Year, sir."

"Ya, ya." The man took the cash and Cam grabbed the tree by its trunk, tossed it onto his shoulder, and headed for Dartmouth Street and Claire. A warrior victorious.

Claire, rolling pin in hand, sniffed the air. "Smells like the cookies are ready, Mrs. Grouse."

"Oh!" Her tenant hoisted herself off the couch where she'd been glued to the news and toddled into the kitchen.

"Would you believe they're still showing footage of Cam and the deer?"

"I'm not surprised. It's a Christmas tale to beat all." She held out her latest creations for inspection.

Mrs. Grouse erupted into laughter.

"Hey, I had to run all over town to get the cookie cutter." She then nodded to the frosting. "Brown. I thought Cam might appreciate it."

"You have a sick sense of humor, child. Remind me never to get on your bad side." She pulled the finished bell cookies out of the oven and set them on top of the stove. "Hand me that wooden skewer, would you? You have to poke the holes in the top while the cookies are still hot or they'll break."

The holes punched, she set the cookies aside to cool and placed Claire's reindeer in the oven. "Cam told me about the woman who wanted him to be a model. Said he'd never been so insulted in his life."

"He had been, but you couldn't blame the woman for trying. He is gorgeous and the camera loves him."

"I'm not surprised. He said you even had pictures made of him."

Claire grabbed the spatula and started transferring the cookies to the cool rack. "I wanted a nice one."

Mrs. Grouse wiped her hands on a dish towel. "Dear, has he told you yet that he's in love with you?"

The pan she'd been carrying fell into the soapy water with a clatter. "He's very fond of me, but doesn't love me." If he did love her, he wouldn't be doing what he was doing.

"And you're okay with that?"

Ah. Mrs. Grouse was apparently aware that Cam now shared her bed. "No, but you can't make someone love you. They either do or they don't." Experience had taught her that much. Her father had loved booze, drugs, and the thrill of the game more than he did her. Her mother . . . well.

"So where's our fearless Highlander now?"

"I've no idea. He said he had to run out and get something."

"You're rather calm. A week ago, you'd have been pulling your hair out wondering where he was."

A week ago, she didn't know for certain that she'd have to get used to him being gone, possibly forever, although she still worried he was getting into trouble.

"Claire, I have something to tell you and I just haven't wanted to."

"Are you ill?" Please, no.

"No, nothing like that. Let's sit."

Settled at the kitchen table, Mrs. Grouse reached for her hand. "You know my daughter is coming."

"Yes. I'm looking forward to meeting her."

"You'll like her. She's very much like you. Independent, feisty. But she wants me to go back with her to California after Christmas."

"That's wonderful. It will be a nice break for you from this dreadful weather."

"Forever, Claire. She wants me to move in with her."

"Oh." The news hurt but made sense. If she were Mrs. Grouse's daughter she'd want the same. "I'll miss you terribly, but you'll be happier in a warmer climate."

"True, but I hate leaving you alone."

Claire patted her hand. "You won't be. I have Cam." Not for long, but then, that was her problem. "Do you know when you'll be leaving?" Hopefully, not too soon. She could only adjust gracefully to one loss at a time.

Looking distressed, she murmured, "She's arranged for movers to come the day after Christmas."

"So soon?" Whoa.

"I know. I should have told you sooner, but I just didn't know how and you were having such problems with Cameron. This short notice must put you in a terrible bind."

"Nonsense. You've seen how well the shop has been doing." It would just take some time to adjust to not having her here. Knowing she wouldn't be able to knock on the door below any time she had need of comfortable companionship. A mother.

Oh well. Life goes on.

Claire rose and gave her a hug. "I'll miss you, but I'm really happy for you and your daughter. You should be together."

Mrs. Grouse dabbed at her tears with the corner of her apron. "You're sure?"

"Absolutely." As tears threatened, Claire sniffled and peeked in the oven. "Woohoo, the reindeer are ready."

Brrrrrrring, brrrrrring.

The tinny loading dock bell continued to grind as Claire hastily pulled the cookie sheet from the oven.

At her side, Mrs. Grouse said, "Hopefully that's not Cam with the sleigh."

She laughed. "If it is, I'll kill him."

Downstairs, Claire peeked through the loading door window, saw Cam stomping his feet, and threw open the bolt. "Why didn't you come in through the—oh, it's beautiful!" He was holding upright a magnificent, nine-foot-tall blue spruce and grinning.

"I didna dare take her in through the shop for fear of knocking something over."

"Good thinking." It would have been a disaster. The lower branches fanned out an easy six feet.

She stepped out onto the platform to give him a hand but he shooed her back inside. "Nay, just hold the doors." He scooped the tree up onto his shoulder, and whistling, headed up the stairs.

Mrs. Grouse gasped, then helped Claire clear a path to the window. As Cam propped it against the glass, Mrs. Grouse placed her hands over her heart. "Oh, Cameron, what a lovely tree."

Claire stepped back to admire it, and Cam came up

behind her, wrapped his arms about her waist and kissed the side of her neck. "Merry Christmas, love."

Love. If only. Growing misty-eyed, she murmured, "It's perfect, Cam. Thank you."

"Ye're most welcome, but bonnie as it is, it still needs lights and such. Ye ken, the doodads and frippery."

"Let's do the frippery after supper." As far as she knew, he hadn't eaten all day. "After we eat, I'll turn on the Christmas carols, you and Mrs. Grouse can doctor the eggnog with whiskey, and we can all get looped while we decorate."

"Brilliant." He kissed the top of her head. "The man said ye likely had a stand for it. Where do ye keep it and the lights and all?"

"In the attic."

Before she could blink, he was gone.

Six hours later, Cam cradled Claire as they cuddled on the sofa, naked as the days they were born, a potent cup of eggnog in hand. "I like yer reindeers."

She giggled. "I thought you would."

"'Tis lovely, the tree. I like yer colored lights better than the white ones I see everywhere."

"Me, too. They're kind of big and clunky, but they remind me of my childhood."

"How so?"

"They once belonged to my mother." She pointed up to the tin star with the bright red center perched atop the tree. "That was hers as well." She pulled his arms tighter about her. "Cam, what did you do to celebrate Christmas?"

"Christmas wasna a day of celebration, but one of penance, much like Lent. Ye labored as ye did on any other day, only harder, if possible. A Yule log was set ablaze and 'twas bad luck for the household should it go out before all turned to ash. But Hogmanay—New Year's—that's a sight. 'Tis the day we exchange gifts with loved ones, feast, dance, and get into our cups."

"You're homesick, aren't you?"

"Aye, at times."

"If you were back in Scotland right now, what would you do?"

"I'd take my time admiring the hills and valleys white with snow, the burns running clear and cold, and the waves crashing on the headland. I'd want to see if there are any MacLeods left on the land that I knew, to ken whether or not there are ships at moorings in the harbor, men still taking their livelihoods from the sea. To stand in the kirk I'd been baptized in, that I was once wed in, and then buried my wife from. To stand beside her and my mother's effigies, mayhap even my brother's and Da's. To pay my respect."

"You've not spoken much of Margie. Did you love her?"

"Ours wasna a match made in heaven but on earth to strengthen a clan alliance. I can say looking back on it she made the best of it, given the bargain she made."

Claire craned her neck to look at him. "Were you unfaithful?"

"Nay, just constantly looking for anything—didna matter what—to get out from beneath the cat's paw, away from her, my Da, and my elder brothers' scrutiny." He chuckled, "I'd rather have been fishing or wielding a sword than spending time studying accounts and fashing over tithes and taxes. I kenned why they insisted I learn such. Life is tenuous at best, and by default, I could have ended up liege, but to my way of thinking, their fashing was a bloody waste of time. The crown kept raising the bloody fines, so what was the point? Ye either had it or ye didna."

She took a sip of her eggnog, her attention again on the tree. "Was she pretty?"

Now why would she want to ken that? "Aye, she was fair and fulsome, but in the way of her time. Ye'd likely not think her so today. She didna have Tracy's glamour or yer intelligence."

"Ah, my intelligence."

"'Tis something wrong?"

"No, I'm smart all right."

But she suddenly tried to sit, and he was forced to wrap his legs about her to trap her where she lay. "Talk to me."

That had been part of his and Margie's problem. They never spoke. They'd simply tup when the mood struck, then go their separate ways.

"Please let me go."

Over his dead body.

He loosened his legs enough for her to spin. When she faced him and tried to rise using his chest for leverage he trapped her again. "Woman, I paid ye a high compliment. What's in here," he tapped her forehead, "and what's in here," he tapped her heart, "are worth a king's ransom to a man with sense. Beauty fades. Babes suck breasts flat and age flattens a rounded arse. A good heart and a fine mind last a lifetime. The fact that ye have fine hurdies and lovely eyes is icing on an already-rich cake that doesna need the decoration.

"'Tis like that tree. 'Twas lovely before the frippery. 'Tis now decorated, so why not enjoy all that as well." He grabbed hold of her arse. "And I plan to enjoy it."

And he did. He just hoped Mrs. Grouse wasna listening. Claire's groaning was loud enough to wake the dead when she lay upon his chest face up and he took her from behind, stroking her breasts and where they joined as he lost himself in her. And he was none too quiet either when later she slid down his body and took him, again swollen with need, into her mouth and over the brink of sanity. And what she could do with her tongue to his balls . . . odes should be written. Made him even happier to be a man.

Less than twenty-four hours after meeting with Tony Delucci, Claire stood in an impressive but cold, black-and-white two-story foyer beside her mirror, her arms out and hands graceful, pointing at her pride and joy like some game show model. "As promised, eighteenth century, silver-lined glass, a solid mahogany frame hand carved by Louie Beauchard himself, above which you have not one but four layers of hand-applied, twenty-four-karat gold leaf. The provenance is in the envelope on the sideboard."

Mrs. Townsend beamed as she ran her hand over the gold leaf. "It's as beautiful as I remembered. I'm right. It will make an absolutely smashing door frame for my dressing room."

Please, don't let me be ill. I have to get through this for Cam. Oh, God, I'm going to be ill.

Claire swallowed the rising bile, nearly choking. When she caught her breath, she murmured, "Sorry, too much eggnog last night." She then took a deep breath. "I'm sure it'll be perfect. Just tell your carpenter to be very careful when he takes it apart. The joints at the corners are dovetailed and glued, unlike most joints today. You don't want to damage the gold leaf." Never mind that a priceless work of art would be destroyed.

Mrs. Townsend nodded and held out her hand. "I'll take it. Please, come into the study and I'll write the check." She then waved *shoo-get-moving* hands at her moving men, who pushed it away down the long corridor before Claire. She would have stood in the foyer until the mirror had rolled out of sight had Mrs. Townsend not said, "Ms. MacGregor, if you please. I haven't got all day."

Bitch.

Cam winced as Mrs. Grouse, contemplating his hair, clicked her shears. "Dinna get carried away now."

She tapped him on the side of the head with the shears. "Stay still and I won't." A moment later, she murmured, "There. This should do."

He held out his hand and she dropped a two-inch curl into his palm. "'Tis perfect. Thank ye."

"You're welcome but what are you going to do with it?" Sounding hopeful, she asked, "Put it in a love letter?"

"Nay, I'm a man of few words." He rose and headed for the door, Mrs. Grouse toddling after him.

"You're not going to tell me, are you?"

Grinning, he carefully pocketed the curl and tapped her nose. "I'll let Claire tell ye."

Downstairs, he found Tracy behind the desk and the shop quiet. "Where's Claire?"

"She said she had some last-minute Christmas shopping to do and asked if I'd cover for a while."

"That was kind of ye." He looked about the shop. "Where's the mirror?" Hopefully it hadna toppled. 'Twas Claire's pride and joy.

"She sold it."

"What?"

Tracy shrugged. "Apparently someone came in, said they had to have it, and she sold it."

"But she loved that mirror."

"I know. I'm as surprised as you are."

"Humph." So why hadn't she said something about it?

The bell above the Velvet Pumpkin's door chimed and the postman walked in, his arms loaded with packages and mail. Seeing Tracy behind the desk, he smiled like a moonstruck whelp, and Cam mentally shrugged. Some men apparently didna ken trouble even when it smacked them upside the head.

As he and the postman exchanged greetings, the

bell chimed again and a small woman of middle years carrying a portmanteau walked in.

Since Tracy was oblivious to all but the postman, Cam said, "Good day, madam, may I be of help?"

The woman pulled off her knitted cap, exposing a short cap of sun-streaked spikes. "Hi, I'm Shelley Grouse, Martha's daughter. Is she home?"

He beamed at her. "Aye, she's home and sitting on pins waiting for ye." He stuck out his hand. "I'm Cameron MacLeod, Claire's friend."

She laughed. "I thought so. You're bigger than I expected after seeing you on TV." Apparently noticing his surprise, she whispered, "Not to worry, Mom's told me all about you. Your secret's safe with me."

"Ack." A bit disconcerted that this stranger from the opposite side of the country should have seen him on TV and recognized him, he muttered, "I'll see ye upstairs."

Climbing the stairs, Mistress Grouse's portmanteau and Claire's mail in hand, he wondered who else kenned what he'd been about.

Ahead of him, Mrs. Grouse's daughter said, "Has Mom told you I'm taking her back to California with me?"

Claire found Cam sitting on the sofa staring at the Christmas tree. "Hi."

He rose slowly and came to her. "Where's the mirror?"

Knowing the question would come, she dropped the videos on the coffee table and not wanting to lie to his face, reached for the mail. "I sold it to a small museum."

"But ye loved it."

"Sometimes we have to let go of things we love . . . for the greater good."

"Humph! Not where I come from."

"Well, sometimes here we just do." She rifled through the bills, tossed them onto the coffee table to examine the lone letter. Not recognizing the address but hoping it might be a query about something in the shop, she opened it.

Dear Claire,

I wanted you to know that I'm out and now living in Chelsea. I have a job and am attending meetings. I've been clean and sober for four years now, not long in the greater scheme of things, I know, but I'd like an opportunity to make up for some of the heartache I've caused you. To apologize to you in person and to perhaps make a fresh start. I did love your mother and still grieve for her. I hope you'll write back. I truly have changed.

Love, Dad

Claire crumpled the letter into a ball. Too little, too late. Her father was a sorry son of a bitch.

"What's wrong, lass?"

"Nothing." Claire shuddered and tossed the wadded letter into the wastebasket. Her father had ruined the first twenty-two years of her life, she'd be damned if he'd ruin the rest of it. Particularly now, when this could well be the only Christmas she and Cam might have together.

Forcing lightheartedness into her voice that she didn't feel, she said, "So, did you leave me any cookies?"

"Aye, but if ye plan to eat more than four, ye'll have to take from yon tree."

It was coated in almond-flavored Christmas bells suspended on fine red ribbon and yards of popcorn garland.

"When were ye going to tell me about Mrs. Grouse leaving?"

Perhaps it was too much to hope that he wouldn't learn about it before he left. "I just found out myself."

Looking none to happy, he grumbled, "Ye'll miss her."

"I will, but I can always rent the apartment again."

"Humph! 'Twillna be the same."

True.

Hoping to distract himself from the crumpled missive lying in the waste basket, Cam moved his carefully wrapped gift for Claire to the opposite side of the tree and stood back to admire it. The saleswoman had done a far more admirable job than he'd managed on Mrs. Grouse's gift, which lay beside it.

He glanced at the basket again. Why had she crushed it into so tight a ball before tossing it away?

"*Humph.*" 'Twasna his affair. He had no business being curious about the missive, much less reading it. But why had reading it made her so upset? She'd turned scarlet. Had someone threatened her in some way? If so, he needed to ken in what manner and take care of it before the sergeant called.

Damn.

He strode into the bedroom, heard the shower running, then returned to the parlor and reached into the basket for the missive. After reading it, he reached for the envelope, memorized the address, and returned all just as he'd found it.

Five minutes later, he looked at the clock. "Claire, we'll be late for midnight mass if ye dinna hustle."

"I'll be right out!"

He yawned hugely. Ack, why would anyone in their right mind wish to attend kirk at midnight when they should be asleep? 'Twas a most bizarre practice. But Claire had insisted. Praying her service wouldna drag on for hours and hours as they usually did at home, he reached for his new down jacket, another extravagance she'd insisted upon over his protests.

Behind him, she said, "I'm ready."

His gaze traveled over her from curls to shiny black boots. "Lass, ye're a sight to behold."

Glowing, she turned in a circle for him, sending her blood-red lace and velvet skirt whirling about her legs. "You like? It's vintage."

He dropped the jacket and strode to her, where he pulled her into his arms, inhaling the fresh sweetness of her. "Ack, ye smell as good as ye look. Are ye sure we have to go? I'd just as soon stay here and relieve ye, piece by lovely piece, of all this bonnie garb."

She laughed and patted his chest. "After mass. You look very handsome in your new sweater."

"Thank ye." He nuzzled her neck. "Are ye sure I canna change yer mind?"

"You could but then you'd be missing something quite wonderful."

"Nay, for I've something most wonderful here."

Grinning up at him, she cupped his face in her hands. "Mrs. Grouse and her daughter await."

"Ack."

She laughed and reached for her keys.

Two hours later, Cam tossed his coat onto the brass hook and helped Claire out of hers. "Would ye believe I can still hear the music?"

"There's nothing like Handel's *Messiah* when it's done right."

He collapsed onto the couch, his arms spreading over the back. "'Twas indeed wondrous. I'm verra glad ye insisted we go."

"Me, too." Saint Patrick's Cathedral was a joy to behold any time but on Christmas Eve, it really was magical. "Now, we get to drink eggnog and open one present."

He frowned as he looked under the tree. "Just one?"

"Yes, just one or Christmas passes too quickly, but it should be a special one."

"Ah, verra good."

When she settled beside him on the couch with spiked eggnog in hand, she saw that he'd selected the gift wrapped in silver paper and elaborate ribbon.

With a shaking hand, she picked out her gift for Cam, the long narrow box wrapped in plaid ribbon, and handed it to him. "You go first."

"Nay, ladies first."

"Okay." Wondering what her gift contained—she'd already shaken the box when she'd spotted it under the tree and knew it didn't jingle—she was now almost afraid to unwrap it.

"Lass, I'll do it for ye if ye dinna make haste." He was smiling but obviously anxious.

She took a deep breath and smiled in turn, then tugged on the ribbon. When she lifted the paper, she found the trademark sky-blue box every woman on the planet would recognize. My God! "Cam?"

"Open it."

Holding her breath, she lifted the lid. Nestled within white velvet, she found an exquisite gold locket. At its center sat five tiny pink pearls surrounding a lone diamond. "Oh, Cam, it's absolutely gorgeous but you shouldn't have." Made of eighteen-carat gold, the pendant had cost a fortune.

He relaxed then, smiling, dimples flashing. "'Tis more, look inside."

Not believing any of this, she pressed on the snap closure and the locket opened. Beneath the glass on the left side, she found the passport photo she'd kept for herself carefully cut to fit and beneath the glass on the right a lock of his hair surrounding the engraved words, *For love, for my life, Cam.*

She burst into tears, and his arms came around her. "Ye dinna like it?"

The man was beyond hopeless. She shook her head. "I love you so damn much."

"Oh, Claire." He cradled her to his chest.

Were all as it should be, that I could admit I feel the same and bind ye to me forever.

And 'twas worth the loss of his broadsword, something that he'd been most proud of, that had been handed down through generations, to make her this happy. He could do naught but hope that the antiquities dealer who'd purchased it treated it with respect.

Sniffling, she straightened and patted his chest. "Dare I ask how you purchased something so exquisite?"

He grinned, "Nay, but rest assured 'twas honestly. Now hand it over, so I may place it on yer neck where it belongs."

It fell precisely as he'd imagined it would, right above her heart. He kissed her, gently but thoroughly, then pulled back. "'Tis almost as lovely as ye."

"Thank you." She picked up the gift she had for him. "Your turn."

"Before I do, I need tell ye something. Why I gave ye the locket." He took a deep breath, so dreading this moment when he would tell her he was leaving. "I canna go on as I have working at the Purple Pussycat and have decided to—"

She pressed her fingers to his lips. "Open your gift."

"But ye need ken—"

She shoved the box into his hands. "Now. You can tell me what you need to after you open it."

Ack. He gave the box a shake. "'Tis a tie."

Clutching the pendant, she shook her head. "Not quite. Open it."

When the paper fell, he lifted the lid then looked at her curiously. "I dinna ken what this British Airways is."

"Look underneath it."

He did and his breath caught. "'Tis a passport." He thumbed through the pages, most of which were blank save for one with a stamp and the one with his picture and name on it. "But how?"

"Let's just say I have friends." She opened the British Airways packet and handed him the contents. Pointing to the fine print, she said, "See, you leave Boston for Gatwick tomorrow at 3:05 in the afternoon. Here is your seat number. You arrive in London at 7:30 the next morning. From there you travel via a shuttle—that's a small airplane—to Edinburgh." She cleared her throat and looked at him, her green eyes glassy. "From there, I trust you can find your way home."

"Home." The word held such import.

She swallowed convulsively as her tears cascaded down her cheeks. "Yes. Home."

He again heard her words as they stood on the library steps holding each other. His throat raw, he whispered, "Ye've kept yer promise."

Sobbing, she nodded and collapsed onto his chest.

Chapter Twenty-two

Claire, her palms sweating and her heart thudding unmercifully, stood at Cam's side as he handed over his ticket and passport to the ticket agent wearing a Santa hat and Christmas earrings. During the night, she'd fretted about whether or not to tell him how she'd come by the passport, fearing it might get him out of the country but might pose a problem getting him into England. In the end, she decided ignorance was bliss, should it not work and the agents at the other end take him into custody and insist he take a lie detector test. This way, he'd pass.

When the woman smiled, wished him a pleasant trip and handed him back his documents, Claire nearly fainted with relief. She caught her breath as she watched the agent slap a sticker on Cam's luggage— all the clothes she'd purchased the day before at Tall-E-Ho's—then led him toward the security check-in.

She stopped some twenty feet from the entrance and pulled him aside, letting a large group of harassed-looking passengers rush past. "You're not armed, right?

You left your knives at my place. You have to go through the metal detectors."

He smiled down at her. "I'm not armed."

"Good. Okay." It still took all she had to keep from frisking him anyway, knowing him as well as she did.

"When you get off the plane, head toward the sign that says United Kingdom Citizens. That's you. And try like hell to get in line with a woman inspector. And smile . . . a lot. Chat with her. She'll love your accent." One look at those dimples of his and the inspector would likely forget what she was doing and pass him through. "And call me the minute you get to London." Once she knew he was safe, she'd tell him how she came by his passport. Warn him not to reuse it. If he really wanted to come back to her, he'd move heaven and earth, go through whatever channels he needed to, to get a legitimate passport. If he didn't . . . well, she would deal with that pain when it came. Right now she could barely keep from falling to the floor in a puddle of grief.

"Claire," he slipped his arms around her, then tipped up her chin so he could look in her eyes. "I canna thank ye enough."

"There's no need. It's been my pleasure—and a hell of an adventure."

"That it has. Ye need ken something, though. After learning about Mrs. Grouse leaving, I met with yer father."

"You *what*? Why? When?" How dare he?

"Dinna be cross. I was having a difficult time thinking ye alone in this place. I wanted to ken what kind of man he was. If he had truly changed as he claimed."

"You read the letter?" *I don't friggin' believe this.*

"Love, I believe he's sincere in his grief. That he now fully kens all he's lost." When she growled deep in her throat and slapped his chest with her palms, he gave her a squeeze. "All I ask is that ye think on it, lass. To mayhap see him just once. Promise me that?"

"Augh!" How could he do this to her, here and now of all times? When he remained silent, only bent at the knees to look her square in the eye, his head tipped in question, his dimples taking shape, she huffed, "All right, I'll think about it, but I won't promise you anything beyond that."

He kissed her, softly then with growing urgency as if they hadn't spent hours making love until the wee hours of the morning. Her fingers dug into him trying to hold him closer. If only she could crawl into him and go with him.

Too soon, he broke the kiss and pressed her head to his shoulder and she could hear his heart thudding. Maybe for the last time. Oh God. Do not cry. Do *not* fall apart.

Into her hair he whispered, "I wish with all my heart ye were coming with me, lass. I'll miss ye terribly."

"I wish I was going as well." But this was something he needed to do on his own. To come to grips with his new reality. She took a deep breath, and with every muscle in her body crying out, demanding she cling, she stepped away. "You'd best get going or you'll miss your flight."

When they'd got in the security line, he on the inside, she on the outside, wishing she could follow him in, to be sure he made it onto the plane, she wrung her hands and told herself this was just as well. She'd likely turn into a blubbering mass if she watched his plane take off.

As he handed his documents to the security guard, she said, "You'll call the minute you can?"

He leaned toward her and kissed her a final time. "I promise."

And then he was gone.

Too agitated to sit, Cam watched the first of those around him step toward the open doorway, hand over their tickets, and then did the same. Palms sweating, he followed his fellow passengers down a low-ceilinged corridor to the airplane. Something he never wished or dreamed to travel in.

Christ's teeth, I wish Claire was with me.

With no small measure of trepidation he stepped over the threshold and was greeted by a lass who smiled at him, looked at his ticket and waved to his right saying, "Enjoy your flight."

Not likely. The very fact that he would take flight in just minutes had his gut in a bloody knot.

It took a moment to find his seat by the window. As Claire had instructed, he found the exit sign and counted the rows to it should he have need for it. As people filed in, many tossing baggage into the over-head compartments, he tried to squelch his anxiety, assuring himself that this many people wouldna be flying were it not safe. He hoped.

A florid man two decades older than Cam settled into the seat next to him. "Hi."

"Hi."

Cam watched as the man secured himself with a belt and quickly reached beneath himself, found his straps, and followed suit. Ack, this didna bode well for what was about to happen.

The man extended his hand. "Jim Lord, from Bristol."

Cam shook it. "Cameron MacLeod, Rubha, Scotland."

"Going home, huh?"

"Aye." For the first time in almost three hundred years. What would he find?

A woman in livery stopped at their side. "May I get you gentlemen anything to drink while we wait for the rest of the passengers to board?"

Jim said, "I'll have a gin and tonic."

She smiled at Cam. "And you, sir?"

"Whiskey."

She listed three and he chose the last.

"Neat or on the rocks?"

"Neat." Sounded less dangerous.

A moment later she handed him a short clear cup and a bowl of nuts. He downed the whiskey in one swallow.

Jim laughed. "Don't like to fly, huh?"

"Nay." Who would? He really should have been more insistent Claire exchange the airplane ticket for one on a vessel. *Accck.*

Too soon all the seats were full, the overhead compartments closed and a disembodied voice welcomed him on board, telling him the flying time to London would be eight hours and a few minutes. Beyond imagining. The last he'd heard, the trip took eight weeks.

As the airplane began to roll, four women in dark

blue livery stood in the aisles demonstrating what was being pictured on his personal TV. When the vehicle thrust forward at unimaginable speed and then leaped into the sky, he decided the ladies' precautions were for naught. Should the airplane decide to plummet back to earth, he'd be splattered across the incredible landscape below like an egg.

Moments later, his breath caught again. He was staring *down* at clouds. Mesmerized by their shape and height, the way the sunlight illuminated the huge columns, he startled when the flight attendant again asked if he'd like anything else to drink. "Whiskey, if ye please. Three, they're wee."

Two hours and twelve wee whiskeys later, he closed his eyes and prayed for sleep only to be jolted awake sometime later by a voice saying, "Mr. MacLeod, please prepare for landing."

He yawned, looked out the window and his breath caught. London lay beneath him, a maze of houses and roadways by the thousands and he was heading straight for them at breakneck speed.

He bolted upright in his seat, his heart beating with a force strong enough to break ribs. To his amazement, his fellow passengers looked not the least alarmed. At his side Jim said, "You sleep like the dead." He jerked a thumb toward the rear. "I feel sorry for those bastards in the back, sleeping upright all night. I flew coach only once and swore never again." He heaved a sigh and started collecting his belongings. "Hell of a day we picked to travel, huh? Gatwick will be a madhouse."

Cam nodded, having no idea what the man was

going on about, and pulled his ticket from his pants, another gift from Claire, to memorize the information about his flight to Edinburgh and saw a number in the lower right-hand corner. $4,489. Sweet St. Bride! Why had he not noticed this when she'd given him the tickets? He'd have demanded she return it and that he travel by sea. Ack!

Jim hadna lied. Gatwick was indeed a madhouse. As people hurried past, he followed Jim to the baggage claim. Waiting beside a movable steel track, Jim asked, "Is anyone meeting you?"

"Nay. I go on to Edinburgh tonight."

"Have a safe trip. Ah, our baggage is finally coming out."

Cam collected his one bag, another gift from Claire, and followed the crowd toward the customs signs. Seeing United Kingdom, he angled left and got in line.

The woman flipped open his passport, looked from the photo to him, and he smiled, flashing his dimples. "Good morning, lass."

She smiled in turn. "Do you have anything to declare?"

"Nay." Claire hadna mentioned a declaration and he could only pray he'd filled the form out correctly.

She scanned the form, stamped the passport and handed it back. "Have a nice holiday, Mr. MacLeod. Next!"

He stepped over the red line and he was in England.

Finding the telephones, he followed Claire's directions, telling the operator her number and that he was calling collect.

A moment later, Claire said, "Hello?"

God, it was good to hear her voice. "'Tis I, I'm in London."

"Cam! Are you okay? Did everything go smoothly? I've been worried sick."

"Aye, all went well, but I nearly choked seeing how much the ticket cost ye. Ye really shouldna have, love."

"I wanted to." After a pause she said, "You need to know something about your passport. Now don't get upset, but—"

"Claire." Cam looked about to be sure no one was listening, leaned into the booth and whispered, "I ken. Ye were sweating bricks, yer eyes never leaving it as it went from hand to hand in Boston."

"Oh." She blew out a breath. "It was such short notice and you have no documents—"

"I understand." His Claire had done a little judicious reiving of her own.

"No, you don't. You can't use it again."

That gave him pause. "I see."

"You'll have to apply at a government office for another in Scotland if you wish to go anywhere outside of the UK . . . England or Scotland."

He frowned, but then if she could manage such, so could he. "I shall apply for another then."

"Good." After a minute she said, "I already miss you."

"And I ye. You'll take care, Claire?"

"Yes, I promise."

"And ye'll give thought to what I said about your father?"

"I'll think about it."

She truly did need to think on it. She was now alone in this world, and if Cam was any judge of men, Mac-Gregor was sincere, a man ill at heart.

Having already said their good-byes, he whispered, "I shall return."

Her voice cracked as she said, "I'll be here."

Ten minutes later, Cam, his stomach growling, waited in line for fish and chips and heard a woman shout, "MacLeod? MacLeod!"

Curious, he looked around and spied a woman frantically waving at him. Christ's blood, 'twas Maggie Wheaton! What on earth was she doing here?

She rushed up to him, her baggage in tow. "I thought it was you! What are you doing here? You naughty boy, you were supposed to call me the moment you got your passport."

She looked over her shoulder and waved an urgent hand at the thin young man trailing behind her. "Come on, Jason." To Cam she said, "I can't tell you how thrilled I am to see you. I mean it. You're an answer to a prayer. Jason really is as sick as a dog."

When Jason joined them, Maggie said, "Jason Jackson, meet your salvation, Cam MacLeod."

Jason, pale as whey save for a bright red nose, eyed him from head to sneakers. "Pleased to meet you." Without waiting for a response, he turned to Maggie, "Does this mean I can go home now. Please? Christ, I feel like shit."

The man, nae doubt handsome under better circumstances, looked like it as well.

"What," Cam asked of Maggie, "do ye mean by salvation?" He had no desire to get tangled up with this woman and her friend when he was so close to being home.

"I mean the opportunity of a lifetime just fell in your lap and you're about to make a shit load of money. Don't scowl at me. I'm talking serious money. More money than you've ever seen in your life."

Serious money? "I'm listening."

"Good." She looped her arm through his. "We need to find someplace where we can sit down and talk."

Chapter Twenty-three

March

Claire stood motionless in a dreary hall before Apartment 3A, her hand raised, ready to knock, but couldn't bring herself to do it. He was home, there behind the scarred door with so many locks she wondered how he managed to find the right keys. Or if any worked. Light seeped from beneath the door, a narrow splash of yellow on otherwise dingy gray linoleum. She could smell onions frying, could hear the faint sound of canned laughter. The man who'd destroyed her mother was watching a television sitcom.

I'm sorry, Cam. I just can't do this.

She shoved her hands in her pockets and turned. Behind her the door opened.

"Can I help—Claire? Oh my God, is it really you?"

Heart beating erratically, she slowly turned. "Hi, Daddy."

The man silently staring at her, a dish towel in his hands, had aged terribly. His thick red hair had all but disappeared and what little remained was sepia. His deep green eyes were now red-rimmed and nearly colorless. Once tall and muscular, he was thin and stooped. A shell of the debonair hustler he'd once been.

He broke out of their mutual stunned surprise first and stepped back, pulling the door wide. "Come in. Please."

She stepped over the threshold and was nearly knocked over by the scent of onions. "Something is burning."

"Oh shit!" As he disappeared around a corner, he yelled, "I was just making supper and haven't quite gotten the hang of cooking for only one." A pan clanged and water hissed as cold met hot. "Make yourself at home."

On what? There was a lonely recliner held together by duck tape sitting before a card table and an ancient fourteen-inch TV with foil-tipped rabbit ears sitting on a cinderblock and wood bookcase. At her feet lay a tattered copy of *David Copperfield*.

A definite improvement over racing forms, which she saw no sign of.

He startled her coming through the kitchen door in stocking feet. "Sorry 'bout that. I never was much of a cook."

No, he'd left that to Mom, along with everything else. For lack of anything to say—what she'd rehearsed for hours on end had simply flown—she asked, "So, how have you been?"

"Good. I'm working at Gino's. As a dishwasher, but I hope to get a promotion soon. Become a waiter maybe." He shrugged as he smiled, showing a gap where his right front tooth should be. "Have to prove myself, ya know. They can't have ex-cons handling the cash right away."

"I understand."

He waved toward the recliner and pulled a cardboard box before it. "Take a seat and tell me a little about yourself." As he settled on the box, his knees nearly poking through his threadbare slacks, he said, "That young man that came around told me precious little. Nice fella, though. Are you two engaged or something?"

"No, we're just friends."

He wrung his hands in the ensuing silence, then said, "Claire, I'm so sorry for all I put you and your mom through. It wasn't fair to either of you. I was a selfish bastard, pure and simple."

She wouldn't argue with that. "You know she committed suicide."

"No." Looking stricken, he murmured, "They said it was an accidental overdose."

"I found her. Christmas morning. Found the letter, the eviction notice. I pocketed it all, then called the police. No way would the church have performed a funeral mass had they'd known, and I was damned if they'd bury her in unconsecrated ground." Anger got the better of her and her tears spilled. "Not after a lifetime of devotion."

He nodded as he wiped his eyes with the heels of his hands. "You did the right thing."

She took a shuddering breath. "So, do you need money?"

"No." He looked around. "This place is cheap and

I get paid weekly. It's not much, but I'm getting by. I just wanted to see you again. See that you were all right. Tell you that if I could, I'd take back the hurt, be a better father to you and a better husband to your mom." He looked out the window. "I never did understand why she chose me over Delucci. He had looks, ambition. And he was Italian like her, which would have made her parents happy. Instead she chose the guy with an easy line and a fist full of useless promises, who brought her to his level instead of rising to hers. That's my sin, Claire. I married above myself and knowing it, destroyed an innocent." He straightened and placed his hands on his knees. "I'm thankful to see you didn't get sucked down too. That you look like her but have her father's grit."

"You knew him?" Her mother had told her little about her grandfather. The few times Claire had pushed for information, her mother had started to cry.

"Yes." He grinned. "Your grandfather was a handsome, hard-working son of a bitch, who could sing the birds out of the trees and loathed me on sight. He owned this really profitable grocery and butcher shop call Mama's, of all things, right in the heart of Little Italy. You know where Church meets Stuart, right there across from . . ."

"We have to do it one more time, Cam. The gull flew right past the lens and ruined that last shot."

"Ack, not again." If he ran into the freezing surf one more time he'd have no balls at all. He huffed and reached for the whiskey flask, the *aqua vita* being the only thing keeping his blood from turning to slush. The whiskey down, he shouted over the surf, "I'm done after this, Maggie. I bloody well mean it."

Maggie looked up from the camera the photographer held out to her. "Cam, just one more, I promise. The rest are great."

If they were all so great, then why the hell did they need another? Ack, he'd never ken these people. And what all this had to do with a man's perfume was beyond any kenning.

He backed into the surf, his legs stinging as wave after wave crashed up against him, and shouted, "Are ye ready? Because ye've only this one chance and I'm out of here."

He'd garnered enough to repay Claire and a bucket more.

When the photographer placed the camera on the three-legged stand, the poor bastard with a huge white reflector waded out to him. As he held it up to catch the setting sun and fought to keep his balance, he muttered, "Thanks for putting your foot down, man. I'm about to die out here."

"Ye are? Humph!" At least the man had clothing on. Cam had naught on but a slip of glossy black protecting his bag of sweeties and it was doing a damn poor job of it. When the photographer finally held up a thumb, Cam cocked a hip, raised his arms, and crossed them above his head as Maggie had instructed. His thoughts on Claire and the last time they'd made love, he looked straight into the camera's all-seeing eye.

Several months later. . . .

Claire jolted awake on the first ring, looked at the clock and grabbed the phone. One of these days, Cam might figure out time zones, but she wasn't going to hold her breath. "Hello?"

"Claire, get your ass out of bed and open the door for me."

"Tracy? Are you drunk? It's—" she glanced at the clock again, "—two-thirty in the damn morning."

"Claire, you are not going to believe this. I'm holding a copy of this month's *Cosmo* and three guesses who's in it?"

Who cared? "Tracy, go home and go to bed." As she started to put the phone down, Tracy screamed, "It's Cam!"

Claire immediately pressed the phone to her ear again. "What did you say?"

"I said it's Cam. Get down here and see for yourself."

Claire's feet barely hit the steps, before punching in the alarm code and jerking open the Pumpkin's front door. "Let me see it."

Coming through the door, Tracy handed over the magazine.

Breath held, Claire flipped pages, and suddenly there in living color, beautiful and nearly naked, looking for all the world like every woman's sex fantasy, stood Cam, waves splashing off the back of his heavily muscled thighs, looking straight at her. In the lower right-hand corner, on the simple but unmistakable, black-and-white designer label were four simple block letters. LUST.

She collapsed onto the nearest chair. "It is him."

"Ya, and he's growing out his hair."

Claire lifted the flap and sniffed the perfume sample. Nice but not anything like Cam.

"There's more, Claire."

"Huh?"

Tracy hauled four more magazines out of her over-sized designer knock-off satchel. "These are all I could afford. I dog-eared the pages."

Claire opened the top one, a stylish men's magazine and there was Cam, leaning against a stone wall, a horse peering over his shoulder, dressed in the height of country gentleman fashion. She opened the next, and there he was again, this time astride a seriously tricked-out motorcycle.

"He's famous, Claire. Next, we'll be seeing him on romance covers and doing margarine commercials like Fabio."

And he'd never said a word about any of this. Without looking at the rest, Claire handed the magazines back. "How did you find these?"

"I saw the bike ad a few nights ago but thought I was seeing things. Then I picked up this month's *Cosmo* and there was no mistaking him this time, so I went to that all-night newsstand."

Claire rested her head in her hands. She'd lost him. To the tall beautiful Tyra and Gisele what's-her-faces of the high-fashion modeling world. It certainly explained why he'd been calling less and less. She straightened, and over the burning at the back of her throat, said, "I believe I'm going to get drunk. Care to join me?"

Chapter Twenty-four

December 2008

Claire handed the last of the weighty paint cans to Victor. "Are you sure about this color? I mean Urban Putty? Looks more like German Mustard to me." The last thing she wanted was for her soon-to-be refurbished rental apartment—what would soon be her father's new home—to look like a damn bratwurst.

It had taken nine months of sporadic, then ever more frequent visits, lots of tears and teeth gnashing, for Claire and her father to come to a peaceful understanding. For that, she'd be forever grateful to Cam.

When the newlywed couple she'd rented the apartment to immediately after Mrs. Grouse had moved to California bought a home, she'd stood in the apartment and thought why not? She had nothing to lose. She hoped.

Victor shoved the cans behind the front seat of the truck. "Claire, who's the designer here? You or me?"

"Okay, okay." Shoulders hunched against the wind,

she climbed into the passenger seat and picked up her list. "Can we swing by the window place and pick up the shades?"

"Sure."

Halfway there, Victor pulled up to a stop light next to an antique shop. Curious about the competition, she studied the window display. Catching sight of a broadsword leaning against a chair, her heart stuttered. "Pull over!"

"Claire, we're in the middle of traffic."

She didn't bother arguing, but bolted out of the truck and ran for the shop.

Inside, the proprietor, a jeweler's lighted magnifying glass on his head, asked, "May I help you?"

"Yes, I'd like to see the broadsword in the window, please."

"Certainly." He stepped out from behind his work station and headed for the counter where he picked up a set of keys. "It's a lovely piece."

Didn't she know it. But then again, maybe her eyes had deceived her. She'd been so lonely for Cam she could barely think straight.

The man held the broadsword out across his palms. "Seventeenth century, hand-forged steel. The stones in the hilt are amethyst and Connemara marble. As you can see, it's been well cared for. I have the provenance if you'd like to see it."

Claire held out her hands. She knew what she'd find engraved on the hilt but still she had to look. "May I borrow a loupe?" He handed her one. And there it was, Sir Cameron MacLeod.

Oh, Cam, you sold the sword to pay for the locket, didn't

you? Damn it. "How much?" If she couldn't have Cam, then she could at least have his sword. The poor teddy bear was taking a beating.

"Forty-five hundred."

"No way." That was twice what she had in her emergency account.

"Miss, it's a masterpiece of period craftsmanship. Forty-five hundred and that's firm."

As Claire placed the sword on the counter, the door chimed behind her and Victor strode in, short of breath and looking fit to be tied. "What's going on?"

"I'm trying to buy a sword."

He looked at it and rolled his eyes. After heaving a sigh, he asked, "Is it his?"

Her throat raw, clutching her locket, Claire nodded. Victor asked the price, and hearing it, groaned. Looking at her he muttered, "I'll take the French armoire *and* the Windsor chair in trade."

He'd just stolen the chair and they both knew it, but Claire threw her arms about his neck anyway. "I love you, Victor Delucci."

"Ya, ya." He pried her arms from his neck and reached for his checkbook. "I'm just grateful it isn't a friggin' reindeer."

Squatting on his haunches, Cam again stared at the breakers thudding against the headland he'd played on as a bairn. At his back was all that was left of Castle Rubha—two listing walls and a pile of rubble—with only a sign where once a busy bailey stood to tell the tale of his loss. It was still true. All that Claire's history books had said. His gaze shifted left to the deep depression in the cliff where on this visit he'd found a few bits of charred timber, all that was left of Tall Thomas's shelter. The last place he could recall being.

Sandra Power had been right. There was no returning.

He stood, took a steadying breath, and brushed the tears from his cheeks. He needed a wee dram.

At the first pub he came to, he asked for a whiskey. When the barkeep handed it to him, he asked, "Are there any MacLeods left here about?" He'd been too upset on his last visit to ask. Surely there had to be a few.

The barkeep scratched his jaw. "I canna think of any off the top of my head. If any would ken 'twill be Peter MacGraw at the Rubha Museum."

Having passed it on his way in, Cam murmured, "Thank ye," drained his glass and tossed three coins on the bar.

The museum, a small whitewashed cottage wedged between a gift and a woolen shop at the center of the village, was well lit. Inside, a few tourists milled about the waist-high glass cases and bookshelves. Cam studied one of the open ledgers in the glass case at the back while an auld man in a modern kilt told visitors where they might find a good meal.

After they left, the thin man with tufts of sandy hair made his way to him, and Cam pointed to the ledger. "This isna right. Here ye list only three bairns. Malcolm had four. Kelsey Mary died of fever when she was but a month auld." Or so Minnie had told him.

The man looked where Cam pointed. "Ye're sure about this?"

"Positive."

The man frowned. "But how? All the records were destroyed when the castle and kirk were razed."

When another couple, cameras about their necks, came in, Cam switched to Gael. "I just do. Are there any family descendants left here about?"

"Nay, the line was wiped out. All died between 1746 and 1748. And before you question that, you should know I'm one of the few left with blood of the original sept and that I've made these records my life's work."

"I'm most pleased to hear it. But all didna die. Cameron MacLeod survived."

The man's eyes narrowed as he shook his head. "Nay, he rode with his clan and died at Culloden."

"Nay, he was drugged and left behind."

The man huffed, quite sure of himself. "I seriously beg to differ. If what you say were true, then I would have found some trace of him by now. I've been at this for forty years. And why do you speak Gael in the auld way? Most men yer age can barely speak the new."

Cam held out his hand. "I'm sorry. I need introduce myself. Sir Cameron MacLeod at your service, and I speak as I learned at my foster mother's knee."

The man's alarm was almost palpable as the furrows on his high brow deepened and his eyebrows rose. "And who might that be?"

Cam waited for the couple who were headed for the door to exit. "*Was* . . . Mhairie Elizabeth Stewart of Rubha, formally of Newark, eldest daughter of Shamus and Mary Stewart."

The man blinked and looking fair peaked murmured, "Yer a ghost then?"

Cam sighed. "Ye could say that."

The man's knees faltered. As his right hand grasped for the oak case, his left clutched at his heart. "Ack, before ye take me, I could really do with a wee dram."

Grinning, kenning precisely how the man felt, Cam waved to the door. "After ye."

Four hours, a hearty meal and a pint of whiskey later, Cam had related his tale and answered a barrage of questions regarding births, deaths, stores, accounts, and armaments—the hours he'd spent slaving over Rubha's ledgers finally being of some use—all while Mr. MacGraw made frantic notes on the pad he'd borrowed from the barkeep.

"So there you have it. I've a British driving license but without real documents I'm a man without a country." Cam propped an elbow on the table and rested his chin in his hand. "Not that anyone would believe I was still alive had the records not been destroyed. Ack."

Mr. MacGraw raised his glass to the light. Studying the amber flashes playing off the whiskey, he murmured, "I'm not only the local historian but also the registrar. I could recreate—with a little shifting of facts—the documents ye need."

Cam jerked upright. "Are ye serious? If ye would, I'll gladly pay ye well for the service."

Mr. MacGraw tasted his whiskey, then tapped the papers before him. "This information is more than payment enough."

Chapter Twenty-five

December 24, 2008

Her elbow propped on the sideboard, her chin in hand, Claire scanned her account spreadsheets. "If by some miracle I win the lottery, I may make it through another year."

She reached for one of the gingerbread reindeer she kept on a tray for customers and bit off its head. Something she'd very much like to do to Cameron MacLeod. She hadn't heard from him in weeks, and then only via a Christmas card, which sat on the wrought iron cardholder next to Tracy's card. A month ago, she would have tucked it under her pillow. But not now. She'd quit smoking. She could quit Cam.

She huffed and picked up Tracy's card. She still couldn't believe her friend had gone back to New York. Tracy's summer stock success wasn't exactly the big time, but it had been enough to stoke the fires of ambition. All Claire could do now was hope Tracy's dreams were realized . . . and send what little money she could spare.

The brass bell above the door clattered, and Claire brushed the crumbs from her lips and smiled only to have her jaw go slack a second later. A huge plush teddy bear, the largest she'd seen in her life, trying to come through the Velvet Pumpkin's doorway.

She came out from behind the sideboard just as a head popped out from beneath a furry arm. "Hi," a pimply-faced teen said, "Are you Claire MacGregor?"

Nodding, she said, "Yes."

"Then this is for you." He shoved the bear into her arms, nearly toppling her, and headed for the door.

"But who sent it?"

"There's a card on the collar."

Grinning at the absurdity of the gift, Claire put the bear on a settee, fumbled with its floppy head and found a card attached to a thick red ribbon.

Usually bears this large were stuffed with straw. Not so this one, which meant it cost someone a fortune. It took a pair of scissors to wrestle the envelope free and open it. "Oh my God." The check was for twelve thousand dollars.

Merry Christmas, Claire. I thought—nay, dare hope—the other bear might be soggy by now. Love, Cam.

Claire dropped to the floor, her eyes welling. The poor bear upstairs did look like a massive wad of mascara-smeared tissue. "He sent a new bear."

She pulled it into her arms and buried her face in its neck, hot tears splashing onto the pristine white fur. Damn you, Cam.

"Does this mean ye dinna like it?"

Her head snapped up. In the doorway stood Cam, tanned, dressed in jeans and a form-fitting leather blazer, his hair brushing his shoulders, blue eyes and dimples flashing. She'd finally lost her mind.

"Cam?"

"Aye. Is there anyone else sending ye bears?" He stepped toward her as she struggled to her feet. "I was rather hoping for a warmer wel—"

She launched herself into his arms, her arms wrapping around his neck, her legs wrapping around his hips, and buried her face in his neck. God, he smelled so good.

With one hand supporting her weight, his other clasped her neck. "Ah, now that's more like it."

He let her huff and sniffle for a minute before saying, "Let me look at ye."

Oh great, she probably looked like a rabid raccoon. But she leaned back so she could look at him and he could look at her.

"God's teeth, ye're a bonnie sight for these world-weary eyes." And then he kissed her. Deep and warm, wet and sweet. He tasted of Doublemint gum. She'd have melted into him had he not lifted his head and grinned at her. "I've missed ye terribly, lass."

"Oh ya? Then how come I hadn't heard from you in months. Where the hell have you been?" She slapped his chest with both hands. "And why didn't you tell me you were modeling? I had to learn it from Tracy!"

He slipped both hands beneath her bottom and grimaced. "It wasna something I was proud of."

"Not proud of? Cam, you're a superstar."

"Humph! I canna go into a restaurant any more without women racing up to me. And the lies they put in the broadsheets about me . . . 'twould make ye hair fry and my mother, God rest her soul, weep with shame. And ye wouldna believe what I go through at airports, lights flashing in my eyes, women shouting and waving like crazed beasts. They even follow me into the bloody loo." He blew through his teeth. "'Tisna a good thing, Claire, not at all."

He shuddered, and she pushed a lock behind his ear. "It's so good to see you again even if you did have to go through hell to get here."

He grinned and waggled a perfectly arched brow. "'Tis good to see ye as well. And I've something verra important to show ye." He set her down and took her hand, heading for the door.

"Wait! I have to tell Dad I'm leaving."

"Yer Da's here?"

She smiled. "Yes, we reconciled, thanks to you. Took some time, but I think it might work out."

He gave her a squeeze, and she dragged him toward the back stairs. On the second-floor landing, she knocked. Her father opened the door, took one look at Cam and said, "As I live and breathe, if it isn't Cameron MacLeod, the man who broke my daughter's heart. I'd deck you but as you can see I have my hands full."

"Daddy!"

He held the tray of cookies out to Cam. "Have a reindeer."

Cam laughed as he took one. "Thank ye. And 'tis good to see ye as well, Mr. MacGregor."

"That remains to be seen."

"Daddy, Cam and I are going out. Will you watch the shop for a few minutes?"

"Sure."

Her heart tripping, Claire pulled Cam toward her apartment. "Come on. I have to get my coat."

Inside her apartment, Cam took a deep breath. Lavender and spaghetti sauce. Pure heaven. He looked around, pleased to see nothing had changed. As Claire reached for her coat, she asked, "Where did you get that fabulous tan? The Riviera?"

He held her coat. "Tahiti. A nice enough place, I suppose, if ye've little to do."

As she sought her purse, he looked into her bedroom, the site of their last lovemaking and was shocked to see his sword mounted on the wall above her bed. Warmth spread through him. He hadn't wanted her to know that he'd sold it and still she'd found it. She truly did still care.

"Wow, I've always wanted to go to Tahiti."

He grinned and took her hand. "Come, 'tis almost gloaming."

Outside, he pressed the button on his key chain and his one indulgence bleeped.

"Cam! Is this yours?"

As Claire ran her hand over the Corvette's glossy red fender, he reached for the door. "'Twas on sale. End-of-year model."

"Wow. You must be doing well."

He shrugged, made sure she was snug in the heated, wraparound leather seat, then jumped behind the wheel and they were off, the global positioning system leading the way. "Tell me, love, what else have I missed these last few months?"

As she brought him up to date, he had difficulty keeping his eyes off her.

"*Eeeek!* Other side of the road, Cam!"

"Oops." He swerved, grinning at the oncoming driver who gave him the finger, and Claire blew out the breath she'd held.

"Are you sure you don't want me to drive?"

"'Twill just take me another minute or two to adjust to driving again on the right."

"Oooh-kay." She checked the tension on her seatbelt. "So how did you get another passport? And how long is it good for?"

He laughed. "Ye're a reiver at heart, lass, ye truly are."

"I most certainly am not." She glanced at him. "Well, maybe just a little and only if it's justifiable." Then she grinned. "So? How did you manage it?"

"I'm now a Sassenach—God help me—in good standing and have a legitimate British passport, good for ten years." Her grin dissolved, and he asked, "What is it?"

"Nothing. So, how long will you be stay—Augh, right! Go right!" She exhaled with a whoosh when they miraculously made it onto the Mystic River Bridge without incident.

"Sorry 'bout that."

"Ya. I was asking how long will you be staying?"

"Depends."

"On your next assignment?"

"Aye."

"When will you know?"

"Verra soon."

"Oh." She looked at the cell phone resting on the console between them, then turned to the window at her side. He dearly wanted to put her out of her misery, but his future rested on what was about to happen, so he turned on the radio and kept driving.

As he took the turn toward Salem, she asked, "Where are we going?"

"You'll see in a few minutes." Taking the coast road, he murmured, "I went home, Claire, back to the sea and Rubha."

"Ah, we're going to see the witch."

They weren't, but he said, "She was right. There isna going back." He told her what he'd found. "The oddest thing . . . it was as if my eyes had to repeatedly see for themselves what my heart already kenned. And still it hurt like hell."

She placed a hand on his thigh, her eyes going soft with pity. "I'm so sorry, Cam."

He shrugged, for there was naught else to say, and entering Marblehead, turned down a small side street. Spying the huge maple trees that marked his destination, he rolled up before them and shut off the car.

He helped Claire out and watched as she stood looking up at the shuttered, gray-shingled house with its dormers and gables and white picket fence. "Lovely. When did Sandra move?"

"I didna ken that she had." He took her hand and walked up the brick path.

Frowning, she asked, "Then whose house is this?"

He stuck the key in the lock and the door swung

wide exposing an airy interior with a view of the ocean beyond. "'Tis yers. Merry Christmas, Claire."

She gaped at him for a long moment before shaking her head in wonder. Mute, she ran her fingertips over the waist-high molding in the parlor, opened cabinets in the dining room, and then stood before picture windows overlooking a lovely brick bailey and the dormant rose garden. Beyond the stone wall, the sea rolled in gentle swells rather than with crashing waves, but the scent of salt was in the air.

"It's more than I ever dreamed of owning, but I can't possibly accept this. It's so large, a family home." She faced him, and eyes glassy, patted his chest. "I love that you want to give it to me, I truly do, but—"

He pulled her close. "Ye dinna find it fair?"

"Are you kidding? It's stunning. Just look at that fireplace and the view . . ."

Verra good. He took a deep breath, and, hands sweating, pulled out the black velvet box that had been burning a hole in his pocket for three months. When he popped the lid she gasped. It was a lovely bit, to be sure. "Claire Patricia MacGregor I love you with every ounce of my being. Will ye do me the honor and be so foolish as to marry this auld man?"

She made a choking sound as tears slid down her cheeks.

"I'll take that as an aye." He took her left hand in his and placed the emerald on the middle finger. "The jeweler and Maggie said I should get ye a diamond, but this reminded me so much of yer eyes, I wouldna be dissuaded." He waited, his gut churning, for her to say something, anything as she stared at the ring.

He was about to explode when she finally said, "Oh. My. God."

What the hell did that mean? Had he made a poor choice? Would she have preferred a diamond after all? Did she love another? *What?*

Claire leaned into him, took a shuddering breath and then another. "Cam?"

"Aye?"

"Yes."

"Yes what?"

She raised her head and his heart soared. She was beaming at him. "Yes to marrying you, yes to the house and yes, I love the ring."

"Verra good." He kissed her soundly, loving the way she moaned as he stroked her, then keened when he reluctantly pulled away. "I've another surprise for ye." He scooped her into his arms.

Giggling, her arms about his neck, her head on his shoulder, she asked, "Now what?"

"Ye'll see." He strode into the bedchamber.

"Oh Cam! It's totally wicked."

"Aye, wicked." He'd found the massive four-poster bed in a London antique shop. 'Twas much like the one that had been in Rubha and had witnessed many a MacLeod birth. He could only hope this new MacLeod bed would see many more. And there was nae time like the present to start. Lowering her to the thick mattress, he settled above her, his weight on his arms. "I've missed ye, love, beyond words."

"Oh, me, too."

That she'd waited this long lonely year and still wanted him was almost beyond imagining. As he undressed her, her hands made fast work of his garments. Finally naked, he rolled onto his side and pulled her against him, her leg falling over his hip. He'd almost forgotten how incredible she felt. Too incredible. Moaning, she pressed her sweet wetness against him and rubbed. Already panting and on the brink, he whispered, "Easy, love, it's been a year and ye dinna want me basting the lamb before it's sheared."

"Right." Claire laughed and pushed Cam onto his back and straddled him, her breath catching as she took his delicious thickness in. "This any better?"

Eyes closed, his hips coming up to meet her, he growled, "Barely."

Her insides molten, needing to rock, she straightened to brace her hands on his thighs and was startled by a flash of light. To her left, behind the partially closed door, she saw a huge baroque mirror leaning against the wall. "Cam, look."

The mirror was every bit as fine as the one she'd sold. The owners would be sick when they realized they'd left it behind.

He grinned, his gaze locking on their reflection. He reached up and stroked the underside of her breasts. "Italian, like ye. Thought we might have a bit of fun,"—he strummed a thumb across her left nipple, sending searing heat through her—"before ye took it to ye shop."

Before she could catch her breath to ask what the hell he was talking about, his hand slipped between her thighs and his thumb caressed her, totally short-circuiting her brain. Without thought but with her every nerve straining for release, she rocked, his every stroke stoking the fire at her core. "Oh, oh, oh . . ."

As his hips came up to meet her, he whispered, deep and husky, "Come to me, love. Come."

Before she could gasp *I am*, she did, back arched and keening, in an explosion of color and sizzling nerves.

Claire collapsed onto his chest, and Cam grinned. He'd forgotten what a noisy wee bit she was when she fell off the earth.

Quite satisfied, he stroked her lovely hurdies, one hand finding its way to the warm wetness where they were joined, he still hard and hot, she all wet and soft. He stroked her there, rocking deeper and deeper, his thighs locked around hers. When her mouth found his and her hands found their way into his hair, he moaned and thrust deeper still, seeking her center. Her tongue thrust into his mouth matching the rhythm of his hips. His release—exquisite—so rocked him, it bordered on pain.

When he finally caught a breath, he cradled her to his chest. "Ye need ken something."

"What?"

"I said good-bye to Maggie."

She craned her neck to look at him. "Truly?"

"Aye, I've had my fill of posing. And I have enough money to see us through until I can find something worthy of a man."

She turned in his arms and cradled his face in her hands. "Hearing this is almost as good as seeing you come through the Pumpkin's door."

He smiled. "Are ye having a Merry Christmas, love?"

"Aye, Mr. MacLeod. You've given me the best gift any woman could have."

"And what might that be?" He'd put money on her saying the mirror. She'd been most fond of hers.

"My very own Highlander."

He laughed and looked at their reflection.

Ye might be ancient, MacLeod, but ye havena lost yer touch.

And with any luck, he'd just given her another Highlander, a wee one.

About the Author

Award-winning author Sandy Blair has slept in castles, dined with peerage, floated down Venetian canals, explored the great pyramids, lost her husband in an Egyptian ruin (she still denies being the one lost), and fallen (gracefully) off a cruise ship.

Winner of Romance Writers of America's Golden Heart and a National Readers Choice Award for Best Paranormal Romance, the Write Touch Readers Award for Best Historical, the Golden Quill and Barclay awards for Best Anthology, nominated for a RITA and recipient of *Romantic Times* 4½ star Top Pick and K.I.S.S. ratings, Sandy loves writing about Scotland's past. She resides in Dallas, Texas with her tall Scot husband and panda-looking pooch Coco. To contact Sandy or to learn more about her, please go to *www.sandyblair.net*